DEAR FRED

Dear Fred

♣ 1857 — 86

K. M. Peyton

THE BODLEY HEAD
LONDON SYDNEY
TORONTO

The author would like to acknowledge her debt to a number of books as the source of facts about Fred Archer that she has used in this story. They include *The Life of Fred Archer* by E. M. Humphris (Hutchinson, 1923), *Men and Horses I have Known* by George Lambton (Thornton Butterworth, 1924), *John Porter of Kingsclere* by John Porter (Grant Richards, 1919), *Memories of Racing and Hunting* by the Duke of Portland (Faber & Faber, 1935), *Turf Memories of Sixty Years* by Alexander Scott (Hutchinson, 1925), and *Fred Archer, His Life and Times* by John Welcome (Faber & Faber, 1967).

British Library Cataloguing
in Publication Data
Peyton, K. M.
Dear Fred.
I. Title
823'.9'1F
ISBN 0-370-30350-4

Printed in Great Britain for
The Bodley Head Ltd
9 Bow Street, London WC2E 7AL
by Redwood Burn Ltd,
Trowbridge & Esher
Phototypeset in Linotron 202 Sabon by
Western Printing Services Ltd, Bristol
First published 1981

To Helen,
Elizabeth, John and Susan,
the grandchildren of
Fred and Nellie Archer

1

She should not have been there.

The two men, the peer and his trainer, sat on their hacks in the cold early morning sunshine, and Laura rode past as if she were, in fact, merely passing, not interested, studying nature. Mr Dawson saw her, nodded, and went on talking.

' . . . a sight, my Lord, the like of which you may never see again.'

Four horses, all belonging to his Lordship, went past at a constrained canter. They were the four best race-horses in England. Laura knew that perfectly well, but had come for a man, not a horse. She watched, seeing only the rider of the dark filly: a tall, slender young man with a sad, thin face turned up into the wind, holding the filly with his magic hands.

Laura's heart turned over with adoration.

Mr Dawson knew she loved his jockey, and smiled at her again, and she rode on with flaming cheeks, pretending to herself . . . half the women in England loved Mr Dawson's jockey—and quite a lot of the men too, for the feats he pulled off—but she was only thirteen, and even when he acknowledged her, it was only as a child. She wanted to marry him desperately. The whole ambition of her life was to become Mrs Fred Archer. He was twenty-two. His birthday was on the eleventh of January. She knew everything about him, from his height (five feet eight and a half inches) to what he ate for breakfast (half an orange and a glass of castor oil).

She rode down the Rowley Mile to see him come by and to be there at the finish in case, in the pulling up and chat and excitement afterwards, he might just possibly notice her and give her the nod of recognition that would see her in paradise.

'I do love you, Fred,' she said out loud. 'I do love you, love you, love you.'

It was a trial, not a race, a private stable trial to test the young filly, Wheel of Fortune. Laura had learned about it from her Uncle Harry next door, who was a trainer. Her Uncle Harry was her father's brother. But her father was only a mouldy artist, a dull moody fellow in thrall to the fashions of the age—he designed door-knobs and hinges and book-plates—very clever, no doubt, and rich, but in no way to be compared with Uncle Harry in his leather boots who gave her ponies, and who dear Fred sometimes came to ride for. Laura spent all her spare time lingering round Uncle Harry's yard, until Albert, or sometimes Gervase, was sent to fetch her. She was allowed to ride out with Uncle Harry but riding alone to the Heath was strictly forbidden. Laura quite often did what was forbidden. It was forbidden to love Mr Archer.

'You don't know what you're saying!' her mother had said, very white and angry. 'A child of your age doesn't know what love is!'

'I do. I love you and Uncle Harry and Priam.' Priam was a horse.

'Yes, that is love. What you feel for Mr Archer is not love. Don't speak of it.'

'What is it?'

'Hero worship. There is far too much of it about as far as Mr Archer is concerned.'

Laura called it love nevertheless.

She presumed the trial was going to finish somewhere near to where Mr Dawson and Lord Falmouth were waiting, so did not want to go too far away, although it was impossible to be anything but conspicuous in the ocean of grass that was Newmarket Heath. She was being very bold, she knew, but she was not acting in ignorance, only in character.

The sound of horses galloping came on the wind, the urgent thudding of hooves on the firm turf that made her blood tingle. There was nothing like it, save the organ in church with all the stops out. She could see the four animals breasting the grass in the distance, coming towards her in a bunch very close together, impossible to see who was in front. Two of them had won the Oaks, the Derby and the St Leger between them, but the one expected to win this time had won nothing yet. 'She's a marvel,' Uncle Harry said, who had nothing in his stables like that, only handicappers. Laura loved the eternal optimism that went with horse-racing, the spring of hope that never failed, every new-born foal a winner. Now, if Fred's filly won, it would be a miracle, like the star of Bethlehem rising over Newmarket Heath. In racing it was happening all the time. Laura's parents dwelt more eloquently on the disasters but Laura knew little of disaster.

The horses were coming close now, their spoky legs covering the ground at a tremendous rate. Laura's little horse started to dance with excitement but she reined him in tightly, biting her lip. The filly Fred was riding lay third, the miracle filly. As he came past Laura saw his hands move up the filly's neck and his legs start to urge her to make her bid, his slender body wholly devoted to coaxing marvels from this horse. The filly started to move away imperceptibly, first past Silvio the Derby winner and then, smoothly, effortlessly, up to the famous Jannette. Laura saw the sweat gleaming on the dark coat, the wild light of the gallop in her eye. Fred's face was grave, taut with concentration. It was a race more important than a public race, a race without the usual swearing and blaspheming, for in trying to win the other three jockeys wanted to prove the fourth the best.

The filly went past clear of Jannette just before the mile post where it was expected of her and then, although Fred dropped his hands to ease her, she ran on, not spent and played out, but still full of going. Fred humoured her and brought her round in a big circle, easing her into a canter and then into a trot. The others followed. Their steam smoked on the clear air. Laura saw the flecks of foam on the jockeys' breeches, heard the excitement in their voices. She had to contain herself to stay where she was as they went back towards owner and trainer. She was not a part of that excitement, only a spectator. She should have ridden on, away, but she wanted too much, and waited. Her mother always said she wanted too much.

The six horses came back together, Fred riding beside Lord Falmouth, the filly relaxed now, shaking her head. They came past quite close and Fred saw her. He turned and touched his cap to her.

'Miss Laura.'

It was what she had waited for, what she had come for, that he should be aware of her, glance at her for one second from those cool, blue-grey eyes. She said nothing, feeling the burning in her cheeks, the bursting of her love. *Love*, mother! It is more than for Priam, for you! She wanted to shout it out.

She rode home behind them at a discreet distance, down into the town where they turned up the Bury road for Heath House. She went on out of town, up the long muddy road between the eternal paddocks to the village where she lived. It was still early, barely an hour past breakfast time. She would have been missed but if she kept out of the way until lunchtime perhaps she could say she had been at Uncle Harry's all the time. She would go there now, to substantiate the lie. To put Priam away, to tell Uncle Harry what she had seen. That Fred had acknowledged her.

'Oh, yes,' Uncle Harry said, smiling. 'He's got lovely manners. That's why all the ladies love him. He's very polite to ladies.' And then, not teasing, 'He's very civil to everyone. He's a paragon, there's no doubt, as much in his ways as on a horse.'

Laura didn't know what a paragon was but it sounded impressive. Uncle Harry did not disapprove of her passion at all, quite the opposite. 'A fine lad to admire, my dear, not like some drawing-room singing fellow. He's like a son to Mr Dawson, and Mr Dawson's never been an easy man to please.'

No, indeed, Mr Dawson's high standards and meticulous ways were a byword in Newmarket. Fred had been appprenticed to him since the age of eleven.

'Cried his eyes out, the little lad, so shy and sensitive he was, and homesick. The other boys were right cruel to him, he wanted his mother so. But put him on a horse—why, he would face anything! They soon stopped laughing.'

Laura could listen to such stories for ever; she knew them all off by heart. Delicate in build, highly-strung, Fred Archer had quickly shown that once on a horse he was a miracle of courage and understanding. He rode his first winner for Mr Dawson at the age of twelve, won the Cesarewitch at fifteen, his first Derby at nineteen and at twenty-two had been champion jockey for five years. His determination and nerve on the race-course were legendary, yet Laura knew that the valet appointed to him by Mr Dawson, a lad of the same age who had grown too heavy to ride, had to go first into the bedroom at night and look under the bed to assure Fred that all was well.

'Well now, it was worth the journey then,' Uncle Harry said. 'And with luck your mother will overlook it, for there's been some excitement over your way this morning.'

'What's happened?'

'You'd better go and find out. I had it from Albert. I haven't been over myself.'

Albert was the butler. Albert passed on everything. The two brothers' houses were separated by a lane which ran into some fields, the old farmhouse and training yard on one side, the artist's new gleaming house on the other. The artist's house was a wonder, designed by Laura's father with the help of Mr Voysey, and London people came to visit it, and famous artists and men of letters came to stay, but Laura used to run to Uncle Harry's and hide in his shabby, doggy living-room, dark with portraits of horses on the walls and mahogany furniture, crammed with discarded boots and saddles, piles of racing calendars and ledgers full of his owners' names and debts. Uncle Harry, unmarried, lived alone there, looked after by a well-worn housekeeper called Martha who lived in a cottage in the lane. His visitors were all horsey and bluff: the corn merchants, his owners, his trainer friends, his mountaineering friends (for he was a mountaineer when he could find time), the local farmers, amateur riders and jockeys to ride work. Quite different from over the road. Laura fitted into both, adjusting her nature to fit. It was no effort at Thorn's Hall, Uncle Harry's establishment, far more an effort at her own home, Dry Meadows.

'This excitement,' she asked, 'will I like it?'

'Well, it's more to your taste, I reckon, than what generally counts for excitement over there—a new shape for a teapot spout or a curlicue for a mantelshelf.'

Harry mocked his brother Philip. Laura knew she should not approve but she did. It was a delicious bond between them. Harry was small (an ex-jockey) but wiry and strong. (Philip was tall and thin and delicate.) He was an active man, quick and direct in his ways. He sometimes found it difficult to be polite to his owners who, he said, were mostly dunderheads. 'Not in the same class as Mr Dawson's, I'm afraid.' Harry knew his station. He was a good trainer, but he was better with horses than with people. His directness could offend. He was not a fashionable trainer. He did not wear a pearl in his cravat and his hands were often dirty, but he was never despondent in disappointment; he had a bubbling, optimistic nature, not subtle and uncertain like his brother.

'He should have stayed in his place,' he said of Philip. 'He'd have known where he was then.'

By place he meant Thorn's Hall, where they had both been born. But Philip had gone off to London to better himself, and only returned because when their father died the land had been divided between the two brothers and Philip, newly trained in design, could not wait to build himself a house. Since then he had regretted bitterly building the house where he had, and he could not sell it, for no one in Newmarket wanted that sort of new-fangled house, and anyone who liked it had no notion to live in such an inartistic town, given over as it was, absolutely, to an animal. Harry was amused, satisfied by Philip's plight, for he had no wish for Philip to move away. If Philip were to move away and take his wife and child with him, Harry knew that a great deal of what made up his own happiness would go too. Much as he enjoyed Laura's company, it was largely because in her every movement and expression he could see her mother Cecily. Laura was as Cecily must have been once: passionate, outspoken, incautious, self-willed. Cecily over the years had found it necessary to repress these unfashionable instincts, and was now considered by most people to be a reserved, dutiful woman of few words, hard to know and harder still to feel any warmth for. But Harry knew differently. He saw her often in company and never by a single glance or hesitation did she reveal what lay beneath the smooth routine of her social and domestic life. She came to him rarely, because of the rarity of the opportunity, but Harry lived for those moments as Laura lived for a glance from Fred Archer.

'Don't tell anyone where I went,' Laura told him. 'My mother doesn't approve of my loving Mr Archer.'

'No, you needn't say. You can still love him but not say.'

'I can to you?'

'Of course. I admire your taste. I only wish you could meet him up here more often.'

'When will he come next?'

'To ride Kimbo on Friday. I'm hoping he'll ride him in the Spring Handicap.'

'And will you let me—?'

Harry laughed. 'You may ride out with the string that day, my dear. If your mother allows it.'

'Don't tell her why. She will allow it, if she doesn't know Mr Archer is coming.'

'She isn't in the habit of enquiring who is coming to ride work, never fear.'

Laura was deeply content with her day's work: one actual confrontation with her hero and another promised for Friday, a rich haul. Her parents had lately been threatening to employ a governess, and Laura knew that her freedom was not going to last much longer; the likely agony of knowing that dear Fred might be across the road at Thorn's Hall and herself locked in lessons with a wretched governess was a terrible prospect. She must make the most of these precious weeks.

She left the Hall and crossed the lane to her own home, going in through the stable archway and the yard—housing only two dull carriage horses—across the vegetable garden and in by the kitchen door. Immediately she was aware of Uncle Harry's 'excitement'. Instead of the usual placid scene—just Peggy the cook rolling pastry and Albert cleaning the silver or polishing boots, happily gossiping—the kitchen was full of people. The gardener was there and the new maid, Alice, and her mother, looking perplexed, and a stranger who seemed to be the cause of the trouble, a boy sitting at the table eating. Wolfing, Laura thought, amazed. Not eating but wolfing, head right down to the plate, elbows out. He was obviously a very poor and common little boy, in clothes so tattered he was not far off being naked, his skin dirty and covered largely by what appeared to be bruises and weals. He was very thin and small, but not as young, Laura supposed, as this made him appear. Perhaps twelvish, she guessed, or even as old as herself, thirteen.

Laura's mother was sending everyone back to their work. Alice departed to do the bedrooms, Percy back to the garden.

'I shall leave him to you, Peggy, and go and ask Mrs Porter if she has any clothes that might fit him. Get him washed, for heaven's sake. I really don't know what Mr Keen expects me to do with him.'

Laura could see that she was annoyed, not liking such interruptions. She was not a motherly woman, and the boy aroused no maternal inclinations in her, merely irritation.

'Your father brought him in from the fields,' she said to Laura. 'He was asleep in Harry's haystack. You can see the state he's in. At least we can feed him and clothe him, and then perhaps find out where he comes from.'

'Perhaps he's an orphan,' Laura said hopefully. She had always hankered for someone nearer her own age in the house.

The boy sent her a sideways glance which she diagnosed as scornful, and bent back to his plate again. Although waif-like in appearance, Laura sensed a quite opposite temperament, a sharpness that was almost aggressive. He had dark auburn hair, curling and rough and dirty, and dark, reddish eyes. Like a fox, Laura thought. Or a tiger. Pulled out of its lair.

'Did he want to come?'

'Your father said he would feed him. I should imagine that was the attraction.'

'He's run away,' Laura said. 'Have you run away?'

The boy did not reply. Laura sat down at the table opposite him and watched him. Her mother went away, and Peggy refilled the boy's plate with mutton stew and dumplings. Freed from the restraint of her employer's presence, the cook relaxed into her usual grumbling acceptance of what was required of her; good-natured at heart, she did not like it to show.

'If he's run away, the sooner he runs back the better. Have you got a name, boy? We'll be expecting some work out of you in return for all this food. You can't live here on charity, you know.'

'What's your name?' Laura asked again, as the boy was silent. The boy shook his head.

'He can't talk.'

'Can you talk?' Laura asked him.

'Yes.'

'But you won't say your name?'

'No.'

It seemed logical to Laura, if he had run away.

'I'll call you Tiger then. My name is Laura.'

'Tiger, indeed! What sort of a name is that?' Peggy sniffed. 'Eats like one, but it's no name.'

'If he doesn't like it, he can tell us another.'

'Very sharp, Miss Laura. Do you want to be called Tiger, boy?'

'If you want.'

Albert laughed. 'What's in a name? He's not stupid. Where are you running away from then? Where've you got those belts from? Your father?'

The boy nodded.

'You probably deserved them. You've been on your way for a while by the look of you.'

'If the missus is fetching him new clothes—and heaven knows, he certainly needs them—you'd best take him out in the yard under the pump, Albert, and get him clean. I don't want my kitchen full of bugs. You can burn his things.'

The boy did not look as if he relished the prospect, but made no protest. He got up from the table, wiping his mouth, and waited while Albert collected soap and a towel from the scullery. Albert, officially the butler, was not a man to stand on his dignity. He was equally at home in his white gloves, waiting on guests at table, as out in the yard scrubbing dirty orphans. 'I don't know what we would do without Albert,' was a stock phrase at Dry Meadows. He had been a waiter in a London hotel, and come up to Newmarket to what he called his retirement, for the racing. But he worked twelve hours a day, not liking to be idle. He never seemed to work very hard, but everything got done. Laura, who spent a lot of her time in the kitchen, could not imagine her home without Albert at its centre, although she could imagine it quite well with anybody else missing, even her mother. Albert lived in, in one of the dormer rooms on the top floor, but Peggy and Alice lived out, in the village. Percy lived in a cottage in the grounds, beside his potting sheds and glasshouses.

Albert came back, tying on his working apron.

'Come on then, Tiger. Let's have a go at those stripes.'

They went out into the yard. Laura wondered if the boy would duck Albert's arm and run for it, but he seemed resigned, standing in the cold April sunshine beside the water-trough, unbuttoning his trousers.

'Come away, Miss Laura,' Peggy said. 'Even that sort of boy's got his pride.'

'What sort of boy?'

'A dirty ragamuffin.'

The only boy Laura really knew, apart from the village boys and Harry's stable lads and a few boring sons of her parents' friends, was her cousin Gervase, who lived with them every school holidays when he was home from Rugby. His parents lived in India and he said he was going to be the Viceroy. Laura did not care for him much. Tiger looked more promising.

'He might be a prince,' she said, 'underneath.'

'Underneath all that dirt?'

'Why did Father bring him home?'

'That's what I'm asking myself, madam. It's all very well to bring 'em home. Getting rid of 'em might not be so easy. I don't want him under my feet down here. All very well for your father.'

'What did Father say to do with him?'

'Feed him, he said. He was near starving, no doubt about that. Your father went for a walk, early, up in the fields where he usually goes, and the boy was asleep in a haystack. Moaning, he was, your father said, but dead asleep. He kept saying something, else your father would never have seen him.'

'What did he say?'

'Your father said he said "charribird". Over and over again.'

'Charribird?'

'That's it. And moaning. And Mr Philip thought he was in a bad way, all covered in those bruises, and freezing cold it was, and the way he was moaning, so he woke him and brought him home. But since then I can't say as he seems to be suffering from anything. Especially now he's fed.'

'What will happen to him?'

'Best ask your father. He's the one to decide. I don't want him here, getting under my feet.'

Laura did. The boy, although rough, was certainly not stupid, and Laura's curiosity was aroused. She was a voracious reader, and had already cast him in the part of a disguised outcast from noble connections. In actual fact, held firmly down under the pump by Albert's large hand, his naked body running with streams of dirty lather, he did not at that moment look princely, merely puny.

Peggy said, 'Miss Martin will be here in ten minutes for your piano lesson, miss. You'd better go and get changed and wash your hands.'

'He won't go before I've finished?'

'I doubt it, if your mother is going to get his clothes from Mrs Porter. That's twenty minutes in the trap just to get there, and then talking, and finding something to fit. Don't you worry. He'll keep.'

Laura, changing out of her riding habit, kept wondering about the word 'charribird' which Tiger had been saying in his sleep. It sounded faintly familiar somehow, but she could not think why. It must be a name, of somebody or something. She tried to place it, but failed. It was very curious.

She laid her habit over a chair and stepped into her sensible brown skirt. In the long mirror she saw her body clothed in hand-embroidered underwear, her breasts just beginning to show. Propped up on the dressing-table was a portrait of Fred Archer, cut from a magazine, arranged so that he was watching her.

'Do you like me, Fred?' she asked him softly. 'If you wait four years or so, I will be old enough to marry you. Please don't meet anybody till then. I do love you so.'

She picked up the cutting and pressed his face to her lips. The paper smelled of mothballs, from being kept in the drawer where her mother was unlikely to look. She held it away from her and gazed at him but, as usual, he never seemed to look at her, but into a distance which brought him no joy. He did not smile and his eyes were bleak. He was quiet, unassuming; he did not speak a great deal in company, and then with diffidence, but every word he uttered about racing and horses was taken as the gospel truth. They said he knew more about the horses he rode, and those he rode against, than the trainers themselves. Laura loved him because there was no one else like him. His very remoteness and his reserve, in spite of the adulation that surrounded him, was his appeal. His deferential 'Miss Laura', his hand to his cap, was more to her than any treat the fondest parent could have devised.

Her mother would have disapproved of her Fred Archer pictures if she had known of them. Laura put it away in her bottom drawer underneath some outgrown clothes, made herself tidy and went down to her music lesson.

*　　*　　*

Cecily Keen drove herself somewhat irritably down to Mrs Porter's, annoyed at her husband's irresponsibility in saddling her with the vagrant boy who in her opinion could well have been left to his own devices. She hoped he would go once he was made decent and his belly filled. She was not good at coping with children—not good, really, at coping with anyone other than at the surface level required of polite society, happiest on her own. She spent most of her time gardening, and her indoor pleasure was to play the piano: two pursuits entirely solitary and deeply satisfying. She ran the house and did the accounts, handled Philip's appointments, made sure he completed his commissions to time, ordered his life for him without any of it occupying her real interest at all; it was her duty. She ordered the meals, saw to the servants, taught Laura her manners and curbed her temperament. 'How cold she is,' they said of her. She knew they said it. 'Cecily is so efficient!' Efficient like a machine, they meant, making no mistakes, no human error. A perfect hostess, elegant, polite, a cool cheek to kiss, a white glove to shake, the flowers beautifully arranged, the wine at just the right temperature . . . they admired, but never drank too much nor laughed too loud nor gossiped, did not enjoy themselves too much. 'There's something about her,' they said, 'that inhibits . . .' She had learned to recognize the admiration and caution in their faces. She did not mind. She had worked hard at it. Dear God, if they knew why!

She had spent all her dull, worthy married life living down her past, and now was terrified for her future, all her long-locked sensuality bursting again in what she considered her middle age, her late thirties. When she saw Laura, the image of herself as a child, frenzied for her glimpses of Fred Archer, she dreaded to see the whole cycle repeating itself. She told herself she was being ridiculous, that Laura's infatuation was nothing compared to the scandals of her own girlhood, that it did not mean the child was showing signs of any abnormal sexual precocity. Yet with her own infatuation for Harry making her life a misery she could not see Laura's development in proportion. It seemed she could see nothing at all in proportion, holding grimly on to this everyday charade of the dutiful wife, the buttoning-down of her emotions exhausting her at times, bringing on migraines and weeping fits that she had to conceal in the deep privacy of her rhododendron shrubbery or in the farthest potting shed when Percy was safely working on the drives. She had not wanted any more passion in her life, latching on to the boredom of country life with Philip as a blessed relief from all that had gone before. And, dull lover that Philip was, she had not wanted another. She had learned to be calm; she had made a cult of being aloof, built steel walls to protect herself. And gradually over the years Harry had infiltrated —so gradually that she had not seen the danger until it was too late. She had not even recognized that he was the sort of man she liked, dismissing her husband's brother as a mere horseman, a rough diamond, insensitive to finer feelings, art, music and November sunsets. Slowly she had learned that he was far from insensitive to several of these things, not least to her own personality, that he had an instinctive sympathy far greater than his refined brother's, that he was funny and that his sense of values seemed to her refreshingly acceptable after the tortured conventions of her own background. Worse, there slowly grew in her physical body an awareness of her brother-in-law that was in no way brotherly. She could not remember when it first started, only the despair with which she recognized it. She had been hopelessly unsuccessful in learning to live with it; outwardly, perhaps, she was successful, but only at the expense of total confusion in the inner sanctum, brain and guts eternally on the verge of volcanic eruption. She seemed to lack the vital resources of the normal adulterer. She knew other women who 'carried on' without any apparent difficulty, but she lacked even the basic guile to deceive her own servants, let alone Philip (in fact, she knew perfectly well, Philip would be far easier to deceive than Albert). If they were unaware of her feelings—and Philip was, although she could never be sure about Albert—it was only through luck, and the blessed thickness of her rhododendrons, not by any skill on her part. She tried her best now not to see Harry, but not seeing him did not seem to improve her emotional state to any measurable degree, in fact rather the opposite. And when, as on Wednesday next week, she knew that Philip was going to London, that it was Two Thousand Guineas day and that Harry would invite her to accompany him, she lacked totally the spine to refuse; she merely commenced to count the minutes to the moment when Harry would bring his phaeton to her door and she would get up to sit beside him. He took enormous pains to keep her in the nicest company on such occasions, having to leave her a good deal of the time to saddle up his horses and talk to his jockeys and owners, but it still constituted a day out with him without causing too many tongues to wag. There were few other occasions.

The artless ease with which Laura flitted in and out of Thorn's Hall was her mother's ceaseless envy. Cecily felt that she went in the nature of a messenger from herself, unaware, and Harry agreed that the child's company was a continual reminder of herself, but Laura's prattle of Uncle Harry was torment to Cecily. She was also envious—though disapproving—of Laura's open adoration of Fred Archer and of her freedom to enjoy it. The child had no inhibitions, would approach Mr Archer with beams of adulation springing from her guileless eyes, while she, the adult, could not meet Harry in company without veiling her gaze in desperate distraction, quite unable to speak freely or to act normally. Or so she felt, but no one remarked on her strangeness. They said she was cold. (They had not said this once.)

Calling on Anne Porter, she found relief in the company of a woman totally devoid of all complications in life, beyond her youngest's teething troubles and her second daughter's refusal to wear a new party dress. Her husband was a trainer.

'Oh, my dear, I can well understand! These little boys are forever running away—either from home to get a job here, thinking they will be a Fred Archer in two weeks or, having got here, back home because the work is so demanding. These stables —they are so hard on the lads! They take them at eleven, little under-nourished shrimps, and expect a man's work out of them. I'm forever at Sidney not to drive them so.'

'I don't have the impression that he is to do with stables,' Cecily said, wondering why that was so. Something to do with the way the boy walked, very upright, putting his bare feet down toes out, like a dancer. Stable boys hunched their shoulders to look like jockeys, and turned their feet in. And then she thought, 'But a *dancer*! How ridiculous I am.'

'Well, he's very small. Perhaps. And independent. Not anxious to please, one might say, only in as far as he was so hungry he was being polite enough to get some dinner. When I get back, you see, he might be gone.'

Anne gave her the slightly doubtful glance Cecily was accustomed to, that suggested she was a little odd. In the old artistic circle in London in which she had grown up it had been quite the norm to be unconventional in ways and dress and speech, in fact *de rigueur* if one wished for success, but in Newmarket such unconventionality as she had been unable to slough off was not admired. Horsey people were very direct and not given to subtlety in their manners and conversation. Women were expected to be brave thrusters in the hunting field and good breeders of children, in both of which departments she was a failure. Anne was a splendid example of the desirable wife.

Cecily enquired after the children, admired some new cut-glass decanters presented by a grateful owner, deplored the new cook's way with poultry and departed in half an hour with a bundle of suitable clothes, worn but serviceable, which she hoped would prove the right size.

The boy, as she had guessed, was still in the kitchen. Cecily deposited the clothes on the table and departed rapidly, before anyone could require a decision from her. There was half an hour before lunch. Alice was laying the table in the dining-room; Philip was working in his studio; Laura had disappeared again (to Harry perhaps, Cecily thought, with the familiar gut-twist of despairing jealousy). She went through the light, sun-washed drawing-room and through the double glass doors into the conservatory. She loved her conservatory and went to it for comfort, finding consolation in the damp, warm smells that came from the rows of banked pots, the chipped terracotta housing monstrous lilies and cyclamen and freesias. From huge urns sprang arches of jasmine and passion-flower to span the roof; velvet auriculas showed strange violet and plum-grey faces from any small space left over; even the mosaic floor was sprouting clumps of moss and a shaft or two of harebell in its cracks under the benches where the moisture dripped from the pots in the evenings. She stood motionless, breathing the strong, humid scents of her flowers, watching how the sun struck down through the burgeoning of the sprays that fingered the glass panes as if they would escape. The sky was very clear and almost transparent, not a cloud in sight, yet it was cold outside, the wind in the east. The thick heady air of the conservatory lapped her in its embrace, secured her from the pains that lay in wait outside, soothed her like a nurse's syrup. It was an illusion she cherished, that she was safe on her own territory, safe amongst her flowers and outside between the walls of the kitchen garden or the banks of her yew-hedges, that nobody save dull Percy would speak to her, that her thoughts could show in her eyes and no one would see, that she could talk out loud and no one would hear. She was herself, pleasing no one, finding endless solace in the eternal, rhythmic duties of the garden. The boy, she thought, if he stayed, could work in the garden, be set the perennial tasks of gravel-weeding, slug-picking, tying up, pinning down, bird-scaring, hoeing. No one would beat him, although he might die of boredom. Oh, the boy! She was worried by him, but not for any good reason she could put a name to. He had been ill-treated, yet his spirit was in perfect shape; he was in complete control. A puny slip of a child, he was in better control than herself.

She watered her flowers, and went in when the gong rang. Laura appeared from the direction of the kitchen and was dispatched after five minutes to see if her father had heard the gong. Cecily sat waiting behind the soup tureen, blank, patient. It was cold in the dining-room after the conservatory, in spite of the fire in the hearth. The flames leaped cheerfully in the scrupulously designed cast-iron confines of Mr Voysey's grate, yet Cecily could find no answering warmth, watching. What was there for her, she wondered? Even if Philip should die she could not go to Harry, her husband's brother, for it was against the law. She had always known the hopelessness of her case. It was not mere convention that held her back, strong though that was, but a legal brick wall through which there was no way. She was not particularly thinking of this, waiting to start the soup, but she was in her habitual state of cold suspension which was rooted in this legal impossibility. There were times when she wondered if, due to the perversity of her nature, she loved Harry because she knew she could not have him. All her life she had wanted what she could not have; in her girlhood she had chosen the impossible, and suffered for it. If now it was legally, if not socially, acceptable to go to Harry and leave Philip, how could she tell whether she would do it or not? Would Harry want it, with his livelihood depending, as it was, on the goodwill of influential people who did not easily condone scandal? She was aware of the questions, but found it impossible to predict the answers. She did not know herself well enough, let alone Harry. In fact, how well did one ever know anyone else, even a lover or a husband? Sometimes she thought she knew nothing, not her men nor her child nor her servants, only her flowers. She had no confidence. But other people did not know this. They merely said she was hard to know, and cold. Yes, she was cold. That part was true.

'Sorry, my dear.'

Philip came to his place, pulled out his carved oak chair (which was nothing like the mahogany and plush dining-room chairs of the average smart house, but an ascetic, mediaevally-inspired piece of uncompromising angularity, although moderately comfortable) and shook open his napkin.

He was, like his designs, angular, delicate and modish. He sniffed at the soup fastidiously.

'Dill?'

'Yes, with celery. They combine well.'

Laura picked up her spoon. 'Uncle Harry says that when Fred Archer was seventeen he rode in the Cesarewitch without a shirt to get down to weight. He came second. And it was a bitterly cold day.'

'Really?'

'He weighed six stone one.'

'Poor lad. I bet he wishes he could make six stone one these days.'

'He never had any dinner. Just dry toast. And he takes some stuff that—'

'Laura dear, I would prefer not to discuss Mr Archer's rather crude methods of wasting over the luncheon table, if you please. The whole of Newmarket knows what he has to suffer. Enough is enough.'

'He's coming on Friday.'

'So I understand.'

'I have to go to London on Friday,' Philip said. 'I shall miss the great occasion—Mr Archer riding up our lane. Are you putting flags out, Laura?'

Laura scorned to reply to this insulting jocularity, and her mother said, 'That boy you brought in this morning, Philip— what am I supposed to do with him?'

'He weighs nothing. Give him to Harry.'

'I don't think Harry is in need of a boy at the moment.'

'Well, someone must want a boy. Or send him on now that he's fed. He's fit, isn't he?'

'Would you speak with him?'

'No, dammit, Cecily, I'm too busy. Surely you can sort him out?'

'Keep him, mother please!' Laura said. 'He can live here. You can adopt him.'

'Laura, think before you say such things! You speak so wildly sometimes, I despair of you. The sooner we find a governess to occupy you the better.'

'Have you done anything about finding one?' Philip asked.

'Not yet.'

'But you said, months ago—'

'I know I said. But I dread interviewing young women, you know how I hate it. I keep putting it off.'

'You must do it.'

'Perhaps you could see them?'

'It's hardly my duty, surely? I will see any that you feel are suitable—how about that? If you are doubtful, we can decide together. But the preliminary sorting—that you must do.'

'*I* will do it,' Laura said.

'You will *not*,' her mother said.

'It will be convenient to have somebody during the holidays when Gervase is here. She can give him lessons too. I think he gets very bored.'

'I think he would rather be bored than have lessons. I would.'

'What you want, Laura, doesn't come into it.'

Laura kicked the table leg. I want Fred Archer to marry me, she thought. But what I want doesn't come into it. I want Fred Archer. I don't want a governess. I want Tiger to stay. I hate Gervase.

'Don't scowl, Laura,' her father said.

'What about Tiger then,' she parried. 'You haven't said.'

'Who is Tiger?'

'The boy you brought home.'

'Oh, for heaven's sake! Send him on his way. I only wanted to see that he didn't starve.'

'He's very small and young, Philip, and has been so ill-treated. It seems callous.'

'It's happening all the time, my dear. We can hardly employ him, can we? How can we know if he's honest? It's not a risk I care to take.'

'Perhaps outside. Percy might use him.'

'If he can, I wouldn't put any objection. See how it goes for a few days. Just for his keep.'

Laura felt her optimism taking hold. The prospects were clearing. If she knew her mother, the governess would be a long time coming. And Tiger, out in the garden . . . a situation full of possibilities.

'Shall I tell them after lunch? Shall I tell Percy?'

'Yes, you may, Laura.' Cecily was relieved.

'I have to finish the decorated panels for the piano at Hulmes before Thursday,' Philip said. 'Time is running very short.'

'I shall see you are not disturbed.'

Laura thought her parents made conversation as if they did not know each other very well.

2

'Good morning, Fred.'

'Good morning, sir, Miss Laura.' He touched his cap to her as if she were the Queen, and dismounted from his hack. Laura, quite unable to speak, took the reins from him, gazing upon the revered features with unblinking eyes.

'A new groom, sir?' Fred smiled, recognizing Laura's condition. 'Is she riding out with us this morning?'

'Yes, she's taking a lad's place for us. She's a fair enough rider for a girl. Learnt it all from me, of course.' Harry grinned in his easy, cheerful way. 'We'll waste no time, eh? Kimbo is ready for you. The lad will bring him.'

Laura, taking the hack to a spare box, was saying to herself, 'It's true! He is here, talking to me, I am going to be with him for the next two hours.' Savour every minute, lose nothing, drink him in, store him up . . . I do love you, Fred Archer! 'Lucky, *lucky* Scotch Pearl!' The well-used hack, sinewy and hard, started tearing at its hay the moment she took the bridle off. She hurried, to get back to Mr Archer's side, going to her horse which was being held by one of the lads. He gave her a bunk up and a wink.

'Mind you don't overtake him, chasin' him so hard.'

Laura gave the lad what she hoped was a superior look and hustled her horse neatly on the tail of her uncle's hack which was leading the string, with Fred at its side. Laura was on a suitably staid seven-year-old named Your Honour, but Fred was riding a very difficult horse called Kimbo, who was considered to be good enough to win all the big handicaps 'if he had a mind to it'. 'Save the old devil hasn't,' Uncle Harry said, and had failed so far to find a jockey to persuade him to change it.

It was awful to think that this wonderful morning, the morning she had ringed on the kitchen calendar with red, blue and yellow stars, was now in the very process of passing. In less than two hours it would be a memory. Laura was aware that she had to absorb every minute of it with great concentration. 'Live for the moment,' as Uncle Harry had advised her mother one very peculiar day in the kitchen garden when Laura had been lying behind a cucumber frame racing a pair of snails. Uncle Harry had had his arms round her mother as if comforting her over something, but what the disaster was Laura had never found out. She just remembered what he had said, and the cheering effect it had had on her mother. She had thought of it since then as very sensible advice, and used it as her motto. She had written it in a few autograph books, with violets round it.

They rode down the lanes to the edge of the town, and up on to the gallops. It was a sunny morning but cold, the wind still in the east and the ground very hard and dry. With the first Spring Meeting starting in three days' time and all the gentry due to flock in with high expectations, the place had a quite definite air of stirring itself for the excitement, of stocking up the cellars and dusting down the pavements. Not much more than a village, Newmarket was proud of regularly receiving the Prince of Wales and being on familiar terms with any amount of Dukes and Lordships; it accepted its foreign princes, outlandish Americans and fussing Frenchmen as part of the normal routine, anxious to please but quite confident of doing so. Having lived in the place all her life, Laura could not credit the dullness of all other comparable towns which boasted no calendar of excitement. She loved the contrast: the long, sleepy winter with slow strings of walking horses with dull coats and cold, hunched boys on top, and then the coming of spring and the quickening of the pulses, the extra trains and the streams of visitors coming down from the station, the carriers' carts converging, the fillies bucking on the gallops and the visiting mares unloading in the sidings, the shop-windows full of goodies. Her mother and father seemed not to care, even saying at times that it was a nuisance, all the visitors clogging up the high street, but to Laura it was a most desirable way of life, the recurring influx. Uncle Harry, for all his disappointments, never failed to get excited about the new season. He was excited now about the meeting next week and quizzing Archer about the likely winners.

'The Two Thousand's very open. The form is altogether. Do you fancy your chances on Charibert? He's gone out to twenty-to-one which is a long price for anything you're riding—on account of his roaring, no doubt. But there's nothing outstanding.'

'He'll get the mile all right,' Archer said. 'Roarer or no. This weather suits him. But you're right, it's very open.'

The name Charibert reminded Laura of the conversation at the kitchen table, the reported gabblings of Tiger in the haystack. Is that what he had been saying? Is that why it had sounded familiar, because it was a horse she had heard of?

'Do you know Charibert?' she asked the boy who rode beside her.

'It's a colt of Lord Falmouth's,' he said.

Laura decided to put the thought aside for future consideration, not wanting to waste her concentration on anything but Fred. He was about to plumb the workings of Kimbo's idiosyncratic brain, the reason for his visit. Kimbo was regarded at home as a jockey's nightmare, being a horse that pulled fiercely to get in front and, once there, stopped trying. Not an uncommon trick, as Uncle Harry remarked, but he had found no one yet who could control the horse sufficiently to time his arriving at the front at the exact spot where the winning-post was waiting.

'I am the winning-post,' Harry said, pulling his hack to a standstill. 'I want four of you to go with Mr Archer'—he flicked his whip at the four selected—'and regard it as a proper trial.'

'Uncle Harry,' Laura whispered. '*Please!*'

He looked at her, understanding, laughing. She was riding astride like a boy, and looked like a boy, her hair scraped back in a workaday pigtail. He knew her time was limited: she was ripe for the governess, stays and knuckling under; she would have to stop her desires shining out of her eyes; turn inward, go under, like her mother. He ached for her, even while he was laughing. She would never have the chance again to ride knee to knee with Fred Archer. He would not deny it her.

'I can?'

'Yes.'

Her horse took off after the others like a rocket, spurred by her passion. Harry knew he should not allow it, knew it was dangerous, ridiculous, but would not resist her. He knew what it was like to want, and the fact that she was only a child made it no different; they were all in the same boat, he and Laura and Laura's mother, and if the child could have her way now, why not? Cecily, however much she might disapprove, was bound to understand his reasoning. Your Honour was an easy horse, and would not run away with her. With such zeal aboard, he might even keep up with Kimbo.

The little bunch of horses hack-cantered and trotted for almost a mile, then turned into a walking line abreast, facing back the way they had come. Harry Keen was a small dot in the far distance, motionless. The bright April grass stretched before them and the horses, turned for home, were stirred up and wanting to go. Laura was frightened, breathless, holding her horse with all her strength.

'Are you all right, Miss Laura?' Fred asked, walking up beside her.

'Yes, yes!'

Kimbo, the strongest puller in Newmarket, was walking like a cat, nose tucked in, yet there was no pressure on his mouth.

'All right to go then?'

Laura had never done more than an exercise canter before, never raced. She knew she had only to sit there tucked in behind the four boys in front, for they were all agog to beat Fred Archer and boast about it over their pots of ale. But Fred was at her side, and the puller was going as kindly as Your Honour himself. Laura wanted to stay with him; she wanted the gallop to last for ever, her heel brushing Fred's boot, flecks of foam from Kimbo's mouth spotting her jacket. She turned her head and looked at Fred, and she could see how Kimbo was pitting himself against him, his eye white-rimmed and furious, could see how Fred held him, like a fisherman playing a shark, by strength, by willpower it seemed, and by humouring him for a stride or two, taking him up again, talking to him. Thin and bony with wasting, he had a steely determination that was a match for Kimbo. The horse's tail switched with fury, but he stayed behind. Stride by stride he matched Your Honour until Laura, glancing up, saw Uncle Harry on his hack only a hundred yards or so ahead. The horses in front were running on, not tiring. In alarm Laura looked back to Fred and saw the reins run out through his fingers. He flung himself forward, the long thin legs clamped down and Kimbo shot ahead as if from a standstill. The timing was perfect, the big horse surging past the others to pass Uncle Harry a head in front.

They all pulled up but Fred made Kimbo run on for another furlong. Laura circled to come back to Uncle Harry, trembling with excitement, not knowing whether to laugh or cry, too breathless to speak. Harry was pleased and called out to her to come up with him.

'You rode that well!'

'He won?'

'Oh, he's a marvel! It was perfection. No one's managed it before.'

He was full of excitement in finding his optimism in Archer's riding justified. Seeing him so exuberant, Laura wondered why her own father was such a dull man compared with his brother. Even when frightfully pleased, he only grunted and said, 'By Jove, how nice.' But Uncle Harry, riding to meet Kimbo coming back, was generous in his praise and made no conventional cover of his satisfaction.

'I always knew, if he could be held up—but you're the only one, Fred! We'll have to work it that you get the ride—if you let me know your commitments. If you'll take it, that is?'

'If I'm free, I will ride him, yes.'

Fred, Laura could see, had not expected to fail. He was cool and relaxed, as if he had been out hacking, very neat in his sober grey coat and tidy neckcloth; the strength he must have exerted on Kimbo was not apparent in his quiet appearance. Nobody knew how he did it on dry toast and sips of champagne. Laura rode back beside him, keeping Your Honour up with Kimbo, occasionally touching the sacred leg beside her with her own. He talked racing with Uncle Harry. He never talked about anything else. They said he wasn't interested in girls.

When they got back she fetched his hack for him and held it while he mounted.

'You make a good lad,' he said, smiling. He thanked her, touched his cap to her again, and rode away.

'There's no one can get a horse up like he can, he's a miracle, yet he never brags, he's always so quiet.' Harry was content to join Laura in the admiration stakes, pleased with the day's work.

'When he's racing, you said—'

'Ah, yes, when he's racing that's another matter. He swears something terrible and he can be as rough as any of 'em. It's a dangerous game when they rough each other up, and they all know, for all he's so quiet, he's got more nerve than the lot of them put together. He hates to lose, you know. He'll show his temper then and no mistake. But all other times, he's a real gentleman.'

'And his brother—'

'Yes, his eldest brother—that's William, not young Charley—was killed last year at Cheltenham, in a fall, and Fred was very cut up about it . . . But that's how it is. Now, Laura, be careful what you say at home. Don't say I allowed you that gallop. It won't help.'

'No.'

'I will send a letter to Kimbo's owner and tell him the good news. We might have a few more winners if Archer was free to ride 'em. No wonder Lord Falmouth gives him the credit, eh? Ah well, we'll see how it goes.'

He was so pleased to have discovered Kimbo's potential that Laura could not help comparing his position with that of Mathew Dawson, the big trainer who Fred rode for, whose owners were Lord Falmouth, the Duke of Portland and other enormously rich men. The stables at Heath House were as impressive as the ducal owners themselves, and the house was trim and sparkling to the last door-knob, new, severe and substantial. But Thorn's was not in the same league as the big yards. It still revealed its rustic origins in half-timbering and thatch and tended to get buried in wild honeysuckle that intruded from the coppice behind it; its stables were converted from old barns, tarred outside and whitewashed within. The yard was a plain square with a walnut tree in the middle. The fodder sheds backed on to the lane, and the house was sideways on, commanding the square—if such a crooked, homely building could be said to command anything. Laura could see very well that, pretty as it was, it wasn't impressive like Heath House or Bedford Lodge, not even as impressive as Dry Meadows across the lane. Harry Keen's owners were mostly farmers and rich tradespeople; there wasn't a title amongst them. They were loyal and got good value, but their horses were only as good as they could afford. They won small races. Harry worked hard and was capable and knowledgeable, but luck had not come his way.

'You need luck, racing.' Everyone said that, even Fred Archer.

Seeing Laura's brooding joy and the look on her face for Fred that he had seen in her mother's for himself, Harry felt a sudden thrust of anguish for the luck that eluded him in other fields than racing. Laura had this effect on him quite often; sometimes he wondered who exactly he loved in this incestuous relationship, for he could look upon Laura with the same feeling as he was able to express on rare occasions to her mother; it seemed at times that he was looking into the same eyes, with the same heart showing, the same frustrations pulsing. He loved Laura's company for its affinity with Cecily's, or so he thought. Just occasionally, as now, he was frightened looking on her, wondering where they were all going. Cooled by the thought, he said to her gently, 'Go along, chicken. Don't let it show too much.'

'No, they get cross,' she said, very prosaic.

He laughed at that, thinking about people in glass houses throwing stones. God almighty, what a tangle it all was! If he hadn't got his work to absorb most of his energies, what sort of a hell would he be living in? He had thought many times about moving away, but he could not move from Newmarket because of his livelihood. Philip maundered on about moving, but doted too much on his bricks and mortar. The situation was deadlock. He was into his thirties now and would like to have married, but there was no way he could look at another woman while Cecily remained to stir his senses at every meeting and Laura reminded him of her every day between. He had come to accept the hopelessness of his situation and lived now for small comforts, the escorting of Cecily, for example, to the Guineas meeting, merely to have her at his side for an afternoon. The greater comforts came his way rarely, and when they did the ensuing sense of loss and despair was so great that he found it hard to conceal. The lads missed little, nor Martha, not to mention Albert and the gang across the road. The circumspection required for the illicit affair was almost impossible to obtain and the feelings of fear and guilt inevitably transcended the fleeting joy. It all seemed to him biblical: to sin, to be punished by remorse. In church on Sunday, in the same pew with Cecily and Philip, the lads and the Dry Meadows servants lined up behind, he felt as if the full weight of the admonitions were directed straight at him, felt his shoulders bowing beneath the load. And yet, in all honesty, his feelings were natural and pure enough; he did not understand why it was as bad as the law and the Church would have it. He felt there could well be more sin in condoned marriage: in Philip drying up the passionate core in Cecily with his pedantic obsession for the tiny details of life, not noticing truly what life was all about. She had frozen beside him, perished by lack of mental nourishment. That was waste, and waste was truly a sin in Harry's eyes. Philip, never having fully comprehended Cecily's way of thinking, had long ago stopped searching for it, and used her as a mere housekeeper and hot-water bottle. There was sin if you like, Harry thought gloomily.

They made a handsome couple in church, this ill-matched pair, and the front of perfect harmony was flawless. In fact it was an actual harmony born of mutual boredom in the other. Philip had always been a complacent, self-centred, small-minded character to Harry's way of thinking, with an inflated opinion of his own worth, which conceit had taken him into the London art circles where his progress into unreality had been encouraged. To spend life as he did worrying about the golden mean of an engraved design on a silver meatdish was another example of Philip's complete confusion about life's priorities. He really was an in-credible ass, Harry had decided many years ago . . . yet in church he looked intelligent and eminently worthy, blond and polished, his skin clear and pink, the picture of a perfect husband. Beside him, even in his Sunday suit, Harry was aware that he cut a much less handsome figure, being so much smaller and less impressive, not so clean and sweet-smelling, less blond and less beautiful. But he could get six horses done while Philip would still be looking for a bucket. It had always been like that, since they were small. And the congregation would kneel and the familiar words: 'Have mercy upon us miserable offenders . . . we have done those things which we ought not to have done . . .' would fall over his bowed head bringing with them an unfailing sense of injustice. Yes, indeed, one needed luck in this life, not only with race-horses.

*   *   *

Laura found Tiger weeding the herbaceous border by the terrace at the back of the house. She sat on the low stone wall and watched him for a bit, but he did not stop or speak to her, although aware of her presence. He was very agile and supple in his movements and weeded for quite long periods without bending his knees at all, which struck Laura as odd. She had been going to engage him in conversation but something about him discouraged her. Although he was so small and doing a menial task, he had, somehow, nothing of an inferior presence, rather the opposite, Laura thought, as if he were used to better things. What, she wondered? Curiosity overcame her doubts.

'Are you going to stay?'

He looked at her sideways. 'For a while,' he said. 'If I suit.'

He seemed to be suiting very well, weeding with more diligence than old Percy had ever shown.

Laura asked, 'What's your name?'

'You said Tiger.'

'Where do you come from?'

He shrugged. 'Cambridge way. North.'

'Cambridge is west.'

'Well, that way. Farther.'

'Why did you run away?'

'I'm not saying.'

'Did you work?'

'Yes.'

'What at? What did you do?'

He shook his head, refusing to satisfy her.

'Gardening?'

'No.'

'On a farm?'

'No.' He straightened up and looked at her directly. 'You will never guess what I did, and I will never tell you who I am, so it's no good you asking. I will never tell anyone, else what is the good of running away? If I tell, everyone will know, and I'll be searched out. Your mother didn't ask, nor Percy, so why do you have to be so nosy?'

Laura was offended. 'You shouldn't talk to me like that.'

'I wouldn't if you were more sensible.'

He bent down and carried on weeding. What he had said was

obviously logical, Laura could see, but it did not satisfy her curiosity. It enflamed it.

'They want you back?'

'Of course they do.'

'Why, if they beat you? They don't seem to like you.'

'I am valuable to them.'

'How?' The amount of work he could do was surely not *valuable*, yet he seemed to be perfectly in earnest. He did not reply, tightening his lips in irritation. Laura glared at him, conscious of the power of his argument, but unable to take her mind away from the mystery. She constrained herself from asking another question while he extracted two dandelion plants with a small fork and threw them in the wheelbarrow and then, with a sudden flash of inspiration, said, 'Who is Charibert?'

'Charibert?' He was obviously shaken by this change of tack, shocked, Laura would have said. She was pleased with the reaction.

'You said it in your sleep. Charibert.'

He went on weeding assiduously, angrily.

'Who heard me then? I sleep alone.'

'My father, when he found you. In the haystack. You kept saying "Charibert". He said you said "Chari*bird*" but I think it must have been "Chari*bert*". He says it doesn't mean anything. But it does, doesn't it?'

He shook his head.

'You're lying,' Laura said.

He did not deny this, but countered with, 'You are the nosiest girl I've ever met. Why don't you go away?'

'I live here. I can go where I like.'

'You are very boring.'

'I'm not. It's just that you don't like what I say.'

'It's the same thing, isn't it?'

Laura supposed he might be right, but did not admit it. She was a little cast down by the interview, finding the boy so prickly and self-opinionated, and dissatisfied by the mysteries. She told Uncle Harry about the boy saying Charibert in his sleep, and suggested that perhaps the boy had been sent to do the horse a mischief, and it was on his mind.

'Dope him, you mean?' Uncle Harry laughed. 'He's not worth

the trouble! No one's betting on him, on account of he's gone in his wind. I was surprised to hear Fred so optimistic. No, it can't be that.'

'He's all mysteries. He won't tell me anything.'

'No. He's afraid he might be sent back to where he came from, I daresay. Someone must be looking for him. Let sleeping dogs lie, Laura. If he gets tired of gardening I'll give him a trial over here. He can't weigh more than five stone, by the look of him. Can he ride, do you know?'

'I'll ask him. I don't see why that should be a secret.'

'I could do with a real lightweight.'

Tiger said he could ride, without elaboration. Laura did not say why she asked, better pleased to have him a gardener, where she could work out her relationship. He fascinated her. She did not want him to go away. He worked a very long day, spoke little, did not complain, ate his meals with Percy and slept on a bench in the tool-shed. What did he think about, Laura wondered? He was extraordinarily self-contained, not like a child at all. Yet he was nervous of being discovered. He said to Laura, 'If anyone comes enquiring, you will not say I'm here?'

'Who will come?'

'My father, if he gets word.'

'Because you are *valuable*?'

'Yes.'

Laura could not fathom it at all. He would not answer her questions.

'I only wanted to say that to you. I don't want to tell you anything else, so why do you keep asking?' Her questions made him angry.

'I would like to be friends, but there is nowhere to start. It's not just being nosy.'

There were no clues. Even his clothes now were somebody else's. He had fitted into the household and made himself scarcely discernible by his way of working obediently, provoking no rebuke, saying nothing and keeping mostly out of sight. Laura knew that her own mother and father had forgotten him entirely, and in the kitchen the extra meal, collected by Percy, was the only indication of his presence. Laura guessed that this chameleon act was his way of staying hidden and unsuspected; he was very afraid of being found out. She could see it in his face; in the fact that he asked her not to reveal his whereabouts.

'I am going to the races on Wednesday,' she said. 'Uncle Harry is taking me. Me and my mother.'

This obviously interested Tiger.

'Do you bet?' he asked.

'Only if Uncle Harry gives me some money.'

'Will he?'

'He usually gives me a shilling or two.'

'Is that all?'

'Yes. He puts more on, lots more, but my mother thinks it's wicked.'

Tiger laughed. 'If your uncle gives you some money, and I give you a tip, will you share the winnings with me?'

Laura considered.

'Are your tips so good?'

'If you promise, I will give you a winner. And you can keep half.'

'All right. I promise.'

'Then put it on Charibert.'

'Charibert! There, I knew! The one you were talking about! Fred Archer is riding him, so I would have chosen him anyway.'

'But you promised to share!'

'All right. I will put a shilling on for you alone. He's at twenty to one, you know, nowhere near favourite. If he wins, it's a lot of money.'

'Good. You should put more on. I would if I had it.'

'How can you be sure?'

He did not answer. 'Don't tell anybody. And don't forget. You will be glad afterwards.'

Laura decided to take her own money out of her moneybox, in case Harry omitted to give her any. She would hate to lower herself in Tiger's estimation by not putting his bet on for him. But she would not say anything about it. As he suggested, some things were better kept private.

It rained in the night. Philip took the gig early to catch the London train. Laura heard the scrunch of hooves on the gravel, and Percy's discreet knock at the front door to say that he was ready, then the slam of the door and the hooves departing. She stretched happily under the sheets, considering the nice day ahead, and Alice brought her hot water in and told her that Albert was betting on Cadogan, but she had told him to put sixpence on Rayon d'Or for herself, seeing as she got no chance to go down to town and put it on for herself. In the bedroom opposite, Cecily could lie in her bed and see Harry's window across the lane without shifting her head on the pillow. She would not have the curtains closed, so that she could lie at night and see his lamp shining on the window-sill. He knew she watched it. When he put it out, they said goodnight to each other, willing it across the dark lane. Even when Philip made love to her she watched for the light. Now, with Philip departed, she lay and listened to Alice fumbling at her door-knob and thought, 'Suppose I say to Alice, go across the road and ask Mr Keen to come here, to my room.' There was nothing to stop her . . . He would come, and walk in through the door and lock it behind him. He smelled of horses. She wanted to see him undressed, lithe and white and hard, not pink and soft like Philip. She wanted him in her bed here, where he had never been and never would come, in her pale blue and white room with its soft carpet patterned with peacocks' eyes. Her bed, Philip's bed (for he designed it) had a mediaeval canopy and curtains of white wool embroidered by the Morris company with pink and jade rushes. She wanted Harry to lie in it pressed close to her, a little heathen intruder in Philip's precious setting, laughing and mocking. He did not care, Cecily thought, as much as she did, although he said he did. He was occupied with his feed bills and his recalcitrant owners, and who to enter for what, and probably slept soundly across the lane from the moment his head touched the pillow until it left it. Not, like her, awake and watching, hearing the barn owl in the small hours. Alice knocked and came in, but Cecily did not ask her.

At twelve thirty Harry called at the door, driving his hack Jester to the dog-cart. Laura was excited and found it hard to stand still; Cecily felt the same, but stood calmly, her hands folded on the handle of her parasol, while Harry pulled up exactly by the doorstep. He grinned down at her and she saw that he, too, was like a boy out of school.

'I've no horses running today,' he said. 'We're just out to enjoy ourselves.'

They climbed up, having to sit close, thigh to thigh, and the dog-cart rocked over the wagon ruts down the lane and came to the road and the long slope down to the town. The big paddocks were full of mares and foals, the hedges flaring with blossom, pungent after the night's rain.

'It's a fine day for it, better than yesterday, with the turf softened at last.'

'Did you go yesterday?' Laura asked.

'Yes. Fred had three winners and a second. He had to get down to eight stone four to ride Pardon, which is tough when you think he was at eight stone ten when he rode Kimbo on Friday. But I suppose he's used to it by now—and he won, which is all he cares about after all.'

'He's not going to win today, I understand,' Cecily said. 'Albert tells me nobody's on Charibert. He told me to put my money on Cadogan, so I might risk a shilling.'

'A shilling! I thought sixpence was your limit?'

'I haven't Philip's restraining presence at my side.'

It was in the thoughts of all three of them that it was far more fun without Philip, although no one was disloyal enough to say so. Laura had noticed that her mother became a different person in the presence of Uncle Harry, far more animated and lively, childish even, and she supposed it was because Harry was much more fun than her father, who tended to pomposity on public occasions. He pontificated on the rails, and liked to meet the right people; he looked out for them. But Harry only met what Laura presumed were the wrong people, and enjoyed himself thoroughly, even when he lost all his money. Philip got annoyed when his cautious bets did not come up. She decided, even so, to say nothing about Tiger's shilling. She was sure now that he was quite wrong to have chosen Charibert.

There was a huge traffic jam in the High Street, everyone streaming out to the Heath, the locals joined by crowds pouring down from the station. Harry coaxed Jester through and got on the tail of a very smart drag thronged with elegant young men which was swathing a successful passage with a good deal of horn-blowing and jocularity.

'We're all right now,' he decided. 'We'll keep tucked in behind and get a straight run down to the stands.'

Laura rather wished she was riding; it was far more fun, but somewhat dangerous when the undergraduates came over from Cambridge and tore about on hired hacks without any respect for those more sober than themselves. On a horse you could watch the start and follow down fast enough to get a good idea of the finish too, but on foot the start was fifteen minutes' brisk walk away. Other race-courses, she understood, were circular so that you saw the start and the finish from the same place, but Newmarket was not so accommodating. It had been designed that way, she understood, to discourage the riff-raff.

They parked Jester and got down to join the throng in the enclosure. Laura was only interested in seeing as much as possible of dear Fred; she loved to see him in his bright silks and immaculate breeches and boots, not the easy, polite Fred who spoke to her at Uncle Harry's, but the strung-up, aggressive racing Fred whom the apprentice jockeys were justifiably nervous of, who sat hunched and smouldering on his horse waiting for the start, gaunt with starvation. She skipped with the joy of anticipation, clutching Tiger's shilling.

She knew every corner of the stands and enclosures and the Birdcage and the best places to see the horses, the jockeys coming out, the winners coming in. Uncle Harry placed her bets for her—'What, on *Charibert*? That's pure devotion, Laura, not sense! But never mind, your money . . . he's gone out to twenty-five to one'—and then she was free to roam and wriggle into the best places, seeking out Charibert where his boy was guarding him, having ridden him over, and admiring Mr Dawson's other runners, Oxonian, Lord Clive and Ringleader, all of which Fred was to ride. Oxonian went out first for a two-horse match, duly won and was quickly auctioned for two hundred and forty-five guineas. The crowds were pressing in for the big race and Laura, small for her thirteen years, could not see over or through. She caught a glimpse of Uncle Harry talking to Mr Jennings, fought her way to him, and asked if she could take Jester down to the start.

'Why, yes, my dear, if that's what you want. But why not come with us into the stands?'

'I shall see more at the start.'

Closer to, she meant, the expression on his face, the impatience in his eyes, his fingers flexed on the reins—not just the passing blur of bunched horses at the finish and a losing struggle to get to the unsaddling enclosure in time.

'Are you sure Jester is safe, Harry?' her mother asked.

'Yes, my dear Cecily, his racing days are long over, and the excitement leaves him unmoved. Laura will be quite safe.' He was laughing and Laura was surprised by her mother's face, usually abstracted with a pucker between the eyebrows, smoothed out in a most uncharacteristic way, so that she looked like a girl, her eyes very bright. Perhaps they have had a glass of port, Laura thought.

'Can I go?'

'Yes.'

She ran. Jester had his face in a nosebag which Laura flung off. He was fastened to the rails with a piece of string; she tore at the knot, snapped it free, and climbed hastily up into the dog-cart. The grass was smooth and the horse cantered gleefully for her out across the Heath towards the gap in the Devil's Dyke, the high chalk rampart which scored the rolling grass. There was a gap in the dyke where the race-course passed through, but the Guineas mile started just clear of it, running straight as a die towards the finish, a heart-breaking mile unmarked for most of its way over the undulating sea of grass. A few clusters of people had congregated there, and the starter, Mr McGeorge, was trotting down on his hack. The race-horses were coming down one by one, little black Visconti, the huge, long-striding chestnut Rayon d'Or, tough little Strathearn, Cadogan and Discord, the favourite. And Charibert, gleaming gold, neat and keen, with the tall jockey in the magpie colours of Lord Falmouth, black and white with a red cap. He pulled up by Mr McGeorge and stood talking to him. Laura coaxed Jester close and watched from her elevated seat, her lips parted in a smile of bliss. She saw how the cold wind cleaved the silk shirt to Fred's ribs, saw how he smiled fleetingly with Mr McGeorge, scratched his nose, moved Charibert across to get the best berth. They lined up nervously, a flickering, ragged line under Mr McGeorge's eye. He raised his flag. Fred had Charibert held together like a steel spring, forelegs prancing; he did not take his eyes off the flag. Other jockeys jostled and cursed and two horses turned round as the flag fell, bumping their neighbours. The line faltered, several horses sprang away and others wheeled round.

'False start!'

The small crowd jeered.

'Come back! Come back!'

Laura's eyes never left Fred, from the perfect release of his chestnut colt into the gallop to his immediate return, scowling, thrusting back to the place he wanted. It was a nervous business, starting a race so important. Laura knew false starts were common, several at times, and the tension mounting, jockeys swearing, horses prancing and bumping. It was rough, and the faces taut and angry. A *business*, Uncle Harry said—pleasure for some . . . for me, Laura thought, holding her breath, watching the flag. As Charibert sprang forward again, her spirit went with him. She groaned, laughed. The bright colours sped away, the fantastic thrumming of hooves on the grass filling the sky. Jester tugged at his traces, prancing to go, and Laura let him follow, but the race-horses were already far away. She rocked in their wake, holding her precious visions of Fred in her mind, praying for his success. Hardly anyone had bet on Charibert; Uncle Harry had been quite right.

Jester cantered up the Rowley mile, enjoying himself, Laura holding the reins with one hand and the side of the cart with the other. The shouting came to her on the wind, the great roar for the winner, but she could decipher no name. People were running across the course. It wasn't the favourite, she could tell by the lack of cheering: an outsider. The roar had been one of amazement, followed by silence, then some ragged clapping. An outsider . . . Charibert perhaps? She leaned forward and flipped the reins at Jester and the cart flew.

'Ten to one the dog-cart!' somebody jeered.

Uncle Harry, having bet on Strathearn, met her guardedly.

'Yes, Charibert! You're in luck, Laura—about the only one who is. You and Mr Wells.'

Mr Wells was a notorious plunger who bet habitually on Fred, in thousands.

And Tiger, Laura thought, climbing down.

'Come, we'll collect your money.'

'I can go on my own.'

'You're too independent by far, Laura,' her mother said. 'Go with your uncle.'

Laura didn't want Uncle Harry to know about Tiger's shilling but now she could not hide it, collecting two sovereigns and a handful of shillings. She had to explain.

'He told me Charibert.'

'That's strange. What does he know about horses?'

'He seemed quite sure. He told me to put more on than just a shilling.'

Harry shrugged. 'Well, Fred was optimistic when I asked him on Friday. Fred and your Tiger . . . I listen to the wrong people, Laura. I shall know next time.'

But he looked puzzled.

Laura wrapped the money tightly in her handkerchief and stuffed it into the breast pocket of her jacket, excited more by the fact of Fred winning than by the money the win had earned her. She went to seek out his next ride and did not join her mother and uncle again until the races were over and Jester was released once more to head for home. Harry took him straight across the Heath and the Cambridge road and into a by-lane to avoid going through the congestion in the town. Laura sat in a dream, etching her fresh visual impressions of Fred Archer into her brain mechanism, so that they would be retained for duller days and long summer nights when she could weave her fantasies of loving in solitude. And Harry and Cecily fell silent, aware that the afternoon had been a facade for being together, and being together had prompted more urgent feelings altogether, hard to ignore in the sensuous gold flushing of the April evening. The damp scents of earthy, burgeoning life seemed to Cecily painfully tantalizing to her quivering sexual inclinations. Years of strict schooling bound her actions, but her senses were as wild, underneath, as they had been fifteen years ago. And fifteen years ago they had been satisfied. Now, she told herself sternly, she was old enough to know better, safely married, biologically fulfilled; her feelings were absurd. Her gloved fingers ground together in her lap. She dared not look at Harry. She looked at his hands on the reins, but could only think of the same hands caressing her. She looked away. The ditches were laced with cow parsley and clumps of yellow flags grew where the water drained out of the paddocks. She kept her head turned away. Nobody spoke.

The cart travelled steadily up the long straight lane. Laura saw nothing but the images in her mind, and Cecily the impossibility of what had happened to her. It was as if she had no will at all. She could not alter anything.

The boys were waiting for them in the yard, eager to know the results. Harry drew Jester to a halt and got down, turning to hand down Cecily and Laura.

'It was Charibert in a canter. Cadogan and Rayon d'Or.'

'Laura, run along and tell Peggy we are home. Tell her Harry will come to dinner tonight. You will, Harry?'

There was a sharpness in her appeal.

'Yes, my dear, of course.'

'Philip will be late. We shall be dull alone, Laura and I.'

It would make it worse, she knew. Dullness was less painful than what she was proposing, but she was too far gone. It is the weather, she thought. The smell of the first honeysuckle was sharp on the evening dew. The sun had gone and it was cold, but with the freshness of a summer night. She could put it down to the spring, her madness, or her cycle, or the star she was born under. Be sane, be dull; think about proper things: advertising for a governess for Laura. She kept putting it off, and Laura was bewitched by Fred Archer as she was bewitched by Harry, and needed her mind occupying, a firm hand. She walked home across the lane and up the gravelled drive. I can do nothing for myself, she thought, but I can help Laura by putting her to her lessons and taking her mind off Fred Archer. God, that a governess could do the same for her! She opened the front door with her key. The hall was cold. A vase of daffodils stood on a marble-topped table, barely open, quenched by Philip's austere architecture. A tall Gothic-shaped window dominated the hall, set halfway up the stairs where they turned back upon themselves, and through it the sky seemed to come in, a deep and luminous blue threaded with pale stars. It seemed to Cecily quite dreadful, filling her house with unfeeling, inhuman space, threatening her with galaxies of frozen stars like lost souls, like hers.

I am being stupid, she told herself, unpinning her hat. I shall draw the curtains and write an advertisement for a governess while waiting for dinner. If I cannot do it, Harry will help me later. He is less pompous than Philip. I shall engage a young and pretty governess and Philip may fall in love with her. I shall encourage him. And then my feelings for Harry will not seem so terrible. Philip will understand if he finds me out. He will become as vulnerable as I am. But she knew she was clutching at straws.

She called Alice to draw the hall curtains and light a fire in the grate. She did not want the chill to fall on Harry when he came. But Alice looked surprised and Cecily knew the cold was an aura of her own making. She went upstairs and changed for dinner and did up her hair afresh. In spite of her day in the sunshine her face was drawn and anxious. She thought she looked old, but her senses would not conform accordingly.

Strangely, when Harry came she felt much calmer.

'By Jove, it's warm in here,' he said, perfectly relaxed. He wore a neat dark suit with the heavy gold chain of his watch, donated by a grateful owner, adorning his midriff. He was delicately made, fine-boned and hard. He was quick; he made up his mind at once, where Philip considered for a week. He said what he thought. When he came, Cecily felt much better.

'I'll tell Peggy to serve the dinner. Are you hungry?'

'We're not waiting for Philip?'

'No. He said not to. He's going to be late.'

She tried to detect whether this news disturbed Harry, but he grinned and merely said, 'Good. I'm hungry.'

Laura came down and they went into the dining-room where the table was laid as usual, the candles lit, a fire burning. Albert and Alice brought the food in and Albert carved at the sideboard while Alice waited.

Harry laughed. 'I do like Philip's ways, Cecily! All this—and when I think how I hack away at a cold piece of mutton in the kitchen, and a couple of potatoes left in the oven by Martha—I have got into rough habits, I'm afraid, and Philip is just the opposite.'

'You should come more often. You always refuse.'

'Ah well, Philip disapproves at heart, although he doesn't show it. He's kind enough. But we bore each other, Cecily.'

'If you had a wife, she would cook you proper dinners,' Laura said sensibly. 'Why don't you get married?'

'Good advice. But I only meet married ladies these days, Laura. I have left it too late.'

His expression was guarded, his eyes fixed on the plate Albert was setting before him.

'Did you get the winner, Albert?'

'No, sir. Cadogan was second. I got my money back.'

'Better than I did then. It's Miss Laura who knows how to pick winners.'

'I picked the jockey.'

'Oh, Harry, don't set her off!' Cecily said. 'I was going to talk about governesses tonight. We really have to see about getting someone suitable.'

'If you get a nice, young, unmarried one, Uncle Harry could marry her.'

'Indeed?'

'I don't think I'd fancy a governess,' Harry said.

'Why not?'

'Always telling you things. How to behave. But very good for you, Laura. High time. I do agree with your mother.'

'She never had one!'

'And look at me, no learning at all. My father taught me to play the piano. That is all I can do. You are getting far too spoiled, Laura. We shall draft the advertisement tonight, after supper. Your uncle shall word it.'

'Wanted, tough trainer for temperamental filly. Must stand no nonsense. Unblemished and sound, looks of no importance.'

'It's not under "livestock", Harry. It's under "Education and Tuition".'

'Poor Laura!'

'Can't we wait until the autumn?'

'No. I did that last year. And then you said until the spring.'

'Life is passing you by, Laura.'

They ate, discussing the day's racing, laughing far more than usual, Laura noticed. When Alice brought in the lemon soufflé dessert, she said to Cecily, 'There's a message come, ma'am, from Mr Keen. Mr Parkinson's manservant brought it up from the station. Mr Keen gave it to Mr Parkinson in London, he said.'

'What does it say?'

'He won't be home until tomorrow night, ma'am. He's staying at Mr Morris's.'

'Thank you, Alice.'

Cecily served the dessert, not looking up. Harry took his and ate politely, in silence. After a few minutes Laura said, 'What's wrong?'

'What do you mean?'

Laura could not explain. She kept her eyes on her lemon soufflé, wondering if she was imagining things. But the silence had a strange, electric quality which disturbed her. It was unnatural, after the laughing and bantering over the first course. She did not understand what had happened to change the atmosphere. She wished she had not said anything. She looked at her mother but her mother was looking at her plate, very distant, very pale. Laura sighed.

'Are you tired?'

'No.'

'Do you want to sit with us in the music room? If you do, you can play your new piece to Uncle Harry.'

'I'd rather not.'

'In that case you must go to bed.'

'Yes.'

She would take out her pictures of Fred and lay them on her covers and leave her candles burning so that Fred could watch her through the summer night. The birds went on singing quite late in Thorn's copse, and she would not sleep. But she was happy enough. She kissed her mother and uncle and went upstairs.

When Alice brought the coffee to the music room Cecily said to her, 'You need not wait up, Alice, nor anyone else. Mr Keen will see himself out. You can leave the tray till morning.'

'Yes, ma'am. Thank you, ma'am.'

She left the room. Cecily picked up the coffee-pot and poured the coffee. Her hand was trembling. It had to be for Harry to say, not her. She had primed Alice not to come back, dismissed the servants. She might as well have locked the door, the way she had spoken to Alice. She had offered herself to Harry, and now dared not look at him.

He said, 'You didn't say what time?'

'What time?'

'What time Mr Keen will let himself out.'

'No. Mr Keen may choose.'

She looked up and saw him smiling. Her hand shook uncontrollably and she poured the coffee all over the table.

'Oh dear, what a fool I am!'

She did not know whether to laugh or cry, she was shaking so much. Harry pulled out a clean handkerchief and got down to mop the drips off the carpet, then remained kneeling on the floor at her feet. He reached out his arms and pulled her to him, burying his face in her lap. She bent down over him, putting her lips to his bare neck, his ears, his cheek, and saying his name over and over.

* * *

It was so difficult, being an adulteress in one's own home. If it had been warmer they would have gone out, down across the lawns over the wet grass, through the shrubberies and down to the stream. But it was impractical and, now the opportunity had arisen, Cecily had a longing to see Harry in her great embroidered bed, so that she could remember him there afterwards, coiled and ribby and sharp-kneed, in the hollow of the feather mattress. Harry would have preferred otherwise, but was too sexually aroused to waste time in argument. If she wished it, so be it. It was immaterial to him, but seemed harder on Philip than it might have been anywhere else. Climbing in, he felt a moment's apology to his brother; one was a decent fellow, after all, and would not have chosen one's own brother to deceive, damn it. But Cecily naked, her hair clouding her white torso loose to her delicious buttocks, was more than his brother had ever deserved. With a sense of wonder and not much of guilt, he went to her, a lithe but delicate lover such as Philip, well-meaning but unimaginative, had never had it in his power to be. Cecily, sharply aware of her thoughts in the same bed that very morning, responded with a sense of wonder, of astonishment and delight at what had come about that transcended mere passion: she felt she was conscious at two levels, wild with plain animal desire and yet above all inhabiting some great sphere of eternal wonder way over and above the body's threshings, which memory she was convinced would endure long after the physical gratification. She adored Harry's unaffected, fizzy love-making. With Philip it all had to be dredged up from deep layers of apathy and inconvenience; it hurt his bad knee, the covers fell off, her nightdress was an abomination to remove . . . the bed was too bloody soft. Cecily lay back and laughed. Harry was spent with his head across her breast, the dark hair flung out, damp and curling. Philip was going bald. She could not help laughing.

Then she remembered Albert in the room above, and stifled her laughter.

'He will think I am mad!'

'He will think you have a lover.'

'As if I would!'

'A lady like you.'

'It's not possible.'

'Well, only when Philip is away.'

'Oh, if only he was away more often!'

Which thought was idle now, but agony in the dawn, when Harry made love to her again and had to leave. It wasn't a joking matter then, holding on to his narrow, sinewy wrists as he dragged himself out of bed, fumbling for his clothes on the floor, thrown anyhow.

'What do you want, little idiot? For Alice to find me here?'

She sobbed, pressing her face into the pillow. He dared not kiss her again, knowing that he was already late; the servants would be stirring in ten minutes, and his own lads had to be kicked out of their beds on time. He was shivering, tensed up, wondering if he was mad to be taking such risks. Even so, he turned back, could not help himself, and she clung to him desperately. But there was nothing to say; it was worse. He knew he should have slipped out and gone while she slept. It was terrible to end it in such despair, but it was acting out the truth, and there was no answer to that.

He was shaken by his own feelings, padding softly down the stairs into the stark, high-arched hall. The embers in the grate were cold. He went through the drawing-room and out through the conservatory, unlocking the door and standing for a moment framed in the bright, scented cold of the April morning. The garden was drenched with dew, every leaf and blade glittering. The sun was coming up over the stream below the lawns, casting long, cold shadows before it where the blackbirds ran, dark against dark, into the tangle of the shrubberies. Harry, used to dawn starts, saw it afresh, as if new-born, and stood for a moment gathering composure. He had not reckoned to pay for such pleasure and delight with the anguish that seized him now; he had not known how deeply committed he was. It had helped, earlier, not to recognize it. He was not that sort of a man, he always thought, not a ladies' man, not given to emotion. But his feelings now were as stark as he had ever known, bewildering in their power. He found it hard to take in. He pulled the door to silently behind him, and leaned against the doorpost a moment, coming to terms.

At that moment the boy Laura called Tiger came round the corner of the house pushing a wheelbarrow. When he saw Harry he stopped. Harry straightened up, startled, but retained enough of his wits not to give himself away too badly. He walked towards him across the terrace, passed him with a brief nod of greeting, and took the path through the shrubbery which led out into the lane, avoiding the stableyard. The boy said nothing, but watched him go. Glancing back, Harry saw him watching.

It did nothing to calm his state of mind at all.

3

Laura found Tiger cutting off dead daffodils at the bottom of the lawn, and gave him his winnings. Tiger counted them out carefully.

'Twenty-five to one,' Laura said.

'That's good. If only I'd had a sovereign to put on!'

'You didn't *know* he was going to win.'

Tiger did not reply. He put the money down his sock, and went back to cutting daffodils.

'You're rich now. You can go on wherever you were going.'

'I'm quite happy here. I would like to work for your uncle.'

'He hasn't got room at the moment.' Laura did not want Tiger to move across the road. She wouldn't be able to talk to him over there as she could in the garden.

'I will ask him, all the same.'

'You can't!'

'Why not?'

Laura thought he couldn't possibly have the nerve but, looking at him thoughtfully, decided she was wrong. He had an inner strength, a confidence, that she found hard to understand.

'Aren't you afraid, on your own?'

'What of?'

'Of—of being on your own, without a home. Of starving. You are lucky to have this job. My parents took pity on you.'

'Yes, but it was only for a few days. I'm all right now.'

'Because we looked after you.'

'I've got money now.'

'Only because you were lucky. You can't always win it like that.'

'I can,' he said calmly.

'Don't be stupid. Do you really believe that?'

Tiger shrugged, impatient with Laura's questions, and said, 'Will you ask your uncle if I can work for him?'

'Ask him yourself.'

'I shall have to, if you won't.'

Laura, afraid she had been unkind, asked Uncle Harry later, when she went across to the yard. Uncle Harry seemed to be slightly short-tempered and Laura thought she had timed it badly, for the effect of her question on her uncle was unfortunate.

'I don't want him here, dammit. I'm not short of boys.'

Laura was amazed at his answer.

'You said—you asked me to ask him if he could ride!'

'Well, I've changed my mind, Laura, I'm sorry.'

'He asked me to ask you.'

'When? When did he ask you?'

'This morning.'

Her uncle was silent, obviously angry. Laura said no more about it, not understanding. Her mother was in a bad mood too, and composing advertisements for governesses.

'Capable, refined young woman as teacher companion to thirteen-year-old girl,' she wrote, but her thoughts were otherwise. She did not want another woman in the house, sensing her secret —seeing, even, as Alice could have seen last night if she had had the wit. She preferred her privacy, and a governess would not be like the other servants, bound up with their own gossip in the kitchen. She would be apart, and bored, and curious . . . who knew to what extent? Cecily wanted to write: 'Unattractive, half-blind woman, hard of hearing, as governess.' Then she remembered Harry's advertisement, and Harry's face across the dinner-table, amused, teasing, found herself smiling, yet knew she was close to tears. She pulled herself together, concentrated her mind on governesses. The woman would have to cope with Gervase too in the holidays, and Gervase was a strange boy, brooding and introverted, not a boy for galloping about the Heath with Harry or going off fishing with the village boys, but a boy unused to women, growing fast, a sex-starved boy, no doubt, in his public school domain, and in a year or two he might find too nubile a governess a dangerous distraction. Cecily would have preferred not to be responsible for Gervase, but Gervase seemed happy at Dry Meadows. He preferred it to being with his grandparents in

London, and seemed to have no desire at all to join his parents in India when his education was completed although he was not averse to being the Viceroy. He was no trouble, and Laura bore with his company without complaint, although she said he was 'no fun'. Poor Laura, thought Cecily, with a truly maternal surge of compassion: the child was short of fun. The governess must be young for Laura's sake, and capable of laughing. How to put that in the advertisement? She doodled with her pencil, her mind wandering in all directions.

Eventually she wrote, 'Capable, refined young woman of cheerful disposition as teacher companion to thirteen-year-old girl. Modern house in rural surroundings.'

She did not want to say about salary, and left it for Philip to finish.

At lunchtime Albert said to her, 'Mr Harry sent a message, ma'am, to say that the young lad you took in—the one Miss Laura calls Tiger, if you remember, ma'am—wants to work at his place and if you are agreeable he will arrange it. He said perhaps he could see you about it.'

'Yes, very well, Albert.' Cecily, having completely forgotten about Tiger, was pleased to have an excuse for seeing Harry again so soon. 'I will walk across after lunch.'

Laura said, 'But he said he wouldn't have him! I asked him this morning, because Tiger asked me to ask him, and Uncle Harry said, "I don't want him here, dammit." '

'Laura!'

'Uncle Harry said it.'

'Well, he must have changed his mind. I shall see.'

She walked across in the afternoon, eager to speak to him again. The yard was tidy and quiet, the boys having their time off until evening stables. She found Harry in the feed-shed, checking a new delivery.

'Albert sent a message.'

'About that boy Tiger? Yes. He saw me leave the house this morning, Cecily. He was on the terrace, starting work, when I left by the conservatory.'

'He's only a child. What would he make of it?'

'Cecily, boys of that age have very naughty minds. I fear the worst. Especially as he came over this morning and asked me for a job. Very bold, wouldn't you say?'

'Yes, I would.'

'He gave me a look, very direct. It was as near blackmail as can be, without actually putting it into words. Give me a job here, or else . . . I agreed.'

'He's no power to frighten you, surely? If he tries anything, you can take him to the authorities.'

'Yes, Cecily, I can. But I don't want him making trouble, and I intend to prevent it. Meanwhile, I just want you to know you've lost your weeding boy.'

'Quite honestly, Harry, he seems too good for weeding. He will be better here.'

Harry went out into the yard and Cecily followed him. She was surprised to see him agitated about something she could not take seriously. At times she could convince herself that Albert and Peggy and Alice must all be witless if they had not divined her secret, but it was impossible to be more circumspect than she was.

'Tiger is different,' Harry said, following her line of thought. 'There is something about him—'

'A child!'

'I have a hunch about him—I shall follow it up. He has his secrets too, which it might pay me to know.'

'Yes—a drunken father who beats him and a mother with a dozen others on her hands and no time—'

'No. That wouldn't give him the sort of confidence he possesses. There is more to it than that.'

Harry decided he needed to be distracted, and pinning down Tiger was a useful preoccupation. The night with Cecily, he decided in retrospect, had disturbed him more deeply than he had foreseen. He found himself spinning out his time talking to her, seeing her back across the lane, lingering in a way that he knew all the time was a public statement of his feelings and yet which he was quite unable to forgo. Knowing that he was being ridiculous helped nothing.

He went back to evening stables and watched Tiger's initiation into the routine tasks. The thin, composed—and yet, Harry guessed, highly nervous—boy reminded him of Fred Archer at the same age, saying little but the brain showing, even then. Archer had had to run the cruel gauntlet of becoming accepted— that was a part of apprentice life in all trades, and perhaps harder in racing stables than in most—and Tiger would have to do the same, although his stoicism would likely be a match for the lot of them. Harry had a head lad called Arthur who stood no nonsense. He used a horsewhip if he was displeased, but never on a horse. Gardening was an easier option by far.

When the horses were all feeding and the boys were free to go for their supper in the kitchen, Tiger came to him and said, hesitantly, 'Sir, I want to ask you if I—' He paused.

Harry waited. 'You'll get no favours.'

'I would like to sleep on my own. It's not a favour. I don't want a room. In the hay will do.'

'What's wrong with the dormitory?'

'Nothing, sir.'

'Why then?'

Tiger looked acutely embarrassed. 'I—I talk in my sleep, sir.'

Harry laughed. 'What about?'

'I—dream.'

'We all dream. What's so special about your dreams?'

Tiger was silent.

Harry, serious now, had a sudden suspicion that Tiger was admitting more than he would have wished, would go no farther, was desperate, in fact, to say no more than he had to. He stood with his head down, very tense, his hands clenched tightly. A faint recollection of a conversation in the Rutland Arms overheard, a few shreds of gossip, came to Harry's mind as he watched the boy. About dreams. He said nothing, turning over his suspicions, not giving anything away. Like Tiger. He felt an affinity with the boy, in spite of the situation between them. This was no ordinary lad applying for a job; there was more to Tiger than the boy wished to reveal.

'Very well, I've no objection. You can use the tack-room.'

The tension gave way to a smiling, childish relief. Tiger claimed to be fourteen, but when he smiled he looked no more than eleven; when he wanted something he had the presence of an adult.

'Thank you, sir.'

He ran. I shall find out, Harry thought; it will pay me. He had no wish to be beholden to a shrimp of a boy, however remarkable.

*　　*　　*

Laura lay in the shrubbery and watched the prospective governesses arrive one by one. Alice opened the door to them and
showed them into the hall where they waited, overlapping at
times, but never speaking to each other. Cecily, as pale and
miserable as the creatures themselves, received them in the morning room, their letters before her, and searched desperately for
conversation and the right questions to ask. Laura, after the first
four, went in round the back way to the kitchen and wept.

'They are awful!'

'There, my lamb, it's not the end of the world.'

Albert took a sugared almond from a bottle on the mantelpiece
and put it on the table before her.

'Where is she going to eat her meals, I'd like to know,' Peggy
said acidly. 'Not with us, I hope.'

'She will have her own room,' Albert said. 'It's usual.'

He was casual and comforting, as always. Laura played with
the gold tags on his lovely watch-chain, and he opened out a large
white handkerchief for her and held it under her nose.

'If—if Fred comes to Uncle Harry's—I shan't be able to go!'

'If Fred comes, Mr Harry will ask you across, I'm sure. How do
you know, your governess might like to meet Fred herself?'

'Have you *seen* them?' Laura asked.

'It's surprising what beats under those grey reach-me-downs,
Laura. I'm telling you. Many an old governess is in love with Mr
Archer.'

Peggy giggled. 'Go on with you, Albert. What nonsense! It's
because of Fred Miss Laura's getting a governess. They think her
head is full of dreams, instead of work.'

'We all need dreams,' Albert said.

'Fred is not a dream.'

'No, don't you fret, Laura. It will come out all right for you.
You're one of the lucky ones.'

'How do you know?'

'I can tell these things. Not like your mother and your Uncle
Harry.'

'Aren't they lucky?'

'Not really, no.'

'You mean, Uncle Harry's horses don't win many races? Only
little races.'

He smiled. 'That's right. He doesn't get what he wants.'

'It's time Mrs Keen had her cup of coffee. She'll be feeling like it, studying all those young women,' Peggy said. 'Set out the tray, Alice.'

Alice took the coffee to the morning room and put it down on Cecily's desk. Cecily, white and anxious, was fingering the credentials of her fifth young lady. A sweat of horror dewed her temples at having to ask such personal questions: how old are you? What is your background? Why did you leave your last post? She thought, looking at the bland, expressionless faces hiding anxiety better than she did herself, have you ever had a lover? Have you ever stifled an unbearable sexual desire beneath the tight lacing of your well-worn corset, disarrayed that rigorous coiffure in an hour of stark passion in a bay-fronted villa in . . .? She glanced at the letter.

'Surbiton?'

'Yes, madam. That is my home.'

Cecily was in despair, attempting to divine a nature behind the stark facades. She was not perceptive. Albert would have done it far better.

'Excuse me a moment.'

She fled. Thank goodness Philip was not in to see her. He was walking by the stream, working out a theme for a tapestry for a billiard room in a country house belonging to a manufacturer of ball bearings. She went to the kitchen, to Albert. She stood in the doorway, breathing hard, distraught. They all looked at her. Laura was sitting on the table, eating sugared almonds.

'I can't bear it,' Cecily said.

Albert stood up, heavily, consolingly.

'There now, ma'am. You can do it perfectly well. It's not so difficult.'

'How do I choose? I cannot tell.'

'The one waiting in the hall now, ma'am, the next one, will do perfectly well.'

'How do you know?'

'She is called Hilda Bell. I know her.'

'You *know* her?'

'When I was in London, her father played darts with me. She lost her last post when the family moved abroad, and I told her

(57)

father that you might be looking for somebody, and that it would be a good post for Miss Hilda.'

'She never said, in her letter—'

'No. I wouldn't have wished to presume, ma'am. If you prefer another, it's of no consequence.'

'No, Albert. If you say she is all right—a great relief to me, indeed. I shall see her straight away.'

Cecily's face smoothed out. She looked ashamed, smiled. 'I am so sorry. I don't know what came over me.'

She had to go away directly, afraid of seeing their smirks. But Albert's words were a blessing: if he said Hilda Bell, Hilda Bell it would be. The awful task would be completed. Philip would stop accusing her, and Hilda Bell would take Laura and her fantasies in hand. Fred Archer indeed! All her problems were solved in a stroke. Perhaps Albert could advise her about Harry . . .

Hilda Bell said she was twenty-three, but it was hard to tell. She had a round shiny face and a severe, scrubbed look, pale blue eyes under colourless brows, pale hair pulled tightly back into a governess's knot. No concessions, Cecily thought. A tight, nervous way of speaking. It is worse for her than it is for me, Cecily thought, worse by far, and softened, relaxed.

'When could you start?'

'At any time, ma'am.'

'On Monday? A month's trial?'

'Why, yes, ma'am.'

It was the wrong way to do it, Cecily supposed, but as she knew Hilda Bell was the one to choose, there was no point in prevaricating. She wanted to go back to her flowers and her shrubberies and her preoccupations, not be tangled with people she had no wish to know. Hilda Bell must keep out of her way, get on with her job of taming Laura, and leave her in peace. Some time later in the day, she realized she knew nothing about Hilda Bell at all.

'She looks like a bull terrier,' Laura said to Uncle Harry.

'Just what you need. Snapping at your heels, keep you up to the mark.'

'You won't fall in love with her. She's not pretty.'

'Thank you, Laura. I wasn't intending to.'

'May I come out with the string tomorrow, before she comes?

She's coming on Monday. I shan't get any chances again. I want to talk to Tiger.'

'I think we might allow it. But talking to Tiger—I don't know about that. Not in his working time.'

'I did when he was gardening. He can ride and talk at the same time?'

The other boys would take it out on him afterwards. Arthur would miss nothing, and find fault to show his disapproval of such favouritism. Laura knew nothing of the delicacies of working relationships. The boy with his uncommon background and strange reticence was having a hard enough time of it without Laura adding to his difficulties. His sleeping alone had set him apart, and his excuses were not accepted. Only by Harry.

'I know why you sleep apart. I know about your dreams. I know who you are, I know everything about you.'

He had made it his business to find out. He had ridden first to Cambridge, made enquiries, and followed the trail farther north in order to confirm his suspicions. It had kept him away longer than he had intended, but he now had as big a hold over Tiger as Tiger had over him. In politics it was called the balance of power. He had come home, summoned Tiger to his office, and locked the door behind him when he came.

'If you wish to continue working here, I want everything plain between us. I am not dismissing you. I am not telling anyone else what I know. But I am telling you that you have no secrets from me.'

Tiger's composure was destroyed by Harry's news. He stood appalled, his eyes glazing with tears.

'I don't want to go back.'

'I didn't say I would send you back.'

'I don't want anybody to know.'

'No. Your name, as far as I am concerned, is Tiger. I shall use no other. You have no father and mother that I know of, should anyone ask me. But the other thing, my lad—it's not exactly a secret, if people know who you are. I had heard of you, you see. These rumours get around. And when Laura told me about Charibert—it came to me then. I think Laura knows too, if she stops to think about it.'

'You can use it if you wish, if you will not tell anyone else.'

The boy spoke with a deep resignation. 'But if everyone knows —I cannot bear it again.'

'No. I have no wish to exploit you, as you have been exploited in the past. But dreaming winners, lad—you can't expect to be considered as other than a desirable property! They are looking for you everywhere.'

The news obviously petrified Tiger. Harry saw the nervous tremors flicker in his facial muscles. He held his hands tightly in front of him, clasped together in instinctive despair.

'I would rather die than go back. They never leave me alone.'

'Naturally. One would have to be unworldly to a degree not to take an interest in your—gift. In fact, if you stop to think of my position, young Tiger, it is difficult. What should I do? If I offer to keep you here, you will assume that I wish to use your prophecies to make myself some money. Is that true?'

'Yes, I think that of everybody.'

'Yet I think you desperately need protection.'

'Not if people don't know.'

'But you give yourself away! Laura knew about Charibert. You do not merely dream, you speak it out loud. For heaven's sake, you are a walking crock of gold to every greedy crook in the universe—the ones you have just left are no exception, and they your own family no less! Yet you say you do not need protection!'

Tiger, white and shattered, wept.

Harry waited for him, seeing only a child. He said, not harshly, 'I will see you are protected. You will have to trust me, that is all I can say. You may have a room of your own in the house with a lock on the door. And if you wish to make money for yourself from your dreams, you must come to me and I shall arrange for you to make your bets in confidence, so that no one will find out about you. And I will bank the money for you so that it will remain a secret, against the day when you wish to go your own way. I cannot offer you more than that. And if you think, by this, that I shall use your information for my own ends, I am not denying that I might take advantage if I can do so without raising any suspicions, but this you must accept. Now sit down and think about it. I am not forcing you. If you wish, you may leave at any time and go on your way.'

Tiger wiped his nose on his sleeve and calmed down at Harry's reasoned speech.

'I want to stay here.'

'I shall not treat you any differently. You will get no favours. But I shall see to the best of my ability that you remain unmolested.'

'If my father comes, or my brothers—?'

'God forbid! I will do my best. I cannot say more.'

Harry poured two glasses of port from his untidy sideboard and gave one to Tiger.

'Drink that and cheer up. And tell me how often you get these dreams of yours, and are they always right? And what else do you dream about besides the winners? I must admit the subject intrigues me vastly.'

'The dreams are always right. Sometimes I dream things that are going to happen. And they always happen. Sometimes it is not even a dream. I just see it. But I don't tell anybody. I never tell anybody. And sometimes it is the horses—that's what they all want to know. They don't care about the other things, just the names of the winners.'

'Of course. There is no money in prophesying anything but winners.'

'I don't dream winners very often. Not often enough to please them—less often than I used to. My grandmother says I will lose the gift—she calls it the gift—when I get older. She used to have it when she was young.'

'Your Nottingham grandmother?'

'Yes.'

'It is very hard to keep secrets of that nature, Tiger. You could be considered a phenomenon. Even down here, I have heard rumours about you. Word gets about. And a fair travels all over the country. You are in a very dangerous situation.'

'People fight over me. My father kept me—he said it was for my own good, when I wasn't working—kept me protected. Protected, he called it that.'

'Confined, you mean?'

'Yes. He liked me best asleep, but he couldn't make me sleep all the time.'

Harry laughed.

'He made me work hard, in order to sleep well. And the work—he said no one could get at me when I was working, so he kept me practising all day, with my brothers.'

'And that's all you did?'

'Work and stay in the van, yes. He locked me in.'

'Until you ran away?' Harry leaned back in his chair, clasping his glass of port. 'It's a strange story, my lad. It explains a few things about you.'

He had never struck any of them as an ordinary child, and nor was he. He tried to be, to fade into his surroundings as well as he could, but he was indelibly marked by his idiosyncratic power and the treatment it had merited him. He was fully aware of his incredible status with his elders, and it had produced in him his kingly self-possession. Yet in truth he was merely an ill-treated, unloved child. The combination had made him the curious tangle of contradictions that he was.

'How old are you, Tiger?'

'Fourteen.'

'That is the truth? It's hard to tell.'

'Yes.'

'You like working here?'

'Yes. I liked the gardening but it was boring. This is more interesting. And I might get a chance to ride in races. I'm very light.'

'That's true. You could be useful to me. But we must understand each other, lad. It's a question of loyalty. It works both ways.'

'Yes, sir. I understand.'

He was intelligent, with the native wit of one who had learned to survive. He could have gone under quite easily, given the circumstances. Scars of battle still showed in the watchful eyes, the natural reticence, the wiry, enduring body. He was hard, sharp, growing fast. He had never played, or mixed with children. He needed ordinariness badly. Young Laura could do him a power of good.

But with the coming of Hilda Bell, Laura's childhood was, in effect, being rounded off. Harry saw that the cloud had already touched her. She came to ride Priam, and cried when she put him away.

'I don't want anything changed!'

Harry too was nervous of Miss Bell's coming, and not sure whether it was entirely transmitted from Cecily, who dreaded the day, or whether there was in his own mind a suspicion that relationships might alter in some way with the new addition. He did not pursue this unease, for speculation was clearly fruitless.

'If she were a servant plain and simple, it would be so much easier,' Cecily said. 'It's this being neither one nor the other that worries me. If Laura eats with us, must Miss Bell eat with us too?'

'Surely you know how other women treat them?'

'All my friends have several children, and so they eat apart and the governess eats with the children. I don't know anyone in quite my situation.'

'Hating it so, you mean?'

'No, I didn't mean that, but that is true too.'

Cecily picked a leaf off one of the rhododendrons and tore it slowly into tiny pieces. 'If you were to fall in love with anyone else, Harry—I'm not suggesting Miss Bell, but the fact of her coming is what puts it in my mind—'

'Laura assures me that I shall not fall in love with Miss Bell.'

'You might. You might fall in love with anybody.'

'I have.'

'I want to say—'

'Yes, I know. You think I should get married. But you don't want me to. Be honest.'

'I wish I could want it. I do want it, for you. I have to say it. You must.'

'You don't want it at all. And we none of us do what is good for us, Cecily. And how could I?'

'You would like to have children. You are wasting your life.'

'Yes, and you. But I prefer it as it is. It is no good talking about it—you know that. There are no solutions.'

'No. But remember what I said.'

'Very well. You want me to fall in love with someone else.'

'I think you should.'

'Like eating greens.'

'Yes.'

She laughed then, and he kissed her passionately under the rhododendron bushes, but afterwards when she went back to the house with her gardening gloves and pruning shears she had the same sense of cold desolation that had touched her the night of the races. The house was empty and silent. She stood at the long windows looking out across the lawns and saw her future as cheerless as the evening.

'I won't let it be this way for Laura,' she thought. 'I was once as she is. And now I am just a shell. There is nothing inside me but regret.'

If she had been a different sort of person, a careless, fearless, active, proper Newmarket woman, it might all have been bearable, but she could not change her temperament. She wanted to fill the empty corners of her life with creation, but she could not conceive (fortunately, perhaps, in the circumstances) and there was only gardening, and the embroidery Philip brought home from Morris's workshop in London, acres and acres of it which disheartened her before she had begun.

'But all their wives and daughters do it, and get paid for it,' Philip said. 'May Morris does it, and Lucy and Janey.'

They sat in circles sewing and exchanging lofty remarks. Cecily had seen them at it. She did not belong there either. She belonged nowhere. She belonged only with Harry in the angles of his thin, strong arms. She always wanted what she could not have, like Laura.

'Laura must be happy,' she resolved. 'Laura must not be like me. She must stop her nonsense about Fred Archer for a start.'

But just before Miss Bell was due to arrive, Laura rode down to Heath House on Priam and waited for Fred to come out with the string. He was riding Wheel of Fortune and Mr Dawson was with him on his hack, and fourteen lads besides. Laura, seeing only Fred, rode up to him and said, 'Please may I ride with you a little way?'

Mr Dawson laughed at her temerity.

'You should take a job with your uncle, riding out. You're bolder than any of my lads.'

'You won't tell my mother?'

'Not this time, my dear, but—'

'I'm having a governess, she's coming on Monday. And then I shan't be able to come out in the mornings any more, so I thought I would come for the last time. If you don't mind.'

'Do we mind, Mr Archer?'

Fred was smiling.

'I don't think so. I'd say it was a pleasure to ride with Miss Laura.'

Laura stored the words in her head, and wrote them down as soon as she got home to make quite sure she would have them for ever. Fred talked work with Mr Dawson, but every so often he would smile at her, or make a civil remark, and all the while Laura watched him unblinkingly. Sitting in his easy way on the mare, he showed no emotion; his impassive face, with its natural melancholy, did not respond with a young man's animation to each passing observation, but remained sombre, attentive, still. But when he smiled he revealed the young man's vulnerability that turned Laura's heart over. She rode home in a dream, and sobbed in Uncle Harry's office.

'After Monday I won't see him any more!'

Having lately left Cecily equally desolated by the imminent arrival of Miss Bell, Harry was moved to wonder why they all brought such penance on themselves.

'If that's what you do left to your own devices—accost Mr Dawson, of all people, and ride without an invitation—it's high time you were taken in hand! It's not at all ladylike, you know, Laura.'

'No, but he didn't mind. And Fred said—he *said*—it was a pleasure to ride with me.'

'He should have boxed your ears.'

But even he could be no sterner, for he loved her boldness.

'Can I talk to Tiger?'

'If you do not stop him working, yes. He should be strapping his horse—although I doubt he'll get much muscle up, the size of him.'

'Is he satisfactory?'

'Perfectly satisfactory, madam. Do you feel responsible?'

'Yes.'

'And so you should.'

'Why does he have a room of his own? The other boys say he has fits. Is that true?'

'Fits? The first I heard of it!'

'Why then? That's what he told them.'

'Did he? The cunning little beggar. He's bright, I'll give him that.'

'What did he tell *you* then?'

'He talks in his sleep.'

'He talks who is going to win races.' Laura dropped the observation as a commonplace, as if it were quite normal.

'How do you know?'

'Because of Charibert. Papa said it's what he was saying when he found him in the haystack. And Tiger said to me he knew Charibert would win. And if he had had more money he would have put it all on. So I suppose his dreams always come true.'

Harry decided he must step carefully. 'Yes, you are quite right. But it's not a good thing for everyone to know.'

'Why not? It's lovely.'

Harry laughed. 'Yes, it is indeed. But a very dangerous gift. People exploit him, you see. That's why he ran away from home.'

'That's what he meant when he said he was valuable?'

'Yes. If he said that, I imagine that is what he meant. His father virtually kept him prisoner, to keep the information to himself, to make money out of it. And unscrupulous people could do the same, if they knew. So it's best that nobody knows.'

'Well, I know.'

'You haven't spoken of it to anyone?'

'No.'

'Then don't, Laura, for his own good. The racing game is bedevilled with real bad eggs who wouldn't scruple to use young Tiger's gift if they got half a chance. Remember that, if you want him safe.'

'He could tell *us*.'

'I daresay he might. But such powers — to know what is going to happen . . . all right with winners, perhaps, but it's not what I would call a happy responsibility. I think you should keep it to yourself.'

'Yes, I will. He can tell me, and you, and that's all.'

'Or nobody, if he prefers.'

'Well that's a bit of a shame, if it's a winner.'

Harry laughed. 'You've no scruples either! Miss Bell is going to have a hard time of it, taming you.'

Laura, on her round of farewell visits, went out to find Tiger.

She had been careful to take no notice of him up to now, perfectly well aware of his needing to go unremarked before his peers, but there was a definite limit to her fund of tact. She found him as Uncle Harry predicted, strapping a horse, standing on an upturned bucket. When she came in, he stopped, pushed his cap back to ease the sweat, and waited guardedly for her approach.

'Hullo.'

'Hullo.'

'You should say, Hullo, Miss Laura.'

'Why should I? Or, if I do, you can say, Hullo, *Mr* Tiger.'

'Oh, all right.' Laura was prepared to let it go. 'I've come to see how you're getting on.'

'I'm getting on very well.'

'Has Arthur given you a thrashing yet?'

'He thrashes everyone who falls off.'

'Have you fallen off?'

'Twice.'

'I haven't fallen off for years.'

'Priam is broken in. That's more than you can say for some of the two-year-olds.'

'Have you had any more dreams?'

Tiger did not say anything. He was standing on the far side of the horse. He laid his arms over the horse's back and rested his chin, watching her coldly.

'Have you dreamed any more winners, like Charibert?'

'I might have.'

'If you tell me, I will put some money on for you.'

'For yourself, you mean.'

'Well, for both of us.' She waited hopefully, but he was not forthcoming. 'It's a pity if you don't. If you tell me, you see, I would keep it secret. Secret as the grave. Hope to die.'

'And if I don't?'

She shrugged. 'I don't know.'

Tiger started strapping again. For all his delicate size he was very strong, Laura noticed. She leaned against the doorpost watching him. He was quite different from the other boys, who were coarse, and would have been saying crude things to her by now, in Tiger's position. She had no wish to be friends with any of the other boys. But Tiger fascinated her.

(67)

'Well?'

It was warm. The sun shone in, drying the washed floor tiles, bringing the smell of hay and summer. She waited. Beads of sweat trickled down Tiger's temples from the band of his cap. His hair curled closely down over his ears, reddish and dusty; the sweat left a pale streak down his cheek and dropped on his shirt. Inside his shirt, the neck open, she could see his body white, covered from the sun. His face was foxy-brown and his eyes gold as a tiger's.

'You want to know what I dreamed?'

'Yes.'

'I dreamed that Fred Archer is going to have an accident. He is going to be badly hurt.'

Laura jerked up from the doorpost.

'You are making it up!'

'You asked me. I'm not.'

'It won't come true!'

'My dreams always come true.' He was not smiling, banging away on the horse's muscled shoulders with his strapping cloth, not stopping.

'It will happen on the Heath, riding work.'

'No!'

Laura was convulsed with an agony of fear and love for Fred. It was as strong as if her mother had died, or Uncle Harry. She could not help herself. She had never felt such anguish. She turned herself to the wall and buried her face in her hands, shaking. Tiger went on strapping his horse, watching her.

'You asked me,' he reminded her.

'I didn't! I didn't! Not that!'

It was all of a piece with Miss Bell coming, the world turning on her, her bright sky shattered. She could not bear what was going to happen.

'I said winners!' She cried, the tears pouring down her cheeks.

Tiger got off his bucket and came over.

'I'm sorry. It was your fault, being so cocky.'

'It isn't true?'

'I will give you a winner, if you stop crying.'

'I can't. Say it isn't true!'

'A chestnut horse with white hairs all through its coat and a white blaze and a black marking on its hindquarters will win the Derby.'

'But Fred?'

'Fred will ride it.'

'And the other thing?'

'Yes. And that will teach you not to ask me.'

Laura ran home weeping. The other boys, noticing, grinned to each other and Tiger went on with his strapping, having climbed in their estimation.

4

Laura, charged by Uncle Harry with keeping Tiger's secret, could tell no one why she looked so miserable, and burst into tears if anyone enquired. Her condition was put down to Miss Bell's coming. A general air of gloomy unease settled over the household. Only Philip went on with his work regardless. 'Splendid that you've taken the step at last, Cecily. You really are a great prevaricator.'

Percy was sent to meet the train with the phaeton, and arrived back punctually with Miss Bell and her luggage. Miss Bell looked smaller than Cecily remembered, in fact not much ahead of Laura herself, and as pallid and nervous as all of them. Great heavens, suppose she turns out to be a terrible mistake! Cecily thought, even as she smiled and advanced to greet her. She would have to go through all this agony again . . . but, remembering that Albert played darts with the girl's father, she put down her panic and shook hands kindly.

'You had a pleasant journey, I hope?'

'Yes, thank you, ma'am.'

'I do hope everything will turn out happily for you here.' Perhaps not the right thing to say, but heartfelt. Cecily felt sure the girl could not be as old as twenty-three. The scrubbed clean look and her pale, innocent eyes made her suddenly seem only a child herself. Cecily had remembered thinking of her at the interview as hard, even steely, but now the severity of her dress and hair gave the effect of childishness, of an orphanage uniform. Cecily struggled to put down her unsuitable impressions, turning to the practical considerations of showing the girl her room, introducing the sullen Laura and, very shortly, escorting her in to lunch. Albert and Alice, waiting on, studied Miss Bell inscrutably over the vegetable dishes as they handed, and Philip made patronizing

conversation to fill the silences, Laura being completely dumb and
Cecily not much better.

'And what made you apply for a post in Newmarket, when
your home is in London?' Philip asked her.

Cecily said, 'Her father is a friend of Albert's, dear.'

Philip gave her a cold look which Cecily interpreted as inferring
that the fact was not a recommendation in his eyes, as it was in
hers, and awaited an answer from Miss Bell.

Miss Bell had no intention of divulging her reason for wanting a
job in Newmarket, but was a practised liar—so necessary to the
job—and made a plausible reply.

'I wanted a country post, sir, a change, and I wanted to live
away from home.'

'Your home is—where? Exactly.'

'Epsom, sir.'

Laura showed her first flicker of interest. 'Do you go and watch
the Derby?'

'I have done, yes.'

'Did you watch it the year before last—Silvio?'

'Yes I did.'

'You saw—'

'Laura, your father was talking with Miss Bell! I am afraid this
will be your biggest task, Miss Bell, to teach Laura the basic rules
about good manners. She is very impetuous.'

'I will do my best, ma'am.'

'You are not too much interested in racing, I hope?' Philip asked.

'Oh, no, sir.'

'I am afraid, living in Newmarket, one can never be unaware of
the sport, but it does attract a very undesirable element to the
town. It is my home, I was born here, but I do not find it a
particularly congenial atmosphere. My brother, on the other
hand, who has a training yard across the road, finds it very much
to his taste. Laura wastes far too much of her time over there,
which your appointment will put a stop to, I hope.'

Laura glowered across the table.

'If I can't go to Uncle Harry's I might as well be dead.'

In front of Miss Bell neither Philip nor Cecily felt able to
remonstrate freely with Laura, none of them quite sure who was
going to take responsibility for such lapses in time to come.

'I am afraid Laura is demonstrating all too clearly the task that lies before you,' Philip said frigidly.

Hilda Bell smiled grimly. 'I am sure we shall manage.'

'I think I told you in the interview that Laura has a cousin, Gervase, who will be with you during the holidays?' Cecily decided to introduce a fresh theme. 'He is a year older than Laura, rather a quiet boy, and will need to learn a few social graces. The public school life is very spartan, I understand, and he is not much used to mixing with other than boys of his own kind. Have you had to do with boys, Miss Bell?'

'Not a great deal, ma'am.' Her lilac-flushed eyelids dropped down demurely as she spoke. She reminded Philip then of the girl he went to when he was in London, and he wondered if she was a virgin, and rather thought not. But he was not much interested in women, save to satisfy the occasional biological urge which Cecily, being so frigid, was incapable of doing. They were not a highly-sexed family fortunately, Harry seeming to do well enough without. For himself, he assumed such desires were sublimated in his creative work. He preferred it like that, amazed by some of the disclosures that were revealed over a drink or two in London in the club or after dinner.

It was a relief to them all when lunch was over. Cecily arranged that Laura should take Miss Bell for a walk round the garden and down by the stream so that they could get to know one another.

'In half an hour. Miss Bell might wish to arrange her things, or change. You will be waiting in the hall, Laura, at half past two.'

Laura went upstairs, locked her door and got out all her pictures of Fred and spread them across the floor and lay sideways over her bed, feasting on them. The thought of the pending calamity marred her usual joy in this occupation. It lay over her mind like a black cloud, an even blacker cloud than that provoked by thoughts of Miss Bell. She wished she could prove that Tiger had made it all up, but she rather suspected the whole strange business was true. Perhaps if she proved his other prognosis wrong . . . she had heard of no horses amongst the Derby prospects with the colouring he described and Fred, as far as she knew, was to ride Charibert who, although chestnut, had no white hairs and no black marking on his quarters. And was not expected to win either. There was no one she could talk to about it, save Uncle

Harry when they were alone, and when would that be now, given her new warder?

They walked by the stream. Without Laura's parents present there was no one either of them had to impress, and neither of them was disposed to impress the other. They had been put together by the will of others, and both knew they must make the best of it. Neither, in the early stages, was inclined to give any-thing away. By the stream they walked in silence, Miss Bell trailing her black hem in the new damp grass, unused to banks of meadowsweet and glades of red campion and the cowpats which she knew Laura was hoping she would step in, aware and wary, hopeful, resigned. Laura was resigned, but not hopeful.

'Shall we call on my Uncle Harry?' she asked. 'You should be introduced.'

No one had said they should not. They both understood this; no one had said they should not, although they both knew that it had been inferred.

'It would be rude not to,' Laura said.

'Very well.'

Laura perked up at once, Miss Bell noticed. They had walked three-quarters of an hour in silence but now, turning back with a purpose, Laura conversed freely.

'You know you have been engaged to keep my mind off Fred Archer? Did they tell you?'

Miss Bell stopped dead at this utterance, but Laura supposed it was the roughness of the track.

'No. I was not told.'

'It's true. But no one can tell you what to think, can they? They can't stop me *thinking* about Fred Archer. I went to see him the other day and tell him that I wouldn't be able to ride with him any more in the mornings.'

'You ride with him?'

'Sometimes. I rode with him last week and he said it was a pleasure to ride with me. And once I rode a trial with him, side by side. He comes to my Uncle Harry's sometimes, you see. I know him quite well.'

Miss Bell appeared to be impressed, for she could obviously think of nothing to say.

'I think he's marvellous.'

'Yes,' Miss Bell said.

'Do you?'

'I—well—he's a marvellous jockey, certainly.'

'I want to marry him.'

'Yes. Who wouldn't?' Miss Bell said simply.

It was Laura's turn to be astonished. It was not a reply to her eternal statement that had ever crossed her mother's lips.

'All that money,' Miss Bell said, 'and admiration.'

'But I love him. It's not the money.'

'Ah, well.'

'I would only marry for love.'

'A very fine ideal.' A trace of bitterness tinged Miss Bell's voice. 'Love isn't everything.'

Laura rather thought that it was but had no wish to argue. Miss Bell sounded amazingly well-disposed towards her way of thinking, not a bit like her mother. It was quite the last thing she had been expecting. She felt much cheered, and when they reached Thorn's Hall even the thought of Tiger's psychic disclosures did not spoil her pleasure in the discovery. Miss Bell was duly introduced to Harry, to Arthur and to Tiger. There was a polite, speculative constraint all round, Uncle Harry being very solemn, Laura thought. She went home with Miss Bell, saw her to her room, and then ran back through the kitchen and yard and returned to the stables.

'What do you think?' she enquired boldly. 'She *likes* Fred Archer, she told me.'

'Yes, all the ladies like Fred,' Uncle Harry said. 'Why should a governess be any exception?'

'Nobody has told her she has to keep my mind off him.'

Harry laughed. 'They will.'

'Tiger says—' She stopped, frowning, and decided better of it. Better to forget. But the other thing . . . 'A chestnut colt with white hairs all through its coat, and a black mark on its hindquarters . . . Tiger says it will win the Derby.'

Harry looked up. They were in his office and he was making out race entries.

'He told you?'

'Yes.'

'He said the same to me, but there's no three-year-old of that description. It's not Charibert. There is, however, a two-year-old I've heard of, belongs to the Duke of Westminster, a colt by Doncaster called Bend Or, that fills the bill. It's worth bearing in mind for next year.' He wrote his name and address on the card he was filling in, and added quietly, 'You're not mentioning this to anyone, I hope?'

'No. Only you.'

Laura knew that Tiger had only told her as a sop, a comforter after the other thing he had said. It had been a present to her. She knew that he had not mentioned the other things to anyone else.

'Well, Laura, it's our secret then. And perhaps next year we'll make the journey to Epsom to see what happens.'

'Could we? Truly?'

'If it's possible, why not? If your mother allows it.'

'Tiger said Fred would ride that colt—'

'So I understand. But your mother will allow you to go, I'm sure, if you behave yourself with Miss Bell and learn your lessons well. It could be your reward, eh?'

'Do you promise?'

'Yes. I promise.'

And it was a date to mark on the calendar, as soon as she could get one for next year, to mark with yellow rings and red exploding stars: Fred winning the Derby. Miss Bell paled into utter insignificance beside such glory.

* * *

Gervase had grown since his last visit, emerging from his cab with his thin wrists bared by a too-short black jacket and shrunken white cuffs, his voice deep and unfamiliar. He had a hectoring of adolescent spots round his jawline and scowled when he saw Laura noticing them. Cecily's heart sank when she saw how badly he needed new clothes; then she remembered Miss Bell, and was relieved. Useful, unremarkable, entirely satisfactory Miss Bell could replenish the boy's wardrobe, his dour uniform and country breeches and evening suit, and she could carry on dividing the irises in the borders, cutting their leaves back after flowering and chopping off the infant rhizomes. Gervase, like herself, was a solitary person, spending hours in his room reading, or wandering off alone with his butterfly bottle or his bird's egg box. Cecily's brother was his father, the military man in Delhi, but in ways and looks he took after the steely beauty her brother had married: not that in Gervase the looks were beautiful. His face was drawn and angular, the cheekbones prominent, the lips uncertain. He had his mother's black curling hair and dark-fringed hazel eyes, but a gaucheness and reticence that detracted, a way of hunching into himself to be unobtrusive. He and Laura had a tacit understanding, instinctive, but did not profess to like each other much. Cecily liked him because he did not disturb her. He was very easy to ignore, in fact seemed to desire it. Harry reckoned to be quite unable to fathom him, thought him unnatural, a 'bookworm' oddity, never wanting to borrow a horse or a pair of skates in the winter, not even a hunter.

'What sort of boy is that then?' he would ask.

'They come all ways,' Cecily said. 'Haven't you noticed?'

'Laura could knock spots off him. And Tiger.'

'Oh, yes. Tiger is your sort.'

Harry knew without being told that Tiger was his favourite, and he had to take care not to show favouritism in the yard. He smiled at Cecily's criticism.

'He's the sort you should have for a son,' Cecily said.

'Oh yes? And who are you marrying me off to now? Not Miss Bell, I hope?'

Cecily shook her head. She had a fond belief that, if Harry were to find a wife, she would, in pure hopelessness, give up desiring him. But because he was always available to her, desiring her in return, her predicament was never to be solved. She could hope for nothing, save that Laura would never suffer in the way she had done. Laura must be introduced to suitable young people. She was dispatched to parties, chaperoned by Miss Bell, accompanied by a glum, mutinous Gervase, but she yawned and would not care about her dress, and when she came home bolted to her Uncle Harry's to complain.

'I don't like those sort of people!'

'What do you mean?'

'I am supposed to like those boys. Those duffers.'

'Are they duffers?'

'Oh, you know—they are stupid.'

Harry had noticed that, given the chance, Laura would talk to

Tiger by the hour. He never mentioned this to Cecily. Laura and Tiger were well-matched in his estimation, but polite society would not consider them so. They were the non-conformers, the naturals, the independents. They were both as sharp as needles. He felt slightly guilty seeing them together. Laura would come and talk to Tiger while he was grooming, which did not hold him up, and the other boys would say nothing. Tiger was treated with respect, even deference, because he could both ride and fight with the best of them, and bore no malice. His apprenticeship was over, the pecking order established. Laura was attracted to him because he was, like Fred Archer, one of Nature's favourites, gifted and brave. Laura was a romantic. Harry loved her for it, and could be frightened for her, if his mind dwelled on it.

Sometimes when no one was near, Tiger would put down his brush and press Laura into a corner of the loosebox and kiss her on the lips. Laura would stand with her eyes shut, tasting Tiger's salty mouth, smiling, not moving, liking it.

'Does Gervase ever do that to you?'

'Good heavens, no!'

'Would you like him to?'

'No.'

'Do you like me to?'

'Yes.'

'When you shut your eyes, are you pretending I'm Fred Archer?'

Laura laughed. 'No.' But she thought it was rather a good idea. 'Do it again, and this time I'll pretend.'

He came up close and she shut her eyes. He was growing and his lips were on a level with hers, and he weighed six stone eight pounds. Uncle Harry said he was never going to make a jockey if he wasn't careful, but, having sweated off a few pounds to ride in an apprentice race, he had decided he would be a trainer instead. 'I couldn't make a habit of that. It's horrible.' 'Fred does it all the time, nearly every day,' Laura said. 'Fred's welcome,' Tiger said. 'No wonder he looks so miserable.' Laura thought of this as Tiger kissed her, Fred sitting naked in his Turkish bath, and a delicious sensation stole over her. She put up her arms and touched Tiger's shoulders with her fingers, felt the hard muscle and bone inside his shirt and pretended it was Fred's back, Fred's vertebrae, Fred's soft dark hair. Her mouth quivered. She felt very strange and pushed Tiger away, opening her eyes.

Tiger was looking angry.

'Were you pretending?'

'Yes. It was lovely.'

'I could tell. You were different.'

'It felt different.'

She could tell that he was jealous. 'It was your idea,' she reminded him. 'You shouldn't have said.'

'No. It was stupid.'

He did not kiss her again until three days after the Cesarewitch, and Arthur, bringing a haynet, saw them over the half door. He did not say anything, but the next morning Tiger got the horse-whip treatment, a stronger dose than Arthur had administered for some time, not since one of the lads smoked a cigarette in the hayshed.

'Your tack is filthy and you never scrub out your mangers,' Arthur said, but they both knew that the tack and the mangers were spotless. Tiger did not say anything, nor hold it against Arthur, for Arthur had his job to do like everyone else, but it brought back memories of the times before he ran away, and he was very quiet for several days. He did not think he had done wrong, but he did not want to anger Mr Keen. Only the shock of the thrashing made him realize how grateful he was for his place, and how valuable was his trust in his employer. He did not want to spoil anything.

All the same, he liked kissing Laura, and thought about it a lot.

5

By the time a year had passed, Laura had decided that Tiger had
told her the dreadful thing about Fred out of spite. Perhaps she
had deserved it, the way she had spoken to him. She had never
spoken to him in that way again. The other prophecy seemed set
to come true, for the chestnut colt with white hairs through its
coat and a black mark on its quarters won all its two-year-old
races and became winter favourite for the Derby. Its trainer,
Robert Peck, was a very good friend of Fred's, and wanted Fred to
ride the colt in its three-year-old races and as Lord Falmouth, who
had first claim on Fred, had no very promising three-year-old that
year he agreed to the proposition: that Fred should ride Bend Or
in the Derby.

'Bend Or is favourite,' Laura told her uncle.

'Yes, but I put our money on long ago, and got a much better
price than they are offering today.'

'Tiger is wonderful!'

'The horse hasn't won yet.'

'He will!'

'We hope so.'

'And we're going down to watch. Mother promised!'

'Yes. It's settled.'

'Me, Mama, you, Miss Bell, and Arthur and Tiger are coming
with the black filly.'

'Your father has decided not to come?' Harry tried not to sound
too hopeful.

'He says not. He's too busy.'

'Do him good, the stick-in-the-mud.' But Harry was relieved. If
Miss Bell could be relied upon to meet her sister, as arranged, and
Laura paired off with Tiger, he and Cecily stood a chance of
enjoying a rare day out. He had entered the black filly for a race as

an excuse to get Tiger to Epsom, for Laura's sake, for it was impossible to take him along socially. Trusting in the boy's powers, Harry found it hard to listen to the racing talk amongst men who, unlike him, did not know who was going to win the big race. For the sake of form he speculated on the chances of Robert the Devil, Mask and Teviotdale, but he did not doubt for one moment that Bend Or was going to win. Talking to Fred was the strangest experience of all, for Fred reckoned that Robert the Devil stood a great chance.

'He'll be the one to beat. He's a cracking horse.'

Harry wanted to reassure Fred, but knew there was nothing to say. Like Tiger himself, he was set apart from his fellow men by this magical conviction of what was to be. It was uncanny and frightening, not a happy gift, Harry decided. Tiger was at times very withdrawn and tense. Six times he had given Harry winners, and he had never been wrong.

Three weeks before the Derby Harry rode out to the Heath with his string on normal morning exercise. Tiger was riding the filly who was to go to Epsom, Black Satin, and had already got into trouble from Arthur for being slow in getting ready. He was in one of his moods, Harry noticed, silent and strung-up, but Arthur made no allowances for temperament. Harry knew Arthur was right, and did not interfere.

When they got on to the Heath there seemed to be some disturbance. A loose horse was galloping in the distance—although that was no rarity—and a small knot of people were gathered at the end of one of the gallops where someone was lying on the ground. Accidents were not uncommon; Harry gave the scene no second glance, but sent his first batch of youngsters away at a canter. He pulled up to watch them go, sitting in his usual place in the great ocean of grass, the sun shining serenely on the familiar scene, drawing out the eternal good smell of damp turf, enticing the skylarks to pour out their songs to the pale ether. Harry's mind was not entirely on his job; it was digressing in a physical appreciation of what his job entailed, thinking that there were not in fact many jobs where one could actually be working with such pleasure and ease, feeling the horse content beneath him, watching his other horses moving with such grace and power up towards the skyline . . . a thud of hooves closing up behind him interrupted his contemplations. One of Mat Dawson's boys was cantering home alone, not a normal habit, and the look on his face prompted Harry to call out, 'What's wrong?'

'It's Mr Archer, sir. He's been half killed!'

Harry wheeled Jester round abruptly and said to Arthur, 'Stay here in charge! I'll go and see what's happened.'

Strangely, his pang of anxiety was more for Laura than for anyone else as Jester rapidly closed with the ominous group. He steadied the horse and brought it to a walk, and saw that Archer was on his feet with Lord Falmouth himself standing close beside him. He supposed at once that the boy had been exaggerating, rumours always being notoriously magnified round the Newmarket scene, but when he got close and saw Archer being lifted by several hands on to Falmouth's hack, he saw that he was, by anyone's standards, a shocking sight. His clothes were ripped and dishevelled and his right arm hung limp, the sleeve of his jacket half torn off and saturated with blood.

'The horse went for him—trod him into the ground and savaged him,' one of the boys told Harry.

'What horse?'

'Muley Edris. Fred got off him, turned his back and—' The boy shrugged. 'He's a devil, that one.'

Fred was sitting on the hack, cradling his right arm with his left, hunched with pain, and Harry could see the blood seeping out between his fingers. Lord Falmouth mounted another horse beside him and turned for home, taking Fred's reins. Harry saw them off, and turned back to meet his string and tell Arthur what had happened.

'I reckon that horse has a long memory. It's had a few thrashings from Archer in its time.'

'There's not many can get it to race at all. It's always been a funny devil.'

'Yes. And a month to go to the Derby. Fred's out of luck.'

When the string came back Harry told Tiger what had happened, but Tiger was silent, passing no comment. He sat white and pinched on the filly in the cold wind and Harry saw that he was shivering.

'What's wrong with you lad? Aren't you well?'

Tiger nodded.

'Ride on then.'

Arthur watched him go and rode behind with Harry.

'He's a funny one too. He sees ghosts, or summat. Sometimes I can't fathom him.'

'Highly-strung. Archer was like it as a lad.'

'We all know that. And not only as a lad. This business will upset him. He'll miss a few races by the sound of it, and likely the Derby on the favourite.'

The prospect would put Fred in torment, Harry knew—not to mention Laura. When he told her what had happened she flung herself in a passion of tears into his arms. He held her and felt her shaking against him, and the knowledge that she was Cecily's flesh confused his feelings in the way he had become accustomed to, so that a part of him wanted to kiss away her tears with infinite tenderness and another part was horrified by the wish and compelled him to hold her away from him and speak to her sternly.

'Tiger told me!' she sobbed. 'He told me!'

'Tiger told you! When? You mean, he knew—'

'Yes. Ages ago. Last year. He told me Fred would be badly hurt on the Heath.'

'Good God!'

The news shook Harry. Tiger's 'gift' was more formidable than he had realized: winners, perhaps, but prognoses of dire events were in another class altogether.

'He shouldn't have told you!'

'No. He told me to upset me, because I was cruel to him.'

'It's a dangerous business. He had no right.'

But what a responsibility, he could not help thinking! What else did the boy know? He called him to his office. Tiger did not want to talk about it. He stood sullen and reluctant.

'Whatever the provocation, you should not have told her. It's a wonder she did not pass it on! If the boys knew . . . it could so easily happen. Believe me, my heart bleeds for your predicament but I cannot do more to help you. No one can. You've to live with it, for better or for worse.'

'I'm sorry. I'm sorry I told Laura.'

'Yes.'

There was nothing more he could find to say, although the sight of the frail figure shocked by the realization of his prophecies he found hard to ignore. Yet neither did he truly want to be more involved, to know what Tiger knew. It was a horrific prospect. He told Arthur not to be hard on him, that he was not well. It was the limit of what he was able to do.

If the boy had prophesied that Fred would win the Derby on Bend Or, this now seemed unlikely. Harry thought that what he had seen of the injury looked bad, and reports substantiated this: Fred's arm was so badly lacerated as to be useless and, worse, as the days slowly passed no great improvement seemed to be forthcoming. Fred visited several doctors, including Lord Falmouth's own consultant in Harley Street, but no magic cure was produced and he went home in despair to his parents in Cheltenham. In equal despair Laura sought out Tiger.

'What you said—he will win—is it true? Is it going to happen?'

'I will not talk about it.'

'But you know.'

'And you know I must not say anything. You didn't like it before, did you?'

'But that was bad news. I would like good news.'

'It is all the same.'

'It isn't.'

Tiger had a way of looking at her now which made her nervous. Tiger as a name had not come to her entirely arbitrarily, she realized. He had not kissed her for a long time now.

'I was so looking forward to the Derby. It won't be the same if Fred isn't riding.'

There was no response, so she added, 'I was looking forward to going with you.'

'I'm still going, to take the filly. So is Mr Keen. It makes no difference to me.'

Laura tried to look pleased, but she was not a good actress. Tiger could see right through her, she knew. She sighed. People did not do what she wanted them to do, and she did not know how to make them.

Her mother was tart with her.

'We're all having a day out at the Derby, Mr Archer or no Mr Archer, Laura, and if he is unable to ride I'm not having you spoiling our day with your sulks. You are being quite ridiculous about it.'

To Miss Bell she said, 'I don't want to hear the subject mentioned any more. Will you please see that it isn't.'

Miss Bell passed the news on to Laura. She was as anxious about the outcome as Laura, and followed the gossip minutely.

'He has come back to Newmarket, you know, but his arm is still in a sling and he is a stone overweight.'

'And only a week to the day!'

'They say it depends most on Mr Peck and the Duke. Fred says he's fit, and they say he's not.'

'Uncle Harry says it will be a close run race with Robert the Devil.'

The speculation exhausted, Miss Bell then remembered her duties. 'You're not to say another word, Laura, else I shall be dismissed.'

Laura giggled.

Uncle Harry kept her discreetly informed, and told her the good news three days later.

'Yes, he is to ride, but to do it he has to lose a stone in four days.'

'It's not possible!'

'With Fred anything is possible.'

Laura passed on the news to Miss Bell.

'Whatever does he do?'

'He eats nothing and takes this terrible medicine like dynamite and spends all his time between the WC and the Turkish bath.'

They stared at each other in awe at this formidable routine.

'But you have to be very strong to ride a race. How can he be very strong after four days of that?'

'I don't know. But Uncle Harry says with Fred anything is possible.'

They both went into a trance picturing Fred in his self-inflicted torment.

'You mustn't say anything,' Miss Bell said.

That evening at dinner Philip said he would accompany them to London on the train, but he would go and stay with Topsy (who was William Morris, Laura knew) and visit the Royal Academy. Cecily looked pleased.

'I shall probably be away two nights. Harry will see you safely home, I trust? He hasn't got to travel with a horse, has he?'

'No.'

'Splendid. You should enjoy it.' His voice was fatherly.

Laura, bursting to tell them that Fred was going to ride after all, kept a strenuous silence, clattering her knife and fork with the strain. She was thinking of the calendar in the kitchen with the yellow stars bursting off the date, and feeling the yellow stars bursting inside her with the excitement. The thought of Fred at his supper (half a dry biscuit and half a glass of champagne), wan from his day's privations, excited her almost beyond endurance. Miss Bell ate primly, eyes downcast, showing no emotion. She showed very little emotion, beyond animation in any conversation concerning Fred.

Arthur and Tiger left for Epsom the day before the Derby with the filly, Black Satin. A string of horses was travelling from Newmarket and Uncle Harry reckoned they would have no trouble walking the filly between Liverpool Street station and Waterloo in company with the others. The two-year-olds were not always too easy when journeys entailed crossing London.

Laura left early in the morning on the day of the race with her mother and father, Uncle Harry and Miss Bell. The train from Newmarket was crowded with the sort of people Philip did not like, mostly friends of Harry's. Philip bought first-class tickets and Harry did his best to ignore his cronies and behave in a decorous manner, but Laura could see that it was only for her parents' sake; he was almost as excited as she was herself. How *boring* her father was, Laura thought, amazed that her mother could prefer Philip to Harry. Studying them with this in her mind, staring from under her lashes at the three adult faces on the seat facing her, she was quite suddenly aware of a shocking suspicion that this supposed state of affairs was not in fact true. She did not know what made her think this; there was nothing outwardly to indicate anything exceptional, her father reading *The Times* and Harry a racing paper, her mother sitting slightly closer to Harry than to Philip. But there was something contained about her mother that Laura had never seen before, as if she, too, had a calendar in her room with yellow bursting stars all round the date, as if she was holding in as great an excitement as Laura herself in anticipating the day's events — and yet, how could it be, when she was not even remotely interested in who was going to win the Derby? Laura had this instinctive feeling that it was to do with Uncle Harry. She did not know why, whether it was anything Tiger could tell her with his prophecies and mysterious insights, or whether it was in her imagination. There was nothing truly to show: her mother's face grave, looking out of the window, very smooth and prim beneath a new hat of grey straw trimmed with white and lemon-yellow flowers, her smooth ash-blond hair piled up underneath so that the hat tilted forwards, shading her eyes. She never gave anything away. But Uncle Harry, lifting his gaze to Laura's, gave her a wink which made Laura's heart leap with love for him: he was so warm and caring about her passions, not crushing like her father. He had dressed very soberly for the day, but there was no disguising his slightly raffish, earthy personality, his eager humour, so en-. dearing to Laura when her eyes had only to move sideways a fraction to note the smooth, prim, boring face of her father above *The Times*, bowdlerized of all emotion save an air of disdain. Up till now her mother too in Laura's eyes had been a cool, inward person, but now Laura was conscious of an unexpected change. My mother is excited, Laura thought; and no, it is impossible. My mother never gets excited. And if she is, what is she excited about? Laura felt a sweaty suspicion in the palms of her hands which was somehow linked up with her clandestine kisses in the stables with Tiger, but she did not understand why. Those kisses had been associated with feelings of guilt. What did her mother have to feel guilty about? Laura could come to no conclusions, and turned her mind away.

The journey seemed endless. After getting off the Newmarket train they had to wait half an hour for a cab, so great was the crush, then the journey to Waterloo took another forty minutes through dense traffic. At Waterloo it seemed as if the whole of London had elected to catch the train to Tattenham Corner. 'But the roads will be worse by far,' Uncle Harry assured them. Philip saw them off, frowning at the drunks who were in evidence already. Laura sensed that he was glad to see the back of them, and set his sights for the altogether smarter environs of Chelsea and its cultivated inhabitants.

The train steamed out through the sulphurous heart of the city and into the country by Norwood and Croydon to the steeply rolling fields and woods that trimmed the downs. The platforms of Tattenham Corner station were crowded with horse-boxes, several unloading. They walked out with the throng and from the station concourse saw the whole panorama of the race-course spread before them, curving away in both directions from the top of Tattenham hill, to their left hugging the crest of the downs towards the starting point and to the right plunging down the valley to the historic bend and the wide green carpet of the finishing straight with the grandstand flying its flag far away at the end. The inside of this great horseshoe was filled already with a mass of humanity and horse-flesh, spectators, bookmakers, gip-sies, showmen and touts, but Laura had eyes only for the sacred turf where Fred would presently speed his chestnut colt on its way. After Newmarket, the only race-course she had ever seen, the undulations and bends of Epsom astounded her.

'Oh, it needs a clever horse,' Uncle Harry said. 'And a clever rider. It's a real test!'

He edged them to one side as a smart drag came past pulled by four chestnuts and heavily loaded with young men. The cabs were bowling out of the station yard but Cecily elected to walk, joining the throng trailing across the course at the top of the hill and heading for the grandstand. A great crush of vehicles was jousting dangerously to take up position by the finishing post, coming from all directions and many at a dangerous pace, but Harry shepherded them safely on to a path which led through the fairground, where the dangers were merely of temptation.

Tiger was waiting for them by the stables where Harry went to inspect Black Satin. Arthur had given Tiger leave for the day.

'You can look after Miss Laura,' Harry told him sternly. 'Mrs Keen and I will stay in the enclosures and the grandstand, but I know that will not suit Laura. She wants to go her own way. And you will be her escort. I am trusting you to look after her.'

Tiger looked suitably sober at the prospect and said, 'Yes, sir.'

'You will bring her back to meet her mother in the ladies' enclosure after the last race.'

'Yes, sir.'

Cecily was looking slightly dubious, but before she could protest Harry said to her, 'Come, my dear, we're all out to enjoy ourselves today. Laura will be perfectly safe with Tiger.'

Laura knew that her father would not have allowed it, but her mother, catching Harry's eye, laughed. Miss Bell had already departed to meet her sister. Tiger, dressed in a new jacket and cap and with a clean white neckcloth and spotless breeches, was looking the very picture of respectability, tailor-made for the task.

'Very well.'

Cecily laughed again. Laura was surprised, but too happy to wonder.

'You are on no account to visit the fair or the booths. Your uncle might take you after the race. But the two of you must keep away from the rough people. You understand, Tiger?'

'Yes, ma'am.'

When they were alone Laura laughed. 'You've got to look after me.'

'What's so funny about that?'

'I can look after myself.'

'Do so for all I care. But I shall get a hiding if I lose you.'

'No. Truly, I prefer it with you. I don't mean it.'

Laura was so excited that she did not want to get wrong with Tiger. She wanted to plan how to see as much of the Derby as possible, the horses in the paddock, the start and the finish.

'You'll have to run like a hare. But it's possible. We shall manage it. Let's go up to the start and have a practice.'

On the brow of the downs at the far side of the horseshoe course the wind blew from the Surrey hills smelling of gorse-blossom and pine-needles. Someone had started a fire in the furze by the start and the smoke rolled across the picnickers. Officials on horseback galloped to call the fire brigade while Laura solemnly examined the sacred turf where Fred would position Bend Or.

'Right here.' There was a marker in the grass, for one and a half miles. 'On the inside.'

She looked to see what Fred would see and was awed by the climb to the skyline. The clouds let through stabs of sunshine and the fire crackled in the wind. Laura laughed.

'I can't believe it!'

She turned round and looked over the valley to where the green river of the course ran straight and clear under the grandstand on the opposite hill. The noise and the shouting bellied soft and loud on the wind, the raucous music of the roundabouts and the thumping of the traction engines, the screams from the big wheels and the helter-skelters. The inside of the downs' curve was a seething nest of urban delights, a city of tents and booths thrown up to offer every sort of entertainment, fraud, spectacle and blandishment. Crowds bent on amusement came in streams over the brow of every horizon. Standing up with the skylarks and the blowing newspapers, Laura saw it all as the ultimate yellow bursting star, filling her gaze with this great prelude to Fred's glory.

'Half of 'em haven't even come to see the races,' Tiger said.

Laura would not be damped. 'If we see them start here, then we must run down the hill and up the other side to see the finish. Is there time?'

'Only if you're on another Bend Or. But we can try.'

They ran, both of them very conscious of the unique freedom of this day, infectious, precious, to be stored away for remembrance. It was in Harry and Cecily too, Laura had noticed, and it was in her relationship now with Tiger, the prickles between them withdrawn. Down the hill, through all the gipsy ponies and the painted vans, the traps and the wagonettes, and laughing and gasping up into the crowds, they toiled back to the grandstand and the green paddock where presently the stars of the racing world would collect. Laura leaned on the rail, inspecting the fine turf.

'Soon! It won't be long. Fred will come here, won't he? He won't be doing anything different?' He was known to, on occasion, she knew, sometimes making his own rules.

'No. Not as far as I know. They have to parade on the course. I don't think he can miss that. Then they go to the start across the valley out of here, the way we came up.'

'Have you seen him yet?'

'No. But I've heard he's very hungry and incredibly bad-tempered.'

There were nineteen runners. Tiger had a card, and Laura pored over it. Fred had made the weight, at what cost she could not guess. His horse had come up from Wiltshire, the Duke was down from Eaton Hall to see his passionate devotion to breeding race-horses vindicated, and these august beings were now beginning to filter out from the stands and stables.

'Fire King and Teviotdale,' Tiger said, as the first horses were led in.

People started to crowd up to the rails but Laura clung like a limpet in front.

'That's Robert the Devil,' Tiger said, as a raking, tall bay was led in. 'He's not pretty but he's powerful. And that's Mask, and Zealot.'

'I want Bend Or.'

'He's not here yet. Wait a bit. There's Mr Peck, his trainer, just coming in, in the grey coat.'

'Uncle Harry knows him.'

'With the Duke, in a topper. And look, there's our horse, coming now.'

The big golden chestnut was unperturbed, looking about him with no more than an intelligent interest, stepping slowly at his lad's elbow. His coat was finely sprinkled with white hairs and the dark blotch on his near quarter stood out curiously, just as Tiger had described. His mane and tail were silvery pale and combed out like silk. To Laura's eyes he looked fit for Fred, the most handsome horse in the field. It was inconceivable that he should not win.

The ring was crowded now and totally closed in by jostling spectators and Laura, accustomed to Newmarket, was aware of seeing it as an outsider, yet all the faces in the ring were the same. She could see Lord Falmouth and Lord Rosebery and Mr de Rothschild and smart little Lord Hastings and Mr Gretton talking to Tom Cannon; Mr Dawson was greeting Charles Wood, the jockey who was standing in for Fred and wearing the familiar magpie colours; Harry Constable and Jim Snowden, little peacock figures, were pressing through to speak with their owners . . . a murmur went up and there was a spasmodic burst of clapping and cheering, and Laura saw Archer appear at the edge of the ring. Quiet and drawn, looking neither to left nor right, he walked across to Westminster and Peck, and Bend Or was brought in to meet them by his lad. Unlike most of the other horses, he stood like a rock while his girths were tightened. Archer patted his neck and was lifted up into the saddle by his attendants, unable to use his right arm to help himself. He exchanged a few more words with the trainer, and then moved the big chestnut out for a circuit of the ring before going out for the parade. The horse came down towards Laura, close enough to touch. She saw the silken gleam of his powerful shoulders, the kind, calm gaze at the hubbub around him, and on his back the tall, painfully slender figure of her revered Fred, his awful pallor accentuated by the resplendent canary-yellow silks of the Duke of Westminster. She felt as if her whole inside turned over at the sight, leaving her giddy with adoration. Tiger was laughing at her.

'Now, if you want to see the start,' he said to her, grasping her by the arm, 'you've got to run.'

Most of the crowd was electing to stay up by the finish, but it was so thick now that by the time they had finished their butting and stumbling over the dusty grass and were heading up across clearer pastures the horses were coming down the valley behind them, stirred up by their canter past the stands, sweating and pulling for their heads. Mr McGeorge the starter was waiting for them on his hack. Laura and Tiger came to the rails as the first horses arrived up on the far brow, filing off the track on to the mown turf. Laura, panting and breathless more with excitement than lack of wind, gazed up into the sun and saw the resplendent gold of Bend Or and his jockey filling her vision in actual fact, as it had filled her daydreams for weeks past, and she called up to him, 'Good luck, Fred! I know you'll win!' But he was no longer the kind, civil Fred on his home ground, but a taut, smouldering frame of nervous tension thrusting his horse into the inside place and holding him there against all the shoving and jostling that ensued, impervious to any outside voice of encouragement.

Laura watched the line form up, Mr McGeorge very calm, the flag in his hand. Fred's eyes never left him. The horses breasted the sea of grass, the legs nervously prancing, quarters squatting. Bend Or stood like a statue, contained, his legs quivering beneath him, poised, held on a thread. She saw Fred's fingers curved, tense, the heavy bandages strapped over his right hand to the knuckle, the horse's silver mane lifting up in the breeze and dropping back to cover the quivering rein. The flag dropped. The line exploded, released as if by a spring. Laura felt the reverberations in the ground; the colours flashed across the grass and the clods flew, tails swirled. The thunder of the hooves went up over the downs like the sound of an engine, and receded, and the skylarks' singing came back, swinging against the sunshine.

Laura was in an agony of nervous tension, as bad as if she was

riding the race herself. 'He must win! Oh, Tiger, he must win!'
Tiger grabbed her by the wrist again and ran her across the brow
of the hill. A big wagonette, deserted, stood with the horses out of
the shafts. Tiger pushed her up on to the driver's seat and scrambled up beside her, and from the elevated viewpoint they could see
the colours moving against the skyline towards the top of the hill.
In another cart nearby a man was watching with a telescope.

'It's Robert the Devil! Robert the Devil, going down the hill like
a good 'un!'

'He can't see,' Tiger said. 'He'll never see what happens round
the bend. That's where it matters. We'll only know when they
come on the straight. We'll see them then.'

When they came into sight again the white and blue sash of
Robert the Devil's jockey, Rossiter, was lengths clear. Fred's
canary-yellow was nowhere by comparison, bunched up with the
trailers sorting themselves out in the straight. Laura clutched
Tiger in agony.

'You are wrong! You are wrong! He will never win!'

Tiger hadn't the conviction to contradict her, seeing how things
were. He knew the Devil was a stayer too, and not likely to fade
away, as the others behind him were now doing fast, the cracking
pace breaking them. But Bend Or was not fading. He came
through with another chestnut, Mask, close behind him, but
making so fast that Mask could not stay with him. The wild
cheering for Robert the Devil which had been ringing across the
enclosures faltered, for the certainty was now in doubt.

'It's not possible!' Tiger was muttering. 'No horse can make up
that much!'

'He will! He will!' Laura cried out. 'He will do it!'

The fiery bright spot that was Bend Or and Archer was moving
irrevocably up the straight closing up the distance at every stride.
Although she could see no details, Laura needed little imagination
to sense the immense power that was driving the chestnut. Robert
the Devil's lead had been unassailable, but it was being assailed.
The vast crowd stood in utter silence, unable to believe what they
were seeing. Laura could see the winning post standing up white
against the sea of frozen faces and Bend Or closing with the bay so
fast it was as if the hand of God was lifting him over the turf. The
horses behind were half the home-straight away, like cab-horses

by comparison. Bend Or locked with Robert the Devil and they passed the post side by side. The crowd rocked with astonishment. Laura wept.

'He has won!'

The man with the telescope said, 'I don't believe it! We must wait for the numbers. Yet I think he has it. I think Archer has it.'

Tiger jumped down.

'Come on, Laura. We must go and see.'

Once more they toiled up the hill. The crowd was stunned with amazement and admiration. Laura heard the exclamations on all sides. 'Only Archer could have done it! What riding!' 'He lifted him home! He just lifted him up!' 'He was shut in down the hill. You wouldn't have thought he stood a chance.' 'What number is in the frame? Is it decided?' The hubbub of conjecture swept over the hillsides, everyone waiting for the verdict.

'Number seven!'

The cry went up, followed by cheering and clapping. The hill was in rapture of excitement.

'Oh, Tiger, he is wonderful! There is no one like him!' Laura was flushed with adoration. But Tiger did not want to argue. He was smiling and pleased, and Laura remembered that he had won a lot of money, his bet having been placed a long time ago.

'You are never wrong,' she said, awed. 'It is exactly as you said. Are you ever wrong?'

'No.'

For Laura, at that moment, life was full of magic. She felt that miracles were commonplace; bliss was in the palm of her hand. She was afloat with the coloured balloons over the grandstand, with the pigeons soaring up to take the news to London.

And suddenly a man stood before them, grinning, holding out his arms to block their path.

'Just a moment, my lad! I never thought the day would come!'

He was powerful and lithe, in young middle-age, wearing flash clothes, handsome, overbearing. With him were two young men who looked like his sons; all had close-cropped chestnut hair and a similar slender grace. They were all just like Tiger.

Tiger ran. Laura glimpsed his face, terrified. She screamed. The man lunged for his son, caught his wrist and wrenched him round, swinging him off his feet, but Tiger twisted like a snake out of the grasp and ran again. Laura rushed into the man's path so that he blundered and almost fell, and in that instant Tiger had dived into an alley up between the candyfloss tents and the gingerbeer stalls and made his escape. Laura ran too, as petrified of the man as Tiger, desperate to be at Tiger's side. She was still child enough to outpace the man, dodging and wriggling over guylines and ropes, seeing where Tiger went, ducking under the wing of an awning over the front of a fortune-teller's tent and diving abruptly behind the cover of a big brewer's dray. Laura cut round the back of the fortune-teller's and met him doubling back. They wheeled with one accord and sprinted up a wide path between stalls of oysters and eels and cockles. Behind them was a hue and cry, several drunks and roisterers having joined in. The stall-vendors cheered them on; one of the brothers appeared at the top of the trampled alley of grass. Laura stopped, shaking with fright.

Tiger thrust her through the dark opening into a large tent. It was full of little tables and chairs, mostly occupied, and doing a roaring trade in seafood dishes. They threaded their way through to the back, panting, and dropped down behind a trestle table laden with plates and glasses. It had a snow-white linen cloth down to the grass, and they crawled under and lay pressed to the ground, close together. Laura could hear her own heart thumping in time to Tiger's and taste the sweat on her lips. She was clammy all over and shaking. She could see Tiger's face very close, beaded with sweat, his nostrils dilated to get breath. It had changed so suddenly. She would have died to save him, she thought wildly, and put her hand over his on the beaten-down grass. The cave under the cloth smelled of hot grass and starch, and their own perspiration. A woman was clattering plates above them. Laura started to cry. Tiger rolled over, stretching out his legs, listening.

'Be quiet!' he hissed.

They heard a voice from the doorway. 'He came in here. There's no way out the other side. We must get him.'

'I'll guard the back, all the same, in case he slips under the canvas.'

'Yes. Go to the far corner. And you, Jem, down the side there.'

'We'll hunt 'im out, mister. We'll flush 'im, the little devil.'

The seafood man could be heard in argument, voices raised, the woman in charge of the crockery joining in.

'This is a respectable place! You can come in here to eat, or else go about your business. We've no time for larks in here.'

'Yes, fine, a plate of cockles then, missus, and plenty of vinegar. Let's come through to the back.'

Laura looked at Tiger, her eyes accustomed to the greenish light that filtered through the cloth. He was lying still, propped on his elbows. They had already examined the view from under the cloth, but the far side of the tent was pegged hard down to the ground, too tightly to crawl under. There was only the one opening. Tiger rolled over on his side and rested his head on his hand.

'It looks like it's all up with me.'

Laura felt the tears rushing up, sliding hot and copious down her cheeks. She could not say anything for weeping. Tiger, strangely, was touched. He reached out his hand for hers again.

'Don't cry, Laura. There's a chance, perhaps. But if not, I do love you, remember. I shall always love you.'

This made Laura cry even harder. She was swamped with pity and affection, choking to try and keep silent.

The vinegar bottle thumped on the table over their heads. They could hear heavy breathing, the clatter of cutlery.

'The little bugger! Wait till I lay my hands on him! He'll not get away.'

'Wait till the missus is serving that lot coming in and we'll get behind the table. He could be lying up behind those beer barrels.'

They could see the boots an arm's length away, the heavy cord trouser bottoms.

'Or under the table.'

'Right. Wait till she turns her back.'

Tiger said to Laura, 'I'll make a bolt for it, when they come round the back. You sit tight. They won't touch you, they won't dare. They'll get after me, and then you can walk away.'

He was quite calm now. Laura couldn't be sure if he had said that he loved her, or whether she was dreaming it. What was happening was certainly very strange, not at all the sort of thing her mother would approve of. The table-cloth was suddenly jerked aside. Tiger leapt out the other side, dragging the cloth with him.

Laura heard a roar and a crash of falling crockery. Looking

through the gap she saw tables and chairs flying in all directions, women jumping to their feet. Tiger ran but his father was faster, and one of the brothers was coming in the doorway. Kneeling in her cave out of the way, Laura saw the fatal collision, and the bodies down and fighting, the proprietor of the tent joining in and his missus advancing with a bottle in her hand. Tiger was fastened in a grip of steel round the back of his neck, dragged off his feet and slapped and punched violently into questionable submission. Laura understood immediately how it was for him, why he had been so grateful for the sanctuary of mere weeding when he had arrived over a year ago. His family evidently took such behaviour in their stride, for his father was laughing now, and giving the proprietor a handful of sovereigns. The brothers had Tiger in a grip which Laura could see was quite final.

'Me boy is nothing but trouble, ma'am. I'm sorry if we frightened your customers. I hope this'll make it right with you.' Another clink of sovereigns.

'My apologies, I'm sure.' He bowed to the dim interior and customers twittered and smiled, quite pleased with the bit of excitement. The man was charming and quite ruthless.

The steamy tent filled Laura's nostrils with the smell of vinegar and canvas, fish, tarred rope and hot, trampled grass. She thought she would never forget the smell, coupling it with disaster, till her dying day. Long after the fuss had died down, she crawled out from under the table and made her way back to meet her mother. She was sick with pity for what she had seen, and lonely, as if the downs were quite deserted. She had never felt more lonely in her life.

6

'There, my lamb, don't cry.'

Albert, as always, was like a rock. 'You had a lovely day, and Tiger will come back, if he wants to.'

'They won't let him!'

'You can't keep a boy locked up, not now he's grown. Not a clever lad like Tiger.'

'You didn't see them! They were fierce and strong—they *laughed*! Lots of them.'

'All like tigers?'

'Yes. They were all the same.'

Albert laughed. He gave her a sugared almond and a large, clean handkerchief.

'You mark my words, he'll be back.'

But Albert did not know why Tiger was so valuable and Laura could not tell him for Uncle Harry had forbidden it, and she cried afresh into the new handkerchief. How did they keep him, she wondered, when he did not want to stay? Did they have a house with barred windows and a bolted door where they locked him? Or a travelling caravan where he was chained like a guard-dog? For they had had a gipsy look about them, something about the brown colouring and the wiry grace of their bodies, an outdoor look. And she was sure their grip on Tiger's thin arms had not eased for one moment since that fatal confrontation in the oyster -tent, save to be exchanged for something more secure. She saw no hope for Tiger at all.

'And what did your uncle have to say about it?' Albert asked. 'For it's his loss. The lad was good at his work.'

'He was upset.'

Laura found it impossible to explain how her mother and Uncle Harry had taken the news. They had been shocked, but there had been between them some strange link—Laura could only think of it as a secret between them, as if they knew something that no one else knew of—and they had taken the news in a slightly absent way, as if it was something that did not directly concern them, as if their secret was far more important. Harry, it was true, had been angry and blamed himself, and said he should have left Tiger at home, but quite shortly afterwards he had changed and was smiling, and had not spoken of it again until they had been coming home in the train. And then he had said to Laura, 'Tiger will come back, I think. Perhaps not immediately, perhaps not even for a year or two but he will come back.'

Uncle Harry had seemed very gentle and quiet and happy, in spite of Tiger. Laura wondered if it was because he had won a lot of money, but did not like to ask. She did not understand how the adult mind worked. Only Albert's. Albert never let her down. Miss Bell was not concerned with Tiger either, but was in raptures over the race.

'There never was a race like it—if you'd seen! Coming down Tattenham hill he was quite well back, and shut in. There was no way through. And then he shouted to Fred Webb that he was coming through on the rails, and there was scarcely a gap at all, but he lifted his leg right up on the horse's shoulder and squeezed in and got through—it was a miracle! And by then he had so much to make up—nobody dreamed it was possible.'

'But anything's possible with Fred,' Albert said.

'And at the end, when he wanted his whip, he had forgotten his arm was no good and he couldn't do anything with it, so he couldn't use it, and he just rode with all his body, with his legs *lifting*, just lifting Bend Or past Robert the Devil.'

'And your money was on him, I take it?'

'I always put my money on Fred,' Miss Bell said.

'Not on the horse.'

'No. The horse had sore shins all the week. He had to have his legs rubbed with brandy every day. So he couldn't come down the hill properly, and that is why he had so much ground to make up.'

'You are giving yourself away, Hilda. For a governess, you seem to know a great deal about horse-racing.'

Miss Bell laughed. 'I learn it all off Laura.'

But Laura already knew that Miss Bell was as besotted as she was with Fred Archer. They talked about him for hours, and Miss Bell had as many pictures in her closet as Laura had herself. Cecily and Philip, Miss Bell's employers, were the only people who did not know.

Laura had eaten a late dinner with her mother in the dining-room, the two of them alone. Laura had kept on crying but her mother had said nothing at all. She had not seemed to exist, it seemed to Laura. Alice had lit the candles on the table, and in the dusky grey room her mother had sat like a white ghost, not moving or speaking. Laura, wrapped up in her day's shocks, had escaped to Albert's comfortable lap and his pinstriped shoulder, warm before the kitchen range. Laura felt secure with him. He was never impatient, wanting to do other things, not when she wanted him. He just sat there, his feet on the fender, and her in his lap.

'You are too big, miss, for that,' Peggy had said a few times, with her sniff, but Albert just laughed.

'Everyone needs a shoulder to cry on. There's no harm in it.'

He had been married, and had six grown-up children. His wife had died and that was when he had moved to Newmarket.

'It's time you were in bed, miss,' he said to her gently. 'It will be better in the morning. Things will turn out all right, you'll see. Go and say goodnight to your mother.'

He took her up into the hall and Cecily was just coming out of the dining-room. She had been alone for almost an hour. The candles had gone out.

She said to Albert, 'I am going out for a walk. You may go to bed, but don't lock the doors. I shall lock them when I come in.'

'Very well, ma'am.'

She did not even look at Laura. She went through the hall, ignoring her hat and gloves and cape, and went out through the front door and down the drive to the lane. The sound of her footsteps faded.

Laura kissed Albert goodnight. She went upstairs. Albert went on standing in the hall for some time. The house was silent. He sighed, and went into the dining-room to clear away.

* * *

Fred Archer stood at the window of his hotel bedroom, listening to the late night revelry that still broke the June twilight of Epsom high street. Celebrating, or drowning their sorrows, the result was indistinguishable by midnight. The paralytic figures wove their way homewards, or fell in doorways, or were conveyed by patient horses back to the city, falling by the wayside all the way from Banstead to Clapham Common. Sated by ale and steaks and more ale, they were happy in oblivion. Most of the toasts had been raised to Archer, but he had merely smiled and been polite, present only from cordiality. It was required from the owners, and expected by Mr Dawson. They had all tucked into their Derby dinners and the magnums of champagne; the table had spilled with roasts of every variety, with lamb and chicken, beef and ptarmigan, woodcock and salmon, with trout and whitebait, sweetbread, turbot, oyster soufflé, quails in aspic, with tiny new potatoes and tender cauliflowers, new carrots and boiled onions in cream sauce, with puddings and tarts and jellies and cheeses and savouries, and wines of every colour and degree, and more champagne, and toasts to the Duke, in champagne; to Bend Or, in champagne; to Robert Peck, in champagne; to himself, in champagne . . . and he had smiled and nodded and sat with a clean white napkin tucked into his best waistcoat, a fork in his hand, and eaten a tiny steak and a tablespoonful of vegetables. Clamped between the hollow, dehydrated walls of his stomach, nausea lay heavily, scarcely controllable; a sweat of revulsion had glistened on his brow. To think of it now made him retch. The Duke and Peck and all his backers could glut themselves stupid on his victory, but he must stay hungry. He must stay drained and parched, like a sun-bleached stick, clapped out, unstoked, powered by nervous energy alone, which was hard to control. Yet he did it by choice. There was nothing else in his life that meant anything at all: to ride winners—and losers were no part of his programme—was the only reason for his existence. He thought about making all his rides into wins the whole time. He did not know why he was driven in this way: he recognized the ambition as a flaw in his character. It was doing him no good. Even now, in June, he longed for the relief of the winter months, to get back to eleven stone and work off his energy in the hunting field. Yet a month ago when the accident had almost decided just such a future for him, he had gone almost out of his mind with despair. There was a madness in him, yet he was praised for his intelligence.

Mr Dawson, his mentor and partner, had suggested that it would do him good to marry, to make a home of his own and raise a family. He had no difficulty in meeting ladies, indeed the reverse. They wrote to him, proposing marriage, by every post; they queued up at railway stations to meet him and waited outside his hotel door. Yet he never thought of women. He lived in an austere room of his own at Heath House and was content with it. Mat Dawson and his wife, childless themselves, treated him like a son. He wanted nothing else.

But sometimes there were moments, like now, when he stared into the future and saw its impossibility. There was a limit to the number of times a body could do what his had done today and get for reward not nourishment but punishment more severe than any he had ever meted out to a horse. But he knew that he was the phenomenon he was just because of this overwhelming desire that drove him. He was acutely aware of its power and the dangers it faced him with. He was too clear-headed for his own good. He was a genius at divining how the equine character worked, but he was equally acute in divining his own.

He undressed in the bare bedroom, exhausted, thankful to God for what he was, for what he had achieved. He prayed on his knees, conveying gratitude for favours received and hope for more to come. He did not pray for comfort, for glory, for money, for ease from his pains, only for winners.

He slept fitfully, plagued by stomach pains and the throbbing of his splinted arm.

* * *

A month later Gervase came home from school and brought a friend with him. The friend was quite different from Gervase: boisterous, active, cheeky and good-humoured. His name was Simister. He was built like a small bull, broad and strong, with thick dark curls on his forehead between where his horns should have sprouted. He had a way of standing, looking up from under his heavy brows, as if watching the matador's cloak, ready to charge. He always seemed to Laura ready to charge, eager to go.

'What do you like to do?' Cecily asked him nervously on his first morning.

'Oh, I like everything. I like walking and bicycling, and riding. Swimming, rowing. Tennis, golf, running, climbing. Especially climbing.'

'Harry climbs mountains,' Cecily said. She knew it was a foolish remark even as she said it, considering the extraordinary flatness of the surrounding terrain and the unlikelihood of Harry wanting to cut off from work at the height of the season to go looking for mountains.

Philip gave her one of his withering looks.

'Are you suggesting—'

'You climbed mountains when I first met you,' Cecily said quickly. 'You went with Harry. It kept you fit, I remember. Have you never thought of taking it up again?'

'It has occurred to me, yes. Young Padfield—he helps with the presses at Merton—he was telling me he was climbing in Corsica last summer. It sounded tempting.'

Cecily was amazed by the success of her conversational gambit.

'You could do with a holiday, Philip, some physical exercise. You are much too taken up with your drawing-board.'

'We might plan it, for the future. If the young people want to go, we could make up a party. Harry too. He never has a holiday. And Laura and Miss Bell—an educational trip for the young.'

Laura was as amazed as her mother. 'I wouldn't want to go,' she said. 'I don't want to go away.' She decided that it was best to make her position clear from the outset.

'You are very quick to make up your mind, miss,' her father said. 'Your education will certainly require some foreign travel before long, whether you like it or not. It's no use talking in that manner.'

Laura kept silence with difficulty, and saw Gervase grinning across the table. The thought of going to a foreign country appalled her.

'It would be great, sir,' Simister said, rushing in happily with his bull's disposition. 'If you should ever plan it, I'm sure my pater would let me come.'

Philip looked pleased. He shone, pink and smooth, in the morning sunlight.

'We'll bear it in mind. I'll have a word with Harry. He was a very fine mountaineer as a boy, as you say.'

Cecily wished she had known him then, wild on the mountains like a chamois. She could see him, slender and fast over the rock, half the size of Simister and twice as agile. If she had met him then, instead of Philip, she would have gone climbing with him and lived in the clouds, bathed in mountain dew, fed on goat's cheese and heather honey, made love on the flowery turf. In those days she had been wild too and had not stopped to think. Philip had spoken to her of his brother Harry disparagingly. 'He is only interested in dangerous sports. He has no culture.' Philip had had culture enough for them all, a shining golden youth at the time, very quick at picking up the artists' patter, letting his hair grow long and wearing his clothes correctly dishevelled. Cecily had married him when she had found herself with child. She had been told as a young girl that she could never conceive. Her parents had been 'Bohemians' and she had been brought up 'naturally'. It had taken her long, hard years to grow out of it. She had never forgiven her parents for the pleasure she had enjoyed in the artistic circles of her youth, admired, indulged, pampered, an artless, irresponsible child posing for 'their' pictures and reading 'their' poetry, holding their hot brows in the long grass and their cold hands at winter firesides—men who should have known better, who peddled carnal desire in a cloak of artistic passion. They called her 'pure lily' and 'beloved child'. Only afterwards, when she had left the precious circle, had she come to realize that they were just dirty old men and she a gullible girl without guidance. Recalling Harry as a mountaineer during those addled days, she could remember him appearing at intervals into his brother's circle, passing through en route for Newmarket or the hunting shires, derisive and unimpressed. He had come to their wedding, not been particularly gallant, had in fact been far warmer a brother-in-law when Laura was born. He had admired the child far more than the child's own father, had always been more of a family man by nature. The pattern of their lives had turned out all wrong and there was no way to right it now.

Simister's ebullience seemed to bring out an expansiveness in Philip that was not usually apparent. Simister had a natural gift for open admiration; he thought the house absolutely ripping and

Philip's designs highly aesthetic, the artist's freedom of self-expression linked so artfully to commercial gain much to be applauded. Philip had always had to go to London to be appreciated up to now and even there the competition was too fierce to be satisfactory, so Simister's awe was much to his taste. Simister had this drawing-out influence on Gervase too, who expanded out of his usual gaucheness into a stammering cheerfulness and took to the bicycle, the fishing-rod and even the tennis racquet under his friend's stimulation. Laura was not so impressed: she kept comparing Simister with Tiger, and every time Tiger's fierce integrity swamped the comparison. She could not forget Tiger's face under the trestle table and his earnest declaration of love, linked to those hard, distant kisses in the loosebox. When he had been there, love had been a small experimental part of the relationship, but now he was gone it was the part Laura remembered. Her love was doomed to depend on shadows; the flesh and blood available and to hand she scorned.

She would sit on the lawn with Miss Bell doing French conversation while the boys, having marked out the tennis lawn and mended the net, exercised their biceps in a match. It was hard not to take any notice of them. Laura, who knew that Miss Bell was three years younger than she had made out to her mother, supposed that the governess even so was too old to be interested in Simister's ploys; she had taken to walking out with Arthur, mainly because he took her in the Rutland Arms and sometimes Fred went there to play billiards and she saw him. She told Laura this but had made her swear not to tell her mother. Fred had never spoken to her yet, and she did not believe that he acknowledged Laura.

'I've only your word for it.'

'Ask Uncle Harry. He will tell you it's true.'

'Perhaps I will. Arthur gave me a racing paper last night. Look, I have it here. It has an interview with Fred. Look it's lovely, the description: "He has wonderful eyes. At first they seem languid, especially when the lids fall over them as he is thinking; but once he becomes interested there comes into them a smouldering fire which illuminates his face. He almost talks with his eyes, they are so expressive." Isn't that lovely?'

'Show me.' Laura took the paper, devouring the heady prose.

'He has been champion jockey since 1874, when he was seventeen. He earns as much money as a Queen's counsel, it says. And yet Uncle Harry says he still has to do what Mr Dawson tells him. He has to attend evening stables, and prayers, and stand to attention when an owner speaks to him.'

'The Duchess of Montrose is in love with him, did you know? Everyone says so. She sends him presents and invitations all the time.'

Laura said, 'So am I. I have been in love with him for years. I shall never love anyone else.'

'It makes it very hard to love anyone else,' Miss Bell agreed.

She gazed dreamily out across the lawn. Percy was weeding the gravel on the far side where it led through the stableyard and into the lane. She saw him stand up and touch his cap, and two figures appeared, walking together in deep conversation. They turned off the drive and came towards her across the grass. Miss Bell thought she was going to faint.

'Laura!' she murmured.

Laura looked up and saw her uncle with Fred Archer. The yellow stars exploded inside her like cannons. She sprang to her feet. Miss Bell was white as paper.

'Uncle Harry!'

'Oh dear, I was hoping to avoid you,' he said, stopping in his tracks. 'That's why I came across the lawn. Your mother will be very angry.' But he was laughing. He said to Fred, 'You're considered a bad influence round here, Fred. Laura is supposed to think of her lessons, and not of racing. Allow me to introduce Miss Bell, Laura's governess, poor lady. Mr Fred Archer.'

Miss Bell got to her feet. Laura looked at her and laughed. She was quite speechless, her face drained, her eyes stark with shock. She put out her hand, saw that Fred's right arm was in a sling, and dropped it again.

'I'm pleased to meet you,' Fred said. 'Please excuse me.'

'Isn't your arm better?' Laura asked him.

'No. It's playing me up again and I'm laid off for another week or two.'

'He's got time to waste. That's why he's here,' Harry said. 'He's come to look at those two fillies down in the marsh meadow. I was taking him the quickest way.'

'Can we come?' Laura asked. 'Oh, yes, we can! You don't mind? You can't!'

'I'm frightened of your mother.'

'You're not! She won't see us! Tell her you invited us, and then she can't say anything.'

'I don't want to get Miss Bell into trouble. But come on, I'll do my best if we're seen. Miss Bell was employed specifically to counteract my bad influence, Fred. You've noticed that Laura isn't allowed to attend trials on the Heath any more? She's got to grow up and be a nice lady. Miss Bell's got the job of breaking her in.'

'You have my sympathy, Miss Bell,' Fred said amiably.

'We were reading in the paper about you,' Laura said, as she was still clutching the sheets in her hand. 'There's an interview— we were just reading it, and then you came.'

'About my smouldering eyes?'

'Yes.'

Fred laughed. 'Mrs Dawson read it to me over the breakfast table. We had a good laugh.'

'So that's how you spend your lessons?' Harry said. 'It's worse than I thought.'

'We were translating it into French,' Laura said.

'Laura!' Miss Bell was shocked.

Harry thought it very funny. 'You'll lose Miss Bell her job, Laura. No one will ever tame you! No, excuse me, Miss Bell, please forgive me, we won't let that happen.'

He could see that she was in a difficult position, and in the trance-like state of shock that Fred was apt to induce in young women.

'Let us go and see the filly by Doncaster that Fred is thinking of buying, and if we are seen I will make sure that I take all the blame. Is that all right? And after that you can get on with your French. Fred needs his mind taking off his troubles. He's missing all these winning rides at Ascot with his arm out of action.'

'But you won the Derby, and since then the French Derby too,' Laura said.

'Yes, I've done too much with it and owners aren't keen on one-armed jockeys. If I don't rest it now, I might not get the use back, they tell me.'

Laura looked to see how expressively his eyes were smouldering at the thought of this dire possibility, and did in fact see a hint
of the melancholy that was a characteristic of his expression. He
was said to be without education, could scarcely read or write,
and yet he never gave this impression, quite the opposite in fact. It
didn't matter, she thought wildly, that she wasn't learning French
in the garden. He had won the French Derby and talking French
hadn't mattered at all.

'When you went to France,' she said to him, 'and rode that
French horse, you couldn't speak French?'

'No.'

'It didn't matter? It was no trouble to you?'

'The horse understood what I was telling him. And when it
came to the finish it was lucky, perhaps, that I didn't know what
they were shouting. They don't like a foreigner to win out there.
They do everything they can to stop you.'

'I wonder you go there,' Harry said, 'the tricks they get up to.'

'It pays well. I make sure of that, else I wouldn't bother.'

They walked across the lawns towards the gate into the grazing
meadows, Laura keeping close and Miss Bell following nervously,
but unable to help herself. Behind them Simister and Gervase had
dropped their racquets and came running.

'I say, sir, is it true? Gervase says you're Mr Archer the jockey?'
Simister was in full charge as usual, sweating and brash. 'You
don't mind—I'd love your autograph, sir. I would be really proud.'

He was groping in his pockets, fishing out a stub of pencil.
Gervase beat at the nettles with his racquet, flushing up with
embarrassment. They were at the gate of the field and Harry was
unlocking the chain.

Fred said, 'It's a bit difficult at the moment. I don't know if I can
manage it.'

'Oh, your arm, sir—yes, that's tricky. But perhaps with your
left—even if it's just a mark. My sister wouldn't half be proud,
sir. If you could—here—'

Persistent, he smoothed the scrubby bit of paper on the top bar
of the gate and proffered up the chewed pencil. Laura watched,
hot with jealousy, furious at Simister's boldness. Fred took the
pencil, not at all put out, and held the paper down with his
splinted hand.

'I doubt if she'll be able to read it.'

But he got the letters down, F. J. Archer, very wandering and crooked, and handed the piece of paper back to Simister.

'That's awfully kind of you, sir. It's really great to meet you. I'm sorry about your arm, sir. I hope it won't keep you out too long.'

'No. I'm hoping so too.'

'Thank you very much, sir.'

Laura glared after the two departing boys, wild with envy at what Simister had achieved. Uncle Harry always said she was bold, but she wasn't one jot as bold as Simister. But she stayed on, hanging over the gate while Harry went down the field to call the fillies up, and Miss Bell stood behind her, her eyes fixed on Fred.

'Uncle Harry took me to the Derby this year. It's the first time I've ever been. I put my money on Bend Or.'

'Then you had a lucky day.'

'It was marvellous!' She wanted to say, *you* were marvellous; Simister would have done.

'Yes, he's a courageous horse.'

'Did you think you'd won? Lots of people thought you hadn't, until the numbers went up.'

'Well, if I'd had two good arms it wouldn't have been such a close-run thing.' He made it sound a casual business. 'People don't like to get such frights when their money's on.'

'Oh, I knew you'd won!'

'Laura the Plunger, we call her,' Harry said, coming up with one of the fillies haltered. 'She needs watching. Steady on, my lass! Stand up now. Her dam is by Blair Athol, won a couple of races as a two-year-old but didn't train on. She got a nice colt by Hermit the year before this one, which Mr Gretton bought. You know it perhaps?'

'I've ridden it, yes.'

Fred caressed the filly with his good arm, feeling her down, and Harry walked her out and trotted her back. Laura hung over the gate, watching with Miss Bell.

'There, I told you, didn't I?' she whispered triumphantly. 'You believe me now?'

'Yes.'

The two fillies wheeled about and the men stood talking, watching their movement. The fields sloped down to the stream, bright with buttercups and at the bottom, where it was marshy, the meadowsweet was flowering in white banks. Its scent drifted up the damp valley. Laura wanted it to last for ever, watching Fred and the playful fillies. When they had walked back with him, she was then as silent as Miss Bell, seeing the perfect moments coming to an end, feeling the torments of longing turning over in her inside. It was impossible for anyone to love a being more than she loved Fred Archer. If he had been just the public man, the brightly-garbed flash jockey with incredible nerve cheered by the whole nation, it would have been a quite bearable, even enjoyable, act of worship, but when he was as well this reserved and gentle man apparently quite unconscious of his glory, a whole new dimension was added. When he had gone, taking his leave politely with his grave smile, Laura was left feeling like seawrack flung high on a stony beach, dried out, stranded, starved and abandoned. As Miss Bell appeared to be in much the same state, the two of them came to the lunch-table so silent and wan that Cecily could not help but notice. However she had no need to ask questions for the bold Simister lost no time in declaring what a stunning bit of fortune to meet Fred Archer and get his autograph.

'Just look here, Mrs Keen, what do you think of that? My sister won't half be bowled over. She's no end cracked on Mr Archer. I never dreamed to meet such a famous fellow.'

By great good luck Philip was having lunch away in Cambridge with a client so Cecily was alone in her disapproval.

Miss Bell explained nervously, 'Mr Keen—Mr Harry— brought him to see some horses, madam. They came across the back lawn, and we were introduced.'

'Oh, he is too bad!' Cecily could not help bursting out. She could see it in Laura's face, pinched-up and distant, the dreamy eyes. She went openly to see Harry after lunch, not caring who saw her.

'You are too bad, Harry! However am I to cure her of her silly dreams when you are so thoughtless? Just when there are suitable boys of her own age to interest her—'

'She has more sense to love Fred than those oafish boys!' Harry was as angry as Cecily. 'What are you trying to cure, Cecily? Your own condition or Laura's? You are ridiculous about her feelings for Fred. There is nothing unnatural in it. Your precious Miss Bell is exactly the same, bowled over—they were reading a magazine article about him when we arrived. You cannot stop nature, not in yourself nor in anyone else. Why do you fight it so?'

'I fight because I never want her to be so unhappy as I have been! And where is happiness in pursuing a dream? Mr Archer will never look at her, she is just a child to him. He has the whole world to choose from.'

'She knows it is a dream. She has too much sense to confuse reality with dreams. Let her enjoy it—and her Miss Bell too! Her dreams did not stop her kissing Tiger out in the stables when he was here. Tiger was no dream.'

'Tiger!'

'Don't worry. The boy was severely disciplined for his indiscretion. I only tell you so that you will see this business in proportion. Kiss me, Cecily. It's not all dreams, you know. There is no need for you to be unhappy, not when I love you like I do. Fred doesn't know the half of it, sticking to his race-horses like he does. Stop worrying!'

He put his arms round her, laughing, and she forgot Fred Archer and laughed too. It was sweet to be loved by Harry, who never wanted anyone else and was always near, and kind. His office was cool, out of the sunshine, and the boys were at lunch, Martha busy serving them; out of the window the yard was quiet, the horses feeding, the dogs laid out under the heavy walnut shade.

'As long as I know you are there—' he said gently.

'And you, Harry. I am stupid, it's quite true.'

'I shall never want anyone else. You must enjoy what there is and never regret what isn't, and then it is all right.'

'If you say so.'

'And this wife and family you are forever wishing on me, it will never happen. I think of you and Laura as my family.'

'You ought to have a son.'

'If it means a wife first, no. I shall do without.' He paused. 'But a boy—I can tell you, Cecily, that boy Tiger was a boy after my own heart. I keep finding myself thinking about him since he's gone. I find myself praying that he will come back.'

'Do you know where he is? You found out who his parents were, I thought.'

'Yes, they are circus proprietors. And do you know what our Tiger does for a living? He's a high-wire performer.'

Cecily was astonished. 'And I put him to weeding! Well, yes, it fits, I thought he walked like a dancer. I remember thinking that.'

'I haven't seen him at it, but I picture him sometimes, poor little devil. He never spoke to me about it, but he knew I found out about his family, who he was. I found out his secrets. But I've never told anyone. Only you, now.'

'He was happy here, I think.'

'Yes. I found it very hard not to show favouritism where Tiger was concerned. If he ever comes back I think I could train him to take responsibility. He could become a partner, in time. That would suit me very well. It's what you mean, I think, about a son, a sense of continuity, for the future. Tiger would be my son.'

'Is that a dream too?'

'Probably. Funny, it's what has happened at Heath House with the Dawsons. Fred went there as just an apprentice, and now Mat has made him a partner. He is the same as a son to the Dawsons.'

'And what has happened to us—it's common enough, I suppose. You are quite right to put things in proportion for me.'

'What you can't change . . . well, it's no use kicking. Take what you can, enjoy it and be thankful. In some ways we're lucky.'

'You can make me believe it now, when I'm with you.'

'Don't worry about Laura, Cecily. She's one of life's survivors. She's strong.'

It wasn't so funny for Cecily finding out that Miss Bell was as besotted with Fred Archer as Laura herself, but she decided to overlook the matter and concentrate merely on keeping the bad news from Philip. The thought of dismissing her for her misguided affections was apalling. Cecily had come to rely on her utterly for keeping Laura occupied, buying her clothes, organizing the boys, driving the trap out on picnics, on expeditions, doing some shopping, buying Laura the right books, mending her underwear. She was unobtrusive, completely troublefree; even Philip could find no fault. She never spoke out of place, never spoke much at all, was perfectly easy to overlook altogether. And she and Laura spent all their days together in apparent harmony. And if it was their mutual adoration of Fred Archer which produced this happy condition, perhaps Harry's advice was correct. Make the best of life's blessings, and ignore what could not be changed. No, the idea of dismissing her and finding someone else was not to be contemplated. Shaken by the very idea, Cecily went to dead-head the roses, her mind blotting out the subject and filling again with dear, sweet Harry. She could not ask for more, given the situation.

* * *

Tiger did not come back.

Simister, liking Dry Meadows, came back quite often, holiday after holiday, a foil for the moody Gervase. Miss Bell organized them, Cecily leaving her in charge, and she did not find them difficult. Simister was invariably polite. His nice manners made him acceptable to Philip, whom he buttered up (Laura called it buttering up) and the occasions he went down to town in the evenings with Gervase and got drunk with the stable-boys and experimented with the local female talent he took care to hide from his hosts. Miss Bell knew, and so did Harry and Arthur and Albert, but they none of them considered it out of the way. It was not necessary for Cecily and Philip to know. To Laura the two boys were like brothers, and she had learned how to resist Simister's tentative unbrotherly advances. She scorned him and made it plain. She was kinder to Gervase, but he did not trouble her in that way. She did not look for boys nor want them, devoted only to Fred Archer.

He had won another Derby on the American horse, Iroquois, and he won the St Leger; he won the City and Suburban and the Epsom Gold Cup on Bend Or; he won the Manchester Cup, the Royal Hunt Cup, the Portland Plate, the Doncaster Cup, the Champion Stakes . . . Laura gave up counting after two hundred by the end of the following summer.

And then she heard the news. It came through the stable-lads at Harry's, and was substantiated afterwards by Miss Bell, via Arthur and the Rutland Arms.

'Fred Archer is courting Nellie Dawson up at Warren House.'

Nellie Dawson was Mathew Dawson's niece, the daughter of his brother John, also a trainer. She was just twenty, a very gentle, pretty girl, highly regarded. Fred was said to be deeply in love. His affair, blessed by both families, was followed with avid interest by the whole of Newmarket. His engagement in the spring was a foregone conclusion. Laura wept. Harry laughed. Albert got out the sugared almonds.

Peggy said, 'There, love, what sort of a husband will he make? He's never there, always travelling. And when he is, he's in the Turkish bath all his spare time. What a man to cook for!'

To make it worse, he was building a house for his bride on the outskirts of Newmarket on the road Laura went by every time she visited town. It was a large, splendid house, nursed in its birth-pangs not only by the architect, builders and incipient owner, but by the Dawsons and Lord Falmouth himself, who was to be seen there at times, discussing embryo drains and porticos. It was to be called Falmouth House.

Laura, passing, pictured herself as mistress of the house, fur-nishing its large rooms, choosing the papers and the carpets, warming Fred's slippers by the fire.

'And I am old enough now,' she said to Harry. 'I am nearly sixteen, old enough to marry. Nellie Dawson looks younger than me. Have you seen her?'

'Yes, she is a little shrimp. But she's sweet and gentle, Laura, not a tartar like you. Fred's got lots of sense.' He was teasing her, full of sympathy. 'You never want to marry idols, Laura. It spoils it. Keep them on their pedestals, out of reach.'

'Why have you never married? Have you got an idol?'

Harry felt himself flinch. He was still treating Laura like a child and she was no longer a child. She was acute and sensitive and had a way of looking at him that made him feel highly vulnerable, exposed. And those aware boys at Dry Meadows . . . his affair with Cecily was highly dangerous, surrounded by adolescent eyes. The children were now more dangerous than the servants. And Harry believed that Albert knew. He trusted Albert's circumspec-tion, but he would never trust Simister. They were all growing up, growing old, and the patterns were working themselves out, for better or for worse. One could not see where the threads were leading. Afterwards, when it was all too late, one would under-stand.

* * *

One weekend in October, when the racing season had come to a close, Harry took Gervase and Simister from their boarding school in the midlands to Wales for a week's climbing. Prevailed upon strongly by Simister, he had been stirred by the memory of his own adolescent attempts on the faces made popular by Whymper, Stephens and their parties, and had agreed to the plan quite happily. Cecily had assured him that it would do him good, and she was proved right. The cloud-shadowed mountains, the steep blue faces of the rock stepping down into wild gullies and empty, sheep-shorn valleys inspired in him the same bold commitment that he remembered. His body was still hard and supple and he revelled in the rock-faces; it was a sport that came naturally to him; his horseman's balance and muscular strength were deployed happily to these fresh uses and the tricks and skills came back as if he had never been away. The two boys, one eager and careless and the other methodical, cautious but on his mettle not to be outdone, made unexpectedly easy companions. They insisted on camping out and as Harry listened to them in the firelight discussing their day's deeds—the two boys that he had thought would be alien—he found that he could relate to them without difficulty. They were not complicated, for all their civilized education; in fact they were predictable and conventional. It struck him as strange when he compared them with Tiger, much the same age, for the untutored boy, brought up without love or privilege, was more naturally sophisticated, far more mature than they were. Sitting out in the sharp night air, his eyes on the moonlit ridges above and the clear October stars, Harry could not help hankering even now for his fairground brat.

When he got back to Newmarket, Harry found that—whether by coincidence or by the pattern he liked to think shaped his insignificant life—the fair and circus owned by Tiger's family was travelling in the vicinity. He half expected Tiger to turn up—the sites were near enough for the boy to get to him within two or three days' walking—but when nothing happened he found that he was too curious to let the matter alone. The next week the entourage would be at Cambridge.

'Would you like to go to the circus?' he asked Laura.

'Yes, of course!'

'Just the two of us. I have a fancy to go.'

Cecily agreed. No one enquired as to the rather strange decision. Laura put on her warm clothes and was picked up by

Harry with Jester to the dog-cart and they departed down the cold lane, pulling the rugs close. The builders were working in Falmouth House, the sound of hammering and whistling echoing out of the unglazed windows, but once past the fatal monument Laura cheered up and became the company that Harry had wanted, chattering and affectionate, taking his mind off the nervous doubts that he could not help harbouring. He had no intention of informing Laura of the object of his sudden interest in circuses, did not know indeed whether Tiger was still part of the act, whether Tiger was even still in this world, but the possibility that he might see him within the next few hours was certainly making him feel surprisingly anxious. He supposed he was afraid of what he might find, remembering the circumstances of the boy's arrival—and no less of his removal—but the thought that he might get the boy back to Thorn's was undeniably making his blood run faster. He realized that he wanted it more badly than he had guessed. There was no question in his mind now of favouritism towards Tiger; Tiger was a boy apart, and if he came back he would have a new standing in the yard—if he was still the boy he had been. And Harry had a qualm, remembering the self-possession of the little boy, wondering how his family had treated him since he had returned to them. A spirit could be broken and Tiger had a highly nervous constitution, plagued as it was by his second sight. Adolescence could well have changed him; he was seventeen now. Harry found that he was anxious. Laura remarked upon his mood and he could find no excuse.

It was a windy afternoon. The blare of the steam-organ music came across the fields above the steady clop of Jester's hooves. People had come from a long way for the entertainment, as they always did on these occasions, and there was a queue of vehicles waiting to pass through the gate, from private gigs to wagons with half a village aboard. They waited, Jester restless and steaming, the big elms threshing overhead against the clouds. The season was over, the circus on its way back to winter quarters, the days growing shorter, yet the excitement was no less. Laura loved the fairground, the thumping of the traction engines generating noise and excitement, the hot smell of oil and the grinding of the roundabouts, the gilt cockerels bobbing on their twisting gold poles, the boy shouting for custom as he swung his way over the twirling platform. Inside the conglomeration that made up the fair, the circus tent was pitched, dominating the site, heaving and restless in the wind, skewered to the ground with a maze of guy-ropes, and anxiously attended by thin gipsy boys.

They parked Jester in the horse-park with his nosebag and made for the helter-skelter.

'There's time.' Uncle Harry consulted his pocket watch.

They climbed up. Laura could feel the helter-skelter quivering, her hair and her hat tugging at their moorings. When she went down the wind blasted her at every revolution, tearing at her skirts, taking her breath away. It was marvellous. They went again, laughing, like being on holiday, and then Harry bought the tickets for the circus performance and they passed into the stream of people going into the big top.

The tent was vast. Once under the entrance flaps, they came into a separate world, a draughty globe of air close and heady with the outlandish smells of unknown animals, damp sawdust and tarred rope. Gaudy tiers of benches encircled the ring, fading up into the pearly gloom of the nether regions. Harry picked places close to the passageway provided for the performers' entrances and exits. The professional atmosphere disturbed him. He looked up instinctively and saw the high wire already stretched, shining taut against the restless ceiling. It seemed to him quite lethal, and made him feel for a moment physically sick, thinking of Tiger up there. He hoped then that the afternoon would draw a blank, rather than that he should have to watch that. He was relieved that Laura did not know, for his feelings were more painful than he had bargained for. He found that he was searching every face, every programme-seller, sweet-vendor, ring-boy and ticket-taker to see if he could recognize the features. He bought a programme and opened it, searching for Tiger's name, but the only reference to the high-wire act was billed as the Daring Diablos, who could be anyone.

He bought Laura a stick of candyfloss. She wriggled with excitement beside him; drama came her way rarely, apart from that of the race-course. Philip and Cecily seldom made the journey to Cambridge to go to the theatre or a concert, and if they did they left Laura at home. Harry knew that Philip was planning for Laura to go to her grandparents in London to 'come out' and 'get finished' or whatever it was that young ladies were supposed to do, but he dreaded the day, found it impossible to relate these gruesome habits of civilized society to his unspoilt child. He had never conformed as a young man to polite society, nor—in her own way—had Cecily, but to Philip it was *de rigueur*: there would be no escape for Laura.

'Oh, I'm so glad we came! It was a splendid idea of yours!' she was saying.

Even before it started the atmosphere was one of contained excitement, the crowd straining in, a band in motley red uniforms launching into some rousing if cacophonous music. The clowns came on, shambling down the passage from the quarters behind; Harry and Laura could look back and see glimpses of tense faces behind the curtains, arranged into public smiles as they emerged. There were liberty horses (flabby by Harry's standards), acrobats and jugglers, two waltzing elephants, a fire-eater and a knife-thrower, some performing dogs . . . as Laura laughed and became flushed with excitement and pleasure, Harry found himself grow-ing cold with apprehension. The crowd cheered and clapped, caught up by the crude glamour of the thrills and trappings, the tension created by the band with its drum-rolls, the ringmaster with his heady introductions. The tent had grown smoky and hot; it groaned and billowed and the great posts trembled; Harry looked up and saw the shining tight wire quivering like a sword-blade. Cold as ice, yet he could feel beads of sweat on his lip.

'Oh, isn't it lovely!' Laura breathed.

He could not agree. He glanced back down the passage as the band crashed into a dramatic silence and the ringmaster stepped forward to introduce the Daring Diablos. Three figures stood inside the slit of the curtain waiting. Harry, wanting desperately to recognize one of the faces, was disconcerted by not being able to. Their eyes were ringed with kohl; they wore close-fitting silver caps which covered their hair and their expressions were uni-formly grim. They were identically slender, brown-skinned, and wore minimal silver costumes scattered with sequins. Any one of them could have been Tiger, or not, Harry could not tell. One was slightly smaller than the others and looked younger. When they moved forward into the ring they came past very close. Laura, glancing sideways, gave a convulsive gasp, leapt to her feet and shouted, 'Tiger!' Harry grabbed at her. The boy looked up, hesitated. Harry saw the face, blank, expressionless, the eyes very wide between the black, drawn lines. The eyes rested momentarily on him and Laura; then the boy ran on into the pool of light to the cheering and the clapping. They had expressed no recognition.

'It *is* Tiger!' Laura was in tears of excitement. 'It is, Uncle Harry—you must have seen! Look at him!'

'Laura, be quiet! How can you tell?'

'The way he moves—'

'He didn't recognize us.'

'Why should he, in that little moment? There wasn't time!'

'He works in this circus. That's why I came.'

'Then it is! You knew!' She was half-crying, half-laughing with shock. 'You knew he was a circus boy? You knew all the time?'

'Yes.'

'You never said! Oh, I knew he was something strange, but he would never say. Valuable, he said. Oh look, I can't believe it!'

The three boys were climbing ropes up to the terrible wire, very smooth and effortless. They came to the small platform at the top, one by one, and stood close together, protected by a little rail. Harry was thrown by what had happened. Laura showed pure delight, but he was torn by anxiety at Laura's indiscretion, which added to his overall fear. The band's drum-roll echoed round the tent and died away and a tense silence gripped the audience. If it had been anyone else, Harry knew he would be enjoying this gut-gripping drama; as it was, he felt screwed up out of all proportion. The roof of the tent was full of moving shadows and wreaths of smoke, no doubt very hot, and in the silence the creaking of the wind-torn canvas made an eerie accompaniment to the first movements of the three figures. One by one they crossed the wire to the platform on the other side. The movements were deliberate and smooth, but around them the canvas strained and groaned. The air was full of motion and the wire trembled when they stepped off it. There was no net to catch them if they fell.

At the next crossing, Tiger was carried between the other two, lying inert, his head thrown back. Three-quarters of the way across he was put down and lay with his spine to the wire, his legs hanging down on either side, his arms behind his head. From this position he pulled himself up on to his feet. He stood upright with his arms over his head, and then bent down so that his hands were on the wire. Laura remembered him weeding in an identical position. Very slowly and deliberately he put his weight on his hands and his legs came up over his head and down the other side back on to the wire. For a moment his body was arched like a hoop, hands and feet altogether on the wire. Then he brought his arms up again, all very slow and deliberate, and made another slow somersault. It was dramatic and beautiful, the small body arching with such precision in the dim, gusty apex of the tent. There was not a sound save the moaning of the wind. When he had made a third somersault, the hoop pivotted and then, very quickly, toppled off the wire, swung under and over and back and came to a halt hanging down, only the heels gripping the wire. The quick movement having broken the spell of concentration, the audience broke out into a roar of rapturous applause. The figure arched again and gripped the wire and swung back to the plat-form hand over hand, and pulled itself up into a standing position. The applause swelled up, with cries of 'Bravo! Bravo!' The figure waved and bowed.

Harry got out his handkerchief and mopped the perspiration out of his eyes. His hands were shaking. The other two boys were doing something else up there, but he did not want to see. He had to rest. Laura was sitting open-mouthed, like a statue, her eyes fixed and brimming with tears. Harry was moved almost to tears himself. He had no idea what he was going to do. The band was making its roll of drums to announce the climax of the perfor-mance, and he was forced to drag his eyes back.

The three of them having completed a manoeuvre together, the two outside figures retreated, one to each platform, leaving Tiger alone in the centre of the wire. Very slowly he sank from his standing position until his hands could grasp the wire, then he eased his legs out from under him so that he was balanced on his hands half above and half below the wire. Very slowly he lay down, the wire across the hollow of his back, and took his hands off the wire and lifted his arms up until they were over his head. In this position he balanced, arched right over, feet down one side and head down the other. And while the drums below went on thrumming out their tense accompaniment, he rolled over, straightening his body rigid, prone, the wire across his centre of balance a fraction above his hips, cutting across the sequined bodice. Three times more, the arms still unflinchingly stretched out, he rolled along the wire, the balance accurate to the vital fraction of an inch. The audience was still and silent, and the drum-roll faded. Tiger lay on his back, arched, motionless against the swaying roof, and the big tent was as quiet as a cathedral. Then, with a quick twist, he had cartwheeled up and over the wire, grasping it with his hands, and in a second had swung back to the platform. The band crashed out in triumph and everyone in the suspended audience gasped out with relief and broke into a great roar of cheering and clapping. The three Diablos plummeted back to the ring down the ropes, and stood together, arms upraised, bowing to the thunder of appreciation.

In this moment Harry knew he had to make up his mind. As the uproar went on around him he weighed the possibilities, knew he would have no second chance. It was up to Tiger. The elephants were waiting to come in; the Diablos took their last bow and came running up out of the ring. The one he thought was Tiger dropped into a walk as he reached the passageway. He came up close to Harry, looked up, hesitated. Harry leaned over.

'If you want to come, I'll wait for you in the lane—Jester and the dog-cart—' There was no time for more, for Tiger did not stop walking. And this time there was no mistaking the expression: the agonized indecision, fear and exhaustion. There was no indication of happy exhilaration at a job well done, not even of satisfaction. The bleak face confirmed Harry's worst fears. Turning to watch his exit, Harry saw the two brothers close in on him as they ducked under the curtain. It did not look hopeful.

Harry knew he could sit still no longer. Laura was bursting with excitement beside him, scarcely able to contain herself.

'Come along!' He grasped her arm and jerked her to her feet.

They scrambled out along the row and turned for one of the exit flaps. A dark-eyed boy pulled it aside for them.

'What did you say to him?' Laura demanded.

'I said we would wait for him in the lane.'

'Do you think he'll come?'

'I don't know. How can I tell?'

'Why should he want to leave all that to be a stable-boy?'

'Did you see his face?'

Laura did not reply.

'Why did he come before?' Harry asked her. 'It was the same then. It's no different now.'

'But what he does is amazing!'

'A great experience for the spectators, no doubt. But for him— it doesn't bear thinking about.' He was harsh in his anxiety. He wanted Tiger.

'What are you going to do?'

'Exactly what I said. Wait and see if he comes.'

They went back to the horse-park and untied Jester. The fair was still in full swing, the field crowded with people and noise. The conditions were ideal for Tiger to make a run for it if he had the inclination. They climbed into the dog-cart and threaded their way back towards the gate and out into the lane. Harry took the vehicle clear of the congestion, and pulled up in a field opening off the road. The afternoon was drawing in; lamps were being lit on the fair stalls and hung in the gateways, flickering in the wind like giant fireflies. The agitated lights, the flurries of yellow leaves driving down into the churned mud, matched Harry's own agitation exactly. Jester, feeling it, pulled and stamped with impatience, his head for home and anxious to go.

'How long shall we wait?' Laura was frightened, remembering the taunting brothers at Epsom.

'Long enough,' Harry said shortly, not knowing.

Laura was a liability if it came to a chase; he did not know what to expect. But if the whole business came to nothing, he knew he would be bitterly disappointed. He got down and lit the lamps on the dog-cart and drew out his pocket watch, holding it to the brightness.

'Sir!'

Tiger was suddenly beside him, out of breath, still in his circus clothes. The sequins twinkled in the lamplight. The cap was gone and the hair clung damply to his skull; the black kohl was smeared over his cheekbones and darkened the eye sockets, so that the face looked gaunt and foreign.

'Tiger? I wasn't mistaken!'

'No. Please—quickly—'

'As fast as we can! Get up. Laura give him the rug, quickly!'

He pushed the boy up into the cart and ran round to the driving side, grabbing reins and whip, as keen to depart as Tiger. Jester leapt into action, equally keen, and Harry let him canter on, pulling out to overtake a stately family wagon and glad to see a clear road ahead.

'Have they missed you?'

'Yes, they are looking. I lay in the ditch till they went down the far hedgerow. They've got the dogs.'

Harry decided to concentrate on the job in hand, not liking the situation at all. Without Laura it would have been less of a worry. He knew how to defend himself well enough if the worst came to the worst. Tiger was shivering against him. Harry gave him the reins and wriggled out of his driving coat.

'Here, put this on.' Jester needed no steering, the road unwinding ahead. Harry put his coat round the boy's naked shoulders and took the reins back into his hands. He was a thief, he supposed, but had no compunction about what he was doing. He did not know what to say to Tiger. The boy was a stranger for the moment, perhaps would remain so. But it was a chance worth taking.

After a few miles they relaxed, pursuit not appearing to be imminent, and Laura thawed out of her state of shock and started to bombard Tiger with questions. But Tiger would not speak, huddled down into his coat.

'You do want to come, don't you?' she threw at him impatiently. 'You *want* to come back?'

'Yes,' he said then.

'Why didn't you come before?'

But he said nothing.

'Leave him, Laura,' Harry said sharply.

They were all cold now, save Jester, jogging up the long home hill, the dead leaves shuffling under the horse's hooves. A few stars came and went between clouds and the bare canopy of branches that arched overhead; and the fields stretched wide and empty on either hand, all utterly familiar to Harry, every blade of grass, every rut in the gateways. Yet nothing was predictable. He did not know what would become of this day's events.

He put Jester away himself and made Tiger help him, sending Laura on into the kitchen to prepare something to eat. He did not want to leave Tiger alone with Laura. Tiger, discarding Harry's coat, rubbed Jester down while Harry fetched a feed. The horse's box was already bedded down and the hayrack filled. When Harry came back with the bucket and saw the horse and the boy together he felt grateful and warm, almost to tears, at his achievement. Tiger had grown taller, but was as thin and slight as he had been before. Remembering his performance, Harry was amazed at the power the slender figure had generated—in self-defence, perhaps, for its life? Harry's emotions were protective. Cecily would have said paternal.

'That will do. Bring the lamp.'

The sequins glittered again. Harry shut the stable door.

'You must come into the house and get fed.' He guessed that Tiger would have preferred to bed down with Jester, but Tiger had to face his new prospects. Harry needed to know what he had grown into.

The kitchen was warm, Laura having opened the fire and lit the lamps. Martha had gone home, the boys were in their own rooms and unlikely to come down. Laura had cut a loaf of Martha's bread and got the crock dish of butter, set the scrubbed table with bowls and spoons.

'Martha left this soup,' she said. 'Shall we have it?'

'Fine.'

Harry fetched Tiger his dressing-gown to wear, and they sat down at the table together. Harry was aware of Tiger and Laura assessing each other, although no words were spoken. He saw Laura afresh, as Tiger must see her after two and a half years, a young woman, strong and direct, but her face still childish with dreams. She was lovely, by her inexperience and her lack of the predatory quality which Harry was nervous of in women. Hilda Bell had this quality and he felt uneasy with Hilda Bell—a way of looking, an appraisal of one's sexual powers. Laura was as transparent as spring water, and it was all innocence. It was what Cecily was so frightened for, this vulnerable openness of Laura's towards what life had in store, as if it was all going to be beautiful. Cecily was convinced it was not. Cecily was not an optimist by nature but her daughter was. By contrast, Tiger's face was strained by the habitual stoicism with which he faced his lot. It was as closed and shadowed as Laura's was open and eager. It was Laura's directness that broke the silence.

'When you're on that wire, are you frightened?' It was a question Harry knew he would never have asked himself.

Equally direct, Tiger said, 'Yes.'

'Terrified?'

'If you let yourself be, yes.'

'Have you ever fallen off?'

'I wouldn't be here if I had.'

'If you're really frightened, how can you do it?'

'You can get used to being frightened. If it's every day, you learn. Lots of practice.'

'Doesn't it go away, with all that practice?'

'It never has, no. How can it, with what you're doing? Being frightened makes you do it well.'

Laura considered this. 'Does everyone feel the same? Your brothers?'

'I've never asked them. I don't know.'

'But if you've done it so long without falling off, aren't you less frightened all the time?'

'My father used to take me up when I was little and hold me by the heels to teach me, and it feels the same now as it did then. Only I don't scream any more.'

Harry hoped this horrific confession was enough for Laura's curiosity. Tiger still had his crushing self-possession, Harry noticed, but there was also the ominous tautness in his manner which Harry remembered on occasions in the past, as if the self-possession was dearly retained, held on to by the finger-nails. In view of what he faced every day, this seemed a reasonable outcome.

'I think you had better go home,' he said to Laura. 'Your mother will be worried if she doesn't know you're back.'

He went to the door with her and said quietly, 'Not a word about what has happened. And when they know Tiger is back, you are never, never to tell anyone about the circus, not your mother, nor Miss Bell, nor any of the lads.'

'Why not?'

'Because it will be talked about, and his father may well find out where he is. He will want him back and he has a perfect right to him.'

'Not to tell anyone about the high wire? Not anyone?'

'No.'

Laura was obviously disappointed.

'It's wonderful to have him back. And you knew all the time?'

'Yes.'

She turned and kissed him swiftly.

'Thank you for today.'

'Keep your side of the bargain.'

'Yes. I will.'

Harry went back to the kitchen. Tiger was still sitting at the table.

'Do you still have your dreams, Tiger?'

'Yes. Sometimes.'

'I have your Bend Or winnings in the bank. You may have them whenever you like.'

'It can stay. Money is no use to me.'

'Do you want your old job back?'

'Yes. I've always wanted to come back.'

'Why didn't you?'

Tiger shrugged, looked down. 'I'm frightened of them. Of being caught.' He was almost inaudible. 'It's worse than the wire. Laura wouldn't understand.'

'You can stay quietly here until they've gone on. No one need know. Are they going back to their winter quarters now?'

'Yes. It's the last two weeks. Back to Nottingham.'

'That's far enough away.'

'Perhaps.'

'I will do all I can to protect you.'

'Why do you want me? Because of the dreams?'

'No. I would rather you didn't dream. I think the dreams are as tough a liability as your father. I don't want your winners. Just do your two horses and ride out, and the boys will keep their mouths shut. You can live a normal life here. It's what you want, isn't it?'

'Yes.'

Harry had not answered the question, nor did he intend to. Tiger went to his old room and slept. He went back to his work, accepted by the rest of the lads, who were strictly warned not to speak of him to anyone. He said very little, kept himself very much to himself; Harry left him alone and told Arthur to do the same.

Laura found she could not approach him in the same way as she had before, openly, bluntly. She was wary of him, impressed, shy. When she saw him she did not know what to say, and he did nothing to help, for he offered nothing. He did not even look at her but turned away if he could. Laura knew that she was in the wrong desiring his company, but his very resistance attracted her. Her feelings towards him were quite different from her feelings for Gervase and Simister. He fascinated her, as he had done right from the start, but now the fascination had strong sexual overtones which confused her. She kept remembering his hand on hers, crouching under the table in the oyster-tent. But now she could not reconcile this silent youth with the boy she had shared that adventure with. And when she recognized how much he had changed, she knew she had changed too.

'I wish I could ride out with you like I used to do,' she said to Harry sadly.

'No, Laura, it wouldn't do.'

'I want to talk to Tiger.' She could say it to Uncle Harry, not to anyone else.

He would not answer, not knowing how it was possible officially. Laura would watch the string go out early in the winter mornings from the landing window upstairs before she went down for breakfast, the boys huddled down on the horses against the sleet-pricked wind. Then she would go down and eat nicely, in silence, with her father behind the sheets of *The Times* and her mother wrapped in dreams, and Miss Bell, inscrutable. Afterwards, in lessons, she did not speak of Tiger with Miss Bell, only of Fred Archer. Fred was being married on the thirty-first of January. Laura had put a black ring round the date on next year's calendar. Miss Bell said the whole year required a black ring, for she expected to be dismissed from Dry Meadows when Laura was eighteen. But Laura thought not until after the foreign tour Philip was planning to Corsica. Nobody wanted to go except Simister, but Philip was determined that they were all to be educated in foreign travel. Harry was to come to organize the climbing expeditions. Cecily had refused to come point-blank. Laura wanted to refuse too, but could not find the courage. She did not want to go abroad, or to London, or to coming-out parties. She just wanted to go across the road to Thorn's as she had when she was little. She supposed she lacked ambition. Her mother said she was wilful.

But when it came to Christmas and the New Year and Gervase and Simister came back, Laura found that she was not missed amongst all the extra work, the comings and goings, the messages to be run. Miss Bell was required to coach Simister urgently in English grammar, Cecily was shopping, and Laura escaped to Uncle Harry's warm kitchen and found him there with Tiger, discussing a horse's injury over mugs of tea. Martha was in the outhouse, washing the boys' shirts and drawers. Tiger stood up to go, but Harry told him to sit down again.

'Get yourself a mug, Laura. Have they let you off the leash then?'

'It's holidays.'

The presence of Tiger muffled her, made her stupid. She dropped the mug, but it didn't break, falling on the rag rug. She blushed furiously. She saw Uncle Harry amused, but too kind to laugh.

'Come and sit down. And you, Tiger.' Tiger was still politely standing in her presence. Stable-boys were drilled in manners, for being correct with visiting owners. She came back to the table with her tea and Tiger sat down when she sat down, not looking very happy about it. It was the first time she had seen him at close quarters since he had come back. He was neatly dressed, wearing a tie and a white shirt and she thought that he had shaved. This gave her a jolt.

'We've owners visiting,' Harry said. He also looked rather smarter than usual. 'We're on our best behaviour.'

'I'm not,' Laura said belligerently.

'No. I've yet to see the day.'

'Are you coming on Christmas day?'

'Yes, after I've had dinner with the lads.'

'For tea? As long as you come—' She glanced towards Tiger thinking of him alone over Christmas. She wanted him to come too. Once she would have said so but she knew better now. The strained look had gone out of his face. Perhaps not doing the high wire was worth any amount of lonely Christmases.

Harry got up. 'I've got to go out and speak to Arthur. I shan't want you for half an hour, Tiger. You can stay here until Mr Absolom comes.'

He went out—on purpose, Laura thought, feeling the agonizing blush coming back, the pulse-thudding embarrassment. She put her face into her tea-mug, hating this lack of control over her stupidity. She could not understand why it happened. Tiger was the same person. So was she. They had been friends before. But now they sat on either side of the table, unable to look at each other. One of the stable cats came out from behind the coal bucket and rubbed itself against Laura's skirts. She bent down to caress it, glad for the distraction. Underneath the table she could see Tiger's breeches tight over his knees, scrubbed gaiters neatly buckled. The amazing ankles that had held him suspended from the wire were hidden in well-polished boots. When she came up he was looking at her.

'Hullo, Tiger,' she said.

'Miss Laura,' he said gravely.

'You wouldn't call me Miss Laura before.'

He actually smiled. 'No.' No excuse.

'Are you glad you came back?'

'Yes.'

He was constrained, polite, as he had never been before. She did not want him to have changed.

'Are you still in love with Fred Archer?' he asked her suddenly. The question came as a shock.

'Yes, of course.'

'He's getting married.'

'Yes, on the thirty-first of January.'

'Are you jealous?'

'Yes. I wish it was me.'

Tiger smiled. It was a hint of the old belligerence, to needle her. 'She's very pretty and he loves her passionately.'

'I know,' Laura said.

'We are all getting the day off.'

'I know. It's a public holiday. They are laying on special trains to come here.'

'And free beer and fireworks.'

'It will be like Derby day. We're going to go early, to get a good view. Miss Bell and me. We want to be outside the church, to see.'

'To cry.'

'No.' One did not cry over dreams.

'I was sorry when I heard—for you. I remembered that time

when you pretended. I remembered how you felt.' Laura remembered it too. He had thought of her then, when he was away. Laura was pleased. She wished he could come at Christmas with Uncle Harry.

But Harry came alone, leaving Tiger in charge of the yard.

'Tiger's got to do the work. He's got to learn the job, so that I can retire in my old age.'

'Why Tiger?' Philip asked.

'He is clever,' Harry said.

There was mistletoe hanging in the hall. Philip took Harry's hat and Cecily came out to greet him. He took her under the mistletoe and kissed her on the mouth. Philip had disappeared into the coat cupboard, but Albert was coming through the hall with a fresh bottle of port on a silver tray and Laura had come out of the sitting room at the sound of Harry's voice. She saw her mother's face over Harry's shoulder, and its expression stopped her in her tracks. Her mother opened her eyes and saw her, and smiled. Laura had never seen a smile like it. She looked past her and saw Albert's face, looking, but quite expressionless. Laura felt as if the floor had moved under her feet. She was stunned, instinctively recognizing what she saw, but unable to reconcile it. Albert was passing on, his eyes on the tray. Harry and Cecily moved apart, Cecily still smiling as if in a dream. Laura remembered pretending it was Fred Archer and how it felt, and thought her understanding must be at fault. She was obsessed with romantic notions; her mother said it was her age. Of course her mother loved Uncle Harry. But *like that* . . .

'Laura, happy Christmas!'

Harry held out his arms to her and she flung herself on him and pressed her face against his cold cheek, burying her head into his shoulder. She clung to him, wanting him to reassure her. She wanted to stay hidden. He held her kindly, kissed her on the cheek and put her away from him, firmly, and said, 'There's nothing wrong.'

She was not sure if it was a question or not, but she accepted it as a statement, and collected herself together. The moment had passed, like the moment in the train on Derby day, and Laura pretended it was just in her romantic mind, because of her age. Her mother was now quite normal, although more cheerful than usual, but as it was Christmas day so were they all. Even Philip. They had tea with crackers and the servants came and helped them pull the crackers and Albert wore a funny hat and joined in a game of charades. Gervase and Simister got very boisterous and after they had acted the title of a play, *Much Ado about Nothing*, with so much bravado that they landed headfirst in the hearth, scorching Gervase's best trousers, Philip suggested that Cecily should play the piano and they should sing some suitable songs. He had a high tenor of which he was rather proud, unlike Harry who was tone-deaf. Laura always refused to sing, but Simister, unabashed, sang 'The Ash Grove' at great length, not terribly out of tune. Gervase, after a glass of port, sang 'The Lass with the Delicate Air' with surprising sweetness and emotion, his usually rather raucous voice softened and vibrant. When it was finished he blushed scarlet at its gratifying reception and relapsed into his awkward, customary embarrassment, going over to the fireplace and gazing into the flames to hide his discomfiture. All singing evenings were rounded off by Cecily, with whom no one could compete, and as she launched without prompting into 'My Love is like a Red Red Rose' Laura wondered if it was only herself who believed that she sang with utter conviction. Harry stood in the crook of the piano, gazing into the strings as if he would count them. Cecily sang looking straight forward, past him, her eyes fixed into eternity. Laura watched them both, for some sign, but they would not look at each other. Judging by their expressions, Laura did not think they dared. She had never seen Harry look like that. Even at the end, when the voice had died away and they started to talk, he did not move, but stayed leaning against the piano, looking—for him—extraordinarily solemn.

After the recital he made an excuse to leave. It was not very late. It seemed as if he could not recover his spirits.

'I'll come with you,' Laura said on an impulse, 'to say Happy Christmas to Tiger.'

'Very well.'

Perhaps it was to forestall her mother, she thought. But Cecily kissed Harry coolly this time, like a sister-in-law. Laura went out with him and across the lane.

'I must do my rounds,' Harry said. 'Then we'll go in for a nightcap with Tiger.'

Laura stayed with him, shivering in the stable doorways as he looked carefully at each horse, holding a lamp up high for the examination. The horses, accustomed to the visit, turned from their hayracks to stare at him, some calmly, some nervously. The shadows flared on the wooden partitions. Harry was very thorough, gentle. Laura loved the ritual. What Harry did, she thought, was much more to her liking than what her father did. She loved the racing life, the constant appraisal of these quixotic creatures, both the beauty and the harshness of it. She could live with it happily.

Everything was in order. They went in. Tiger was sitting by the range reading a racing paper. He got up quickly but Harry said, 'Don't go. Laura has come to wish you a happy Christmas. Get the glasses out, Laura. We'll drink to it.'

Laura did as she was told.

'They've all eaten up out there. Everything looks fine. No problems?'

'No, sir.'

Laura set the glasses out and Harry fetched the port from the front room where he entertained owners. They took the drinks to the hearth and Harry said, 'Happy Christmas, Laura, and may you see many of them. Happy Christmas, Tiger, and may you stay here for ever.' They all drank. Martha had tied mistletoe to the washing rack that hung from the ceiling. Harry gestured towards it, kissed Laura kindly and said, 'I've got some work to do in my office before I go to bed. Will you see Laura home, Tiger? And then lock up?'

'Yes, sir.'

He went out. Laura, warm now and stirred by the day's celebrations, looked at Tiger, wanting him to kiss her. She wanted it very badly. But he stood silently, his eyes dropped to the hearth-rug. He was only a fraction taller than she. His hair curled closely to his skull, cropped short; it was all she could see, and the lowered eyelids, the tiger-red lashes fringing the cheekbones.

'Tiger.'

There was no one to thrash him now, if he kissed her. Laura knew that Uncle Harry wanted Tiger to kiss her.

He lifted his head. When he had kissed her before he had been commanding and bold, but now she saw that he was very nervous.

She thought of him on the high wire, and the drums rolling, and of his being frightened; she did not want him to be frightened and nervous. She wanted him to be the Tiger she first knew. She realized she did not even know his name.

'Tiger,' she said again, and moved forward and put her lips to his. She felt them quiver, but no more. She pressed hers against them, and moved her mouth down across his cheek to his jaw, into the hollow underneath, feeling the roughness, resting her head there. He did not move. It was very pleasant, her face pressed in there, smelling him, the feel of their flesh together, friendly. She was quite satisfied. She felt as if they were friends again.

But when she came out, backed away, smiling, he was not smiling. He looked strange. He looked even more nervous than he had before.

'What's the matter?'

'What do you want?' he asked.

'I want you to take me home.'

'I didn't mean that.'

She did not understand.

'Is that all?' he asked.

'Yes.'

He went and fetched his cap. He was withdrawn, not at all Christmassy. She could not imagine him singing round the piano like Gervase and Simister. He was not like any of them. They went out and walked down the drive and across the lane. The lights spilled out from Dry Meadows, golden cracks between the Morris draperies, glittering on the frosty grass. Tiger took her to the front door. Laura hoped he might kiss her goodbye, but he only said, 'Goodnight, Miss Laura,' and went away.

Laura was bitterly disappointed.

7

As the day of Fred Archer's wedding came near, Laura realized she was not alone in marking the day on the calendar, either in black or in yellow. For all the heartbroken ladies, there were as many rejoicing stable-lads looking forward to the holiday and the celebrations to break the monotony of winter work. The town was aware of little else and all the talk was of wedding arrangements and of the fabulous array of presents, the solid silver dinner service from Lord Falmouth and the pearl and diamond bracelet for the bride from Prince Batthyany; of bridesmaids and invitations and parties to watch the fireworks.

Even Cecily knew she could hardly keep Laura away from the festivities. Fred had donated a live bullock, sent to him by Lord Hastings, to be roasted for the stable-lads, and everyone went to see it arrive at the station, where it broke free and caused a greater entertainment than anticipated. After it was killed it lay in state at the back of the Waggon and Horses in the High Street and everyone went to view it and pay their last respects. The atmosphere in the town was like a carnival, and Laura and Miss Bell went down at the smallest excuse to pick up all the gossip.

'They are going to Torquay for the honeymoon,' Miss Bell reported, and they both went into a trance picturing themselves arriving at the Imperial on Fred's arm, the red carpet laid out and the staff lined up to greet them.

'Anyone would think it was royalty,' Philip said disapprovingly, reading of the special train that was to wait in the Newmarket siding, but Cecily said calmly, 'It's what the public wants. I daresay they would prefer it otherwise themselves. Miss Dawson is a quiet little girl and I will say for Mr Archer, he has never had his head turned by the adulation he receives.'

Laura was given permission to go down and watch the wedding

in the company of Miss Bell and they had privately arranged to meet Arthur and Tiger. It was very daring, but in their current mood of delicious despair, watching Fred slip through their fingers, it seemed appropriate. If one could not have Fred, at least life could go on. Hilda Bell found Arthur amiable enough, if not exciting, and Laura, not saying a word, privately thought Tiger as fascinating as ever, for all his new reticence. She longed to tell Miss Bell about the high wire, but accepted that it was impossible. She was afraid that Tiger's undesirable family might come to Newmarket for the wedding junketings but Tiger assured her they would not, as it was midwinter and the circus fixed in winter quarters.

'And if you were still there,' she asked him, 'what would you be doing? Nothing?'

'Practice all morning, maintenance and repair the rest of the day. It's very dull in winter.'

'Do you ever wish you were back? It's dull here in winter.'

They were in the feed-shed, Tiger cleaning up after a delivery, and Laura sat on one of the bins, picking out husks with her teeth, keeping her feet out of the way of the broom. She was bolder about coming to Thorn's now, because of Tiger, and so far no one had remonstrated. She knew that if they did her uncle would stick up for her. There was nothing to lose, if she was to be dispatched to her grandparents for 'the season' in the autumn, which was the current plan. Tiger had been promoted, and besides doing his two horses he spent some time in the office learning his way about the books. Harry said he was quick, but he had never received any formal education. In the evenings Harry was teaching him to write a fair hand. Laura had seen the screwed-up sheets in the hearth, Harry's careful copperplate copied line for line. She made no mention of what she had found out. Tiger still dreamed occasionally and still had his own room, and Harry kept an account book especially for him, locked in his safe. He said Tiger was rich as young lads went, but Tiger never showed any interest in his money.

Laura had several times tried to draw him out about the circus, but he was not forthcoming.

'You always want to know things,' he said. 'Asking questions. I don't ask you questions all the time.'

'You know all about me.'

'Well, you saw what I did. There was nothing else. Just the travelling, and the setting up and the taking down, the practising and the performance. I was all work.'

He was cautious of her, careful not to get too close, but he spoke more freely and in the same old abrasive way, half scornful. Laura did not mind her treatment, respecting him, pleased to have him talking again. She was looking forward to being with Tiger, as well as to the agony of seeing Fred married.

On the morning, she was strung up with excitement. Miss Bell was the same, and they had to avoid each other's glances over the breakfast table. It was politic to be careful. They said nothing, escaped to their rooms and dressed warmly for the ordeal. Percy drove them down to the town and dropped them at the end of the Ely road. The streets were full of traffic and people; three hours before the wedding everything was at a halt round the church; one hour before, all the guests were in place and the church overflowing. They were reported to be standing on the pews inside, for a good view, and in the street the police were having difficulty in keeping the road clear.

Laura watched for Fred's arrival in a dream. She was numb with cold. She was aware of this day as a milestone: the end of dreams, the beginning of reality. It was starting, with the carriages arriving and the cheering preceding them all down the street from Heath House and Warren House. She did not want to look, feeling only the cold. Miss Bell, white-faced, gave an ecstatic moan. Fred got down from his carriage with his best man, Mr Jennings, and the cheers were so great that he had to stop and acknowledge them on all sides. The crowd strained and buffeted round the churchyard. The policemen heaved and swore and several hats went.

'It is awful,' Laura whispered, pinched and shivering.

Miss Bell's large bulging eyes were glazed with tears.

Tiger and Arthur were laughing. They were all pushed together, moving with the crowd, cold breath clouding their cheering. The bride came with her father, accompanied by five bridesmaids in flame-coloured dresses: a small, child-like figure, awed but smiling beneath her veil. Laura could scarcely bear to watch her; she looked younger than herself, which she found outrageous, and no better equipped to bear such glory. Tears of sheer indignation pricked her eyelids.

She could not join in the general banter and chatter that enlivened the long wait during the ceremony. She stood looking down at the gutter, thinking of Fred taking that little girl into his arms and kissing her. And afterwards into his bed. She was ignorant of what constituted the act of love, for human biology was not part of Miss Bell's curriculum, but she knew it took place in bed. She had seen stallions serving mares and knew the reason for the strange performance, but could not relate such a tussle to the human condition. If they had been alone, she would have asked Miss Bell. No doubt Fred knew what to do even if he had had no girl-friends before, and Miss Dawson's mother would have told her what to expect, for she understood that the great secret was revealed to a girl on the eve of her wedding by her mother. To think of it made her feel hollow in the stomach, thirsty in the loins; it made her shiver. She could not stop shivering.

After what seemed a very long time, the bells burst out above their heads, the church doors were flung wide and the wedding party came out into the cold morning. The bride's veil was flung back; she looked shy, ecstatic, colouring up to the enthusiastic cheers that greeted her.

'What a lucky couple!' a woman said behind Laura. 'They want for nothing!'

Fred came down the church path to the waiting carriage with the bride through a rain of rice and confetti. Pigeons wheeled up through the bare trees and the bright spots of the confetti danced in Laura's vision. She felt Tiger's hand tighten on her shoulder. He let out a strange cry and shrank away from her, but could not move for the people pressing up. Laura, distracted, saw that he was looking at the bridal pair as if he was seeing something quite terrible: beads of sweat stood out on his forehead; his lips were white and his mouth twitched uncontrollably. Tears started to run down his cheeks.

'Tiger!'

Laura was horrified, her attention diverted. Arthur, standing on the other side of Tiger, took him by the arm urgently.

'Steady on, old man! Hold up. Take his arm, Miss Laura. He's going to pass out.'

Tiger was swaying, his eyes glazed. 'No,' he said. 'No. No.'

But he was not limp and fainting. His body was rigid, his gaze fixed on Archer. The footman was closing the carriage door. The cheers welled up, with cries of good wishes, and the crowd began to break up, moving with the bridal carriage. Tiger shrank back, turned away, started pushing his way against the crowd to get out, and Arthur and Laura tried to keep with him, shoving and trampled against the tide.

'It's one of his fits,' Arthur said.

But down the street, out of the press, Tiger's urgency left him and he stopped, leaned against a wall as if completely exhausted, his head flung back. The expression on his face, of shock and grief, was agonizing.

'What is it?' Arthur was asking. 'What's wrong with you, fellow?'

Tiger shook his head. He turned his head away from Laura, not wanting her to see it, struggling to gain control of himself. He leaned against the wall, hiding his head in his hands, and stood silently crying. Arthur was puzzled and impatient, but Laura knew what it was. In the distance she could hear the cheers following Fred Archer and his bride up through the town. The bells pealed out clear and commanding to the sharp winter sky, but her feelings had turned to ice. Miss Bell came along, having lost them in the crush, looking far-away and pink-eyed.

'What's the matter?'

'The lad's had a sort of fit, I reckon,' Arthur said. 'It's the gipsy in 'im. He gets taken queer sometimes.'

Laura said, 'You can leave him with me. I'll take him home. I know what to do.'

'I don't like it,' Arthur said. 'I'll fetch Mr Keen. He's got Jester in the dog-cart down at the Rutland. You wait here.'

Laura did not argue. She felt a hundred years old, aware, perfectly in control. Miss Bell was useless; she knew nothing. Laura stood by Tiger, knowing there was no hurrying such a matter; he had to come back to himself in his own time, Tiger of the strange talents, of the dreadful vulnerability. But the reason for his present agony was something she dare not look in the face. It was in her mind, clouding every corner, but it had no edge, for she would not look at it. She could not bear the idea. She kept staunchly turning her mind away, concentrating on the lines in the pavement, the muddy hem of Miss Bell's skirt. People were coming back from the church, staring. The church bells seemed harsh and mocking.

'What is it?' Miss Bell kept saying, frowning. She was adrift herself, not wanting to be concerned for the distraught boy, yet conscious of doing her duty. 'It's not right to be waiting here in the street, Laura. I think we should go on. Arthur will come back.'

'I cannot leave him. You may go on if you wish.' Laura knew that she had grown out of governesses, in a stroke.

By the time Harry came back in the dog-cart with Arthur Tiger was able to turn away from the wall, the tears dried. But his face was like a mask, and he was wracked with convulsive shivering like a fever victim. Arthur got down and they helped him into the cart. Harry wrapped the rug round him, asking no questions.

'I'm coming too,' Laura said.

She climbed up, huddling close, and Harry turned Jester for home. Laura could feel Tiger's body shaking beside her. He sat with his head in his hands and Laura could see her uncle's face over Tiger's bent head, very non-committal, hiding his concern. And me too, she thought, I am very cool, I am not a child. I know what has happened, yet I am very composed; I am like my mother. I am strong. There was some confetti caught in the braid round the bottom of her dress, she noticed, little specks of colour, bright as jockey's silks.

They reached home, not a word being spoken, and Harry took Tiger into the kitchen and sat him in the chair by the fire, still wrapped in his blanket. He seemed spent and limp, conscious yet oblivious, his head thrown back, eyes shut, the tremors taking him every few minutes like the shaking of an invisible hand. His face was white and covered in sweat, yet he was cold.

'What happened?' Harry asked Laura.

'Nothing happened. He was watching Fred and Miss Dawson —Mrs Archer—as they came down the path to their carriage, and suddenly he let out this awful cry and could not watch any more . . .' It was hard to keep her voice steady. 'He saw something,' she said. 'Something dreadful.'

She saw the look on Harry's face, an echo of Tiger's own distress, but he would not acknowledge the truth of the situation.

'I'll get him to bed. He must sleep. I'll get him a draught out of the cupboard, and you fill a hot bottle. He can go on the couch in the study. There's a fire burning in there.'

Practical concerns occupied them. They undressed Tiger and put him to bed in the study. He did not protest but moved in a daze, completely uncommunicative, unseeing. Harry pulled the curtains, made up the fire, and Laura fetched blankets from the bedroom. Tiger lay prone, his head buried in a cushion, his arms round his head, the convulsive shivers seizing him every few minutes. They left him, shut the door.

Laura felt spent herself, sick with fear.

'What did he see?' she asked.

'Laura, don't.'

'He must not tell me. But I shall never stop wanting to know. All the time, until it happens.'

Harry knew reassurance was out of place, for he could not hide the fact that his thinking was the same as Laura's. They were thrown together in their predicament; there was no one else to share it with.

'Poor Laura! It's a bad day for you. What can I say? Stay here if you wish, and Martha will get us something to eat.'

Laura did not argue, but sat by the fire while Harry called Martha to prepare them a meal. The place was empty, all the boys having the day off after exercise. Martha put the food out; Laura went to the table with her uncle and Martha went back to her cleaning. Laura and Harry sat opposite each other, the meat and vegetables between them.

'What did he see?' Laura said.

'You must put it out of your mind. You must not let it upset you. In time you will forget it happened.'

'No. I shall always know something terrible is going to happen to Fred.'

'Don't, Laura.'

Harry could not hide his own distress. They picked at the food, not attempting any more conversation, and in the town Mr and Mrs Archer left the wedding reception for the station where a special coach was waiting for them. Shunted on to the London train when it came, it was greeted by waiting crowds all the way to London, like a train with royalty on board.

In the evening Harry took Laura to the fireworks and the ox-roasting on the Severals.

'I shall never forget this day,' Laura said.

She sat in the dog-cart watching the fire and the orange-lit, grinning faces of the boys reaching for the hacked meat that sizzled over the flames. The grass underfoot was crisp with frost, the smell of roasting meat unlikely in the cold air. Drunken singing and shouting echoed from the High Street and the crowded inns; the stables were overflowing with visitors, carriages and traps parked in every gateway. Harry drove Jester slowly up the hill over the hoof-trodden grass, away from the noise and the lights, and they watched the fireworks break out in canopies of glittering coloured lights. Rivalling the frosty stars, Fred rode in triumph across the heavens and from the watching crowds sighs of amazement rolled up the hill. 'Archer's up'—the current catch-phrase to indicate satisfaction—hung in the aftermath of a myriad coloured explosions above which the moon sailed in bright astonishment at her company. Laura had never seen anything like it since Tiger in the dome of the circus tent.

They watched in silence, alone, Jester taking them across the dark acres of turf that spread from horizon to horizon. It was an ending, Laura thought, a day to go on her calendar as a milestone, not with yellow rings nor yet with black, but with grey for acceptance, for compliance with a scheme of life over which she had no control.

8

They did not speak about what had happened again. Laura knew that Tiger had seen Fred's death, and that it was terrible, and that it was locked in his mind irrevocably. She knew that he was bitter at having revealed his frailty—he considered it a frailty—but only she and Harry knew what it meant. Arthur and Miss Bell merely thought that he had 'come over queer'. Although nothing was said, Laura was very much aware of a bond having been formed between herself, her uncle and Tiger by the events of the day, the tenuous link of mere compatibility being strengthened into a deep and powerful relationship to which she could put no name. Perhaps Harry had not changed, but she felt that both she and Tiger had emerged from some sort of chrysalis over the winter months, turning into their true colours out of the confusion of childhood, the process sparked by the experience they had shared on the day of the wedding. Laura's dream-love for Fred was now something apart; she loved him no less, but had dropped off her fantasies with the sloughing of her cocoon. She could face up to the realities of Falmouth House, even the knowledge—and there was no doubt in her mind about this fact—of the dreadful events that were to come; she could consider the situation without panic. Her child-love had turned into compassion. It was the same feeling as on the day of the wedding, when she had realized what was happening; she felt a hundred years old, out of a normal age-span altogether.

But her tutor, with Fred's marriage, seemed to go into a decline. She could not bear to pass Falmouth House.

'Your father will dismiss me in the autumn, and what shall I do then?' she asked Laura bitterly.

'And what shall I do in the autumn?' Laura cried out. 'I do not want to go to London! It is no worse for you! Mother will find you another place, and you have Arthur, and there is Corsica.'

Everyone except Laura was looking forward to Corsica with some excitement. Even Harry, having influenced the date so that he was missing only a few minor meetings, was boyishly making climbing plans; Philip was booking hotel accommodation and travelling tickets, poring over timetables of packet boats from Marseilles to Ajaccio, and Cecily was grimly reading catalogues of sportswear. She, like Laura, wanted no part in the Corsican affair but she, unlike Laura, was free to please herself.

'Yes,' said Hilda Bell. 'I am looking forward to going to Corsica. But what of my future when I come back?'

'And what of mine?' Laura asked, but she knew she was stronger, altogether more buoyant than Miss Bell. Fred's marriage had decimated Miss Bell. She cried in her room every night. Her pale, scrubbed-looking face was crumpled with despair.

'I hate going to interviews for new jobs. It's like being sold in a fair. They look at you, they ask you personal questions. And new places, horrid children. It was nice here. I like it here. It will never be like this again.'

'You will get married.'

'There is no one to marry.'

'What about Arthur?'

'Arthur is coarse. He doesn't want to marry anyway.'

'Perhaps you will meet someone in Corsica.'

'Perhaps.'

'Perhaps Nellie and Fred will have children and you can be their governess.'

'They say Nellie is expecting. Dr Wright has been calling.'

This stopped Laura short, causing her an unexpected lurch of anguish. She asked Tiger about it at the first opportunity.

'Have you heard it said? That Nellie is expecting?'

'No, but it's probably true. Do you wish it was you?'

'Tiger!'

'The way you love him—'

'You don't know the way I love him. It's not like that. You don't know.'

'Why do you think I don't know?'

Laura could not answer him, confused by her retorts. He had always answered her back, since he had first arrived, even as a gardener. She did not consider him a servant any longer. She knew he was, in a sense, Uncle Harry's adopted son. She thought she knew now why Uncle Harry did not look for a wife, and had taken Tiger for a son. But she could not talk about love with Tiger.

Tiger said, 'Could you love me?'

Laura was amazed, wondering if she had heard correctly. She remembered being under the table in the tent, and Tiger's declaration long ago. She felt the blood burning in her cheeks, and none of the coldness with which she had spurned Simister and Gervase. It was true that Tiger was forever in her thoughts, his image teasing and tantalizing her, and that the memory of those experimental kisses in the loosebox had the power to make her feel very strange, but these facts were no answer to his question.

'How can I tell?'

'Would you come out with me?'

'My mother would not allow it.'

'She's not watching you all the time. One evening, we could walk across the fields, and talk. I don't mean to the *theatre*.'

The usual scorn withered her feeble attempt at a refusal.

'When?'

'This evening. When you've had your dinner.'

'I'll try and come.'

Her father was away in Cambridge and would not be back until late.

'Mr Keen said he was going out this evening. I will be free when we've done evening feeds. I'll meet you by the field gate.'

'Very well.'

Laura was excited by the appointment, in spite of her reluctant answer. She kept thinking about it all through the afternoon, not being able to guess how it would be—talking. She had talked often enough with Tiger, but always in passing, on the way to somewhere else, with other people nearby. Tonight they would talk without end, trailing through the banks of meadowsweet and buttercups down in the marsh fields where Fred had come to see the fillies two summers ago—no, three summers—when Tiger had been a circus boy and she had been a child, long ago. It seemed long ago. Now Fred had a smart house full of new furniture and beautiful paintings and gave dinner parties and soon would be a father. Life was overtaking them. Fred was twenty-seven. He was getting old. And she turned her mind away from the terrible things she knew, that Tiger knew.

Her mother had dinner early; she was going to call on Mrs Adams at the bottom of the village who had once done the laundry at Dry Meadows and now was dying of some long-drawn-out and tedious disease. Very convenient, Laura thought, not wanting to know about dying. It was a warm evening, almost midsummer, not yet a hint of dusk, but only the over-ripe fullness of the late sun, gold and thick, casting long shadows across the fields. The fields were bare and hard-grazed, baked gold. Tiger was not waiting impatiently, agog, but was lying spread-eagled on the grass, his hands behind his head, eyes shut, a stalk in his teeth. Laura leaned on the gate and looked down on him. He had not changed but was in his working clothes, although his shirt looked clean. He looked delicate, so fine and small, but Laura thought he was made of steel. She wanted to see him do his act again.

'Will you show me? Do you remember how?'

It was easy enough to talk, after the initial greeting. Tiger did not look any less scornful than usual, did not take her hand nor breathe heavily, but walked ahead of her down the field, still sucking his grass.

'Have you put a wire up for me then?'

'No. You can do it in the trees, like a monkey.' She laughed. 'Turn a somersault for me.'

'It would be easy, on a branch. As good as the floor.'

'Will you?'

'I haven't come out to climb trees. I'm courting.'

'Have you told my uncle?'

'He's gone out too. I didn't have to ask. Do you think he would mind?'

'No.'

'No, I didn't think so either, else I wouldn't have asked you.'

'And if he'd forbidden you?'

Tiger did not reply. Laura followed him, nervous, intrigued. She wanted him to kiss her. She kept thinking about it. After that, she didn't know. She wondered if he had ever loved a dirty gipsy girl. They were going down the beaten path beside the stream into the woods where the sun had a struggle to get through. The gold light came down in splotches and medallions, glittering. The stream was idle with summer, deep and cold, and the path went close, and then away into the trees, to glades where the grass was dry and beaten down.

'People come here,' Tiger said, stopping. He looked round. 'It's a good place.'

'What do you mean?'

'Lovers, I mean.'

'Oh.' Laura was looking up, squinting into the shafts of light. The trees went up, converging, struggling against each other for the sky. They were hazels, very straight.

'Look, there's a branch,' she said. 'A perfect branch, for you.'

It arched out strongly some fifteen feet up, like a sprung bow. Tiger considered it.

'It's too easy,' he said. 'Not worth bothering.'

'I would like you to.'

Perhaps, because he was taking her out, he wanted to please her. She could see him torn, despising the branch because it was too easy.

'No one else could do it, even on the branch,' she pointed out.

'It's stupid,' he said.

'Please.'

He sighed then, but obligingly took off his boots and socks. His feet were very fine with long, agile toes. He climbed the tree by merely walking up it. Laura could see his toes spread out, curling for a grip, and his fingers clasped round the trunk, moving up steadily. He came to the branch, pulled himself on to it and stood up straight, not holding anything, looking down at her.

'What do you want?'

'A somersault.'

Tiger stood in silhouette against a fading sky, a backdrop of bright leaves. To Laura he was haloed in gold, arched incredibly backwards, hands and feet all on the branch. He lifted his feet up quite slowly and stood on his hands, perfectly straight, looking down on her.

'Like this?' he asked.

'Yes.'

'Why?'

'It's beautiful.'

To her, it was magical. There was a great beauty to it, the

delicacy of the control of the body, the slow arching of the spine into the circle, the extraordinary command of the boy against the sky, the branch gently dipping to his movements. Nobody, she thought, has ever been wooed like this before. The satisfaction of seeing the human body extending itself, of seeing its infinite possibilities, fascinated her. It was perhaps the same fascination as she felt for Fred Archer, the man whose body too was capable of such feats of power and courage. Perhaps, she thought, I can only love men who can do these things. The idea made her laugh. I shall never marry a grocer or a clerk; I have no use for artists; I must be married to a body that can enchant me by its physical skills. The idea was fresh and exciting and funny.

'You are beautiful!' she shouted up.

He was coming back, turning the slow, poised somersaults. He stopped, hooped and still, and looked down at her.

'So are you.'

She shook her head, laughing.

He was laughing too, still in his circle. 'Come up. Everything is different up a tree.'

'I can't.'

'I will help you.'

But her white dress made it very difficult. She could not go home with bark stains all over it. Tiger found an easier tree nearby, with more obliging branches, and he went first and pulled her up after him. He found her a comfortable seat against the trunk and broke off the surrounding twigs that caught in her hair, and sat beside her.

'I wouldn't do this for just anybody,' he said.

'Nor would I.'

'Don't ladies climb trees then?'

'No. My mother would never climb a tree.'

The sun was almost gone amongst the trees, but they could see the deep gold of the far fields through the dark leaves. The shadows of the big elms stretched from the top hedgerow to merge with the darkness of the stream at the bottom. The damp scent of the flowering rushes filled the cool shadows. With Tiger close to her, Laura now felt constrained. She was very aware of his physical body, although it was now relaxed and his attitude in no way intrusive. He did not seem inclined to kiss her at all.

(146)

A green woodpecker was shrieking close by.

'There's someone coming,' he said.

Laura listened, worried.

'They won't see us up here.'

Laura wondered what her mother would say if she could see her in her present position. She could hear a cracking of branches and the murmur of voices, spasmodic.

Tiger whispered, 'Keep still, and they won't see. People never look up.'

There was a footpath along the stream, but it was rarely used, travellers preferring the top path through the field when bound for the next village. The voices did not sound like village boys. They were soft, gradually coming nearer. They were laughing. Laura was puzzled.

'It sounds—'

The green woodpecker's mate shrieked and Laura saw the bright flash of departing wings. The indignant cry echoed through the woods.

She knew then.

'Tiger!'

'Hush,' he whispered. He put his arm round her, for her sudden shivering. 'It's all right.'

'No.'

She could see them now, at an angle through the branches below, her mother's familiar grey silk dress soft in the shadows, her mother laughing, Uncle Harry's arm round her, her mother's cheek laid against his. They separated as the path narrowed, came out together into the open patch and lay down. The grey silk skirts billowed and subsided and fell in a circle like a water-lily in the pool of trodden grass. Looking down, Laura saw the two figures drawn together, the laughing finished.

'Tiger!' She felt herself panicking.

He came close, pressing her to the trunk, half blocking off her view.

'Don't look,' he whispered. 'You don't have to.'

'I do!'

She wanted to see what was happening, hating what she was seeing but excited by it, astonished. Yet having known it, she realized. But *seeing* . . .

'Don't,' Tiger said.

But she could hear such strange sounds, a sobbing of joy. She lifted her head and saw the leaves moving below her, blurring her view, and the bodies moving beneath them, naked, locked together, coming and going under the dark leaves. The white bodies gleamed between darkness. She saw her mother's face, and the look which she had seen only once, intensified, in a rapture of joy. Her marble mother, austere and secret, crying out and gasping with her love—she had to watch, stricken in her tree like a bird frozen to the branch. Tiger did not move, nor say anything. He was looking too, frowning and breathing quickly, very still. Laura remembered the stallion and the mare, and the man chivvying her away. Was it the same, this gleaming dance of flesh on the stream bank? Seeing her mother stripped not only of her grey dress but of her grey, secretive nature made Laura wonder if this is what she had been hiding all these years under her silence, her lonely ways, her love of solitude. This was another person, yet it was her mother. Laura felt suspended out of time, as if watching a story played out by actors. And yet she had known, she told herself, known but not admitted. She did not admit these things until they were thrust into her notice and she was forced to look. Tiger said she did not have to look, but she knew that she did. She wept for knowing, but dared make no noise, and buried her face against Tiger, biting on his bony shoulder. He sat motionless, his arm round her, and the sun disappeared and the dampness rose up from the stream, the midges biting, the nightingales singing, a dog barking from the village. Harry and Cecily lay talking softly, laughing, propped on their elbows. They were like two children, carefree, careless. Laura and Tiger froze and stiffened in the tree, their childhood finished.

Afterwards, Laura could not face Tiger, for his knowing.

'But I've known for years, ever since I first came here,' he said angrily.

'How can you say that?' Laura could not stop shivering for cold and cramp, dropped down from the tree in the summer darkness, damp with dew, her face streaked with tears and moss and bark stain.

'Mr Keen knows I know. I saw him, when your father was away once, he spent the night with your mother in the house.'

'He *couldn't*!'

'He found out about me, so that I wouldn't give him away. He had a hold over me, and he knew that it was mutual—I had a hold over him. That's why he kept me.'

'That's not why! He loves you, that's why! He went looking for you, didn't he?'

Laura was vehement in her state of shock, wanting to excuse her uncle but not her mother. She turned her anger against Tiger.

'You knew about tonight—you took me there on purpose! You said it was for lovers—that's what you meant!'

'I didn't! I didn't know it was *them*.' Her injustice stung him. 'Why do you have to be angry with me? It was your idea for me to turn somersaults, wasn't it? I didn't want to go tree-climbing, did I?'

Laura went back through the meadows, crying, and Tiger stalked by the hedgeside, insulted. Laura, amidst all the tumult in her mind, wondered if he had ever lain with a gipsy girl or a Newmarket tart. He seemed to know all about it. There was a part of her mind which kept escaping from the general shock which it seemed perfectly right to be experiencing: it kept hiving away in wonder to dear Fred, to Tiger, even to Simister and Gervase . . . these subjects one never spoke of . . . the sobs became uncontrollable.

'You can't go home like that,' Tiger said, stopping.

Laura did not want to go home at all. Albert, she thought. Hilda Bell. Fred.

'Oh, look—it's stupid—stop it.'

Her mother!

'For heaven's sake!' Tiger stood in front of her and pushed a large handkerchief into her face. 'It's not the end of the world. People do it all the time.'

She felt dizzy and sick and cold as ice.

'Do what?'

'That. What they were doing. Mating.'

'Why?'

'They want to do it. They enjoy it. You—you too—you wanted it, at Christmas, when you kissed me. What's the difference?'

'But kissing isn't—isn't—.' What?

'It is. It's the beginning. When you feel like loving someone.'

'But I didn't want—' The recollection of the look on her mother's face stopped her words. Nobody would choose to forgo such bliss.

'You did want. Don't be stupid.'

'No!' Tiger's bluntness appalled her. She turned away from him and ran, pushing her way through the hedge into the wild part of the garden. She went into the house through the conservatory and fled up to her room, flinging herself on the bed in a storm of weeping. Her weeping was for self-pity, she realized afterwards. Nobody heard her. Miss Bell was out with Arthur; her mother was out with Uncle Harry; and her father was with his client in Cambridge. She did not see her mother again until morning, at the breakfast-table. She was serene, cool as ever, her face expressionless. Laura, seeing her, found it hard to believe what she had seen the night before. 'Two-faced' . . . the adjective was absurdly apt: it kept buzzing in Laura's head. Her eyes were swollen with crying. She could not speak, even when asked what was wrong.

Her father said jocularly, 'It must be this trouble her Mr Archer is in.'

'For not winning the Derby?' Cecily replied. 'It's a hard life, when being third brings such acrimony.'

'He was on the favourite.'

'The favourite, no doubt, because he was on it.'

'They say he didn't try, so that the horse his brother's money was on would win. They're a crooked crew, these racing men.'

'But not Fred, surely? His honesty is part of his appeal.'

Her mother's eyes were calm, talking of honesty. Laura knew they were only talking about Fred Archer to draw her out, and would not be drawn. She went back to her room, not able to face anyone. Albert sent Miss Bell up with three sugared almonds on a saucer.

'What's wrong with you? Was it Tiger, last night?'

'No.'

'What then?'

A week later, when Laura had got over the shock, she told Miss Bell what she had seen. She had to tell someone, discuss it with someone, and there was no one else. She felt desperate for reassurance.

'Tiger said people do it all the time.'

'But only with their husbands, surely!'

'Have you ever? With Arthur?'

'No.'

Miss Bell was as shocked as Laura had been.

'What about your father? Does he know? He can't.'

'No, of course not. But Tiger says he's known about it ever since he first came here five years ago.'

'Do *they* know he knows?'

'He says Uncle Harry does.'

'Perhaps that's why he's so well-treated—not like an ordinary lad.'

'He's not ordinary,' Laura said crisply, tempted to tell her about the high wire.

But Miss Bell was thoughtful in a way that made Laura nervous.

'You mustn't tell anyone what I've said!'

Laura realized she had given Miss Bell a lever over her mother, as Tiger had one over Uncle Harry; she could compel her employer not to dismiss her in the autumn. But she felt no compunction. She was sorry for Miss Bell and her drab prospects; Miss Bell lacked courage in looking forward, and the charm and vivacity to make friends. She was turning in on herself, soured by the melting of her dreams, the passing of her youth. She was shrewish about dear Fred and Nellie, coarse about Nellie's pregnancy. Uncle Harry had once said she lacked class, using the term as he would apply it to a horse: implying a quality of mind, rather than a mere pedigree. Laura felt she had grown out of her and would be glad when they parted, after Corsica.

'I wish I hadn't said anything.'

'I won't pass it on.'

'I thought you'd know about—about—'

But there was nothing she could put into words, even when the opportunity arose: impossible to ask Miss Bell whether it was true, as Tiger said, that when she had wanted Tiger to kiss her she had wanted all that as well. 'All that' summed up the vast abyss of her ignorance. She could not reconcile the lovely anticipation she had enjoyed, meeting Tiger and walking down through the meadows with him, watching him high on the branch against the bright evening sky, with the passionate consummation she had watched. She could not bear to meet Tiger now, and yet was more aware of him than ever before. He treated her with such abrasive scorn, yet she knew she held the power to hurt him. He was so confident and straight and capable; yet at the same time she had seen him thrown by his visions into near-hysteria. His vulnerability was something he could not overcome, whatever his strength of mind. And she loved this weakness in him which he covered by his aggressive self-containment.

Nor could she meet Uncle Harry any more. She avoided Thorn's Hall assiduously, and looked forward to Gervase and Simister coming home; even to Corsica, in spite of Uncle Harry. She wanted to get things right in her mind; a breathing space was necessary.

9

Laura spent the first week in Corsica crying. She felt oppressed by the towering conifers of Vizzavona and could not stop thinking of home, of Tiger and Fred and Uncle Harry. Uncle Harry broke his ankle two days before the party was due to leave, and had to be left behind. A horse kicked him in the yard, and Laura was there and saw the bone sticking through the flesh. After that nothing went right: the hurried rearrangements ... Philip was in two minds not to go, but Simister badgered him unmercifully, and Harry said they could hire a guide for the climbing, so the business went ahead. Philip, Laura, Miss Bell, Simister and Gervase departed for foreign climes, taking the packet from Dover, the train to Marseilles, the packet to Ajaccio and a train to Vizzavona and the Hotel de la Forêt, *tous conforts*.

The Hotel de la Forêt was a gaunt, shuttered pink building slumbering amidst dense forest some hundred yards up a stony track from where the mountain train to Corte stopped at the Café de la Gare, Vizzavona. There were said to be wild mountains above the forest, but Laura was not interested. The attics of the hotel were full of bats, which clattered in the shady peaks of the shingled roof. It was unbearably hot and her skirts and underwear and stays clotted her body unbearably. Miss Bell was supposed to teach her French and all about the flora and fauna, but Miss Bell hated French and knew nothing about flora and fauna, and went to drink absinthe with Philip in the smoking room, while Simister chatted up the Corsican peasants in his perfect Rugbeian French, which they could not understand, and Gervase sulked, besotted with cheap wine from the Café de la Gare.

Laura was left alone, marvelling at a landscape so foreign to the Newmarket heaths, and the killing heat, like a drug, drawing out the resinous odours of the heavy brooding forest which crushed them in on all sides. Accustomed only to the healthy breezes of Newmarket, Laura could not accommodate herself to her new environment. She lay on the bed, gasping and sweating, the light coming through the closed shutters like spears into her eyeballs.

After five or six days, the revolt seemed futile. The body acclimatized. She threw out her stays and petticoats and acquired a black peasant skirt from the chambermaid in exchange for a high-necked lace blouse. She wore nothing underneath it and felt much better. The chambermaid brought her a blouse of cheap cotton, loose-fitting, and Laura bartered a bracelet for it, and tied her hair up in a coarse scarf and felt she had made a big improvement.

Simister had arranged donkeys to take them into the mountains, and a pair of guides, brothers called Giovanni and Pasquale. Giovanni was swarthy and workworn, a man of few words but competent; Pasquale, much younger, was lissom and smiling, eyes like black olives that missed nothing. Laura thought he was beautiful but dared not speak to him. There was something elemental about him: graceful and animal-like. He made Gervase and Simister look like duffers. Hilda Bell decided that she wanted to go climbing too. She said to Laura that it would be terribly dull the two of them staying in the hotel alone, and she asked Philip if they could go. To Laura's surprise he agreed. He took them to a place in the next village in the mule cart and he bought them a pair of boots each. He was a changed person, no longer sour and pedantic, but laughing and boyish. His blond hair had grown dishevelled, his pink skin burned red and blistered, and he wore a white handkerchief knotted at the corners in the heat of the day and peasant sandals. He chatted to Miss Bell and called her Hilda as if she was one of the family. After a little while they all called her Hilda, even the boys. Hilda seemed to Laura to bear no relation to the Newmarket Miss Bell, the tense, scrubbed look giving way to a smiling, burnished content. She was secretive and withdrew from Laura.

Gervase told Laura that Hilda was 'making eyes' at Philip. He was rather drunk at the time, dozing off his over-indulgence in a bed of pine needles behind the hotel. Laura sat beside him and squashed ants. Gervase did not notice the ants although they ran over his open collar and down on to his chest. Laura had found herself rather thrown on Gervase since the holiday, he being the only one beside herself with reservations in his enthusiasm for what they were doing. Drink improved him, for his gaucheness and normal lack of self-confidence were no longer apparent; his early sulks, due to an ingrained guilt at his pleasure in drinking, had given way to his present delight in the power of the vine. The sulks, like the lack of confidence, could be quenched by a greater intake. He then became serene, charming and funny.

'Why aren't you always like this?' Laura asked him.

'Drunk, you mean?'

'No. Just nice.'

'I need to be drunk just to be like most people are all the time. It's awful.'

'Simister's beastly when he's drunk. He's pretty beastly when he's sober too.'

'What, old Simister? I thought he was terribly popular.'

'He's so busy and enthusiastic all the time. I find him very boring. He's the only person who is just the same out here as he was at home. Everyone else has changed, you and Hilda and my father.'

'That's because I am drunk and they think they are falling in love with each other.'

'You *are* drunk! However could they!'

'Quite easily, I should think. There's nothing else to do.'

'Do people fall in love because they are bored?'

'I think it's quite common, yes.'

Her mother was bored, Laura thought. Was that the reason she loved Uncle Harry? But Miss Bell . . . with her father! It seemed ridiculous to Laura.

'And your mother,' Gervase said. 'You know about your mother?'

'Yes.'

Gervase smiled. Laura wondered whether the great improvement in him was due to alcohol, or whether he was growing up. *She* was said to have improved with maturity; perhaps the same applied to Gervase. Certainly, closely considered, he had lost his angular, spiky look, and his spots. His face was firmly modelled, nose straight, chin firm. The skin was tawny and freckled and the eyes, examined coolly, were distinctly fine, large, of a deep secretive hazel and fringed with very decent lashes. His hair was long and poetic, grown free for the holiday with the same casual abandon as Philip was exhibiting in his knotted handkerchief, and she, Laura, in her peasant clothes. He looked athletic and decisive, but she knew he was not.

When they set out early for the mountains, he was his old self, morose and subservient to the enthusiasms of Simister, moving without grace in his heavy boots. He would not smile at Laura, unamused by her suggestion that they stopped in the next village for some wine. She remembered his graciousness, the curve of his lips and the fine secrets of his eyes when he was released from the knowledge of his inferiority by intoxication. He is locked up, she thought. So was her mother, and Tiger, and perhaps herself.

Walking took her mind off her introspections, for it was hard and it seemed they had a long way to go. From the next village they branched out on to a track that followed the valley of the Manganello and for the first time they were out of the claustrophobic trees and had long views of the way ahead of them, the dusty white path winding along the side of the steep hillside, passing the occasional stone hut wreathed in vine, or flock of goats. It was very hot. Laura could feel the sweat trickling down her thighs beneath her skirt, waist and breasts prickling under the coarse cotton, but she liked the feel of the effort. It was animal-like, to sweat and pant. Gervase and Simister stumbled and grunted, but Giovanni and the beautiful Pasquale strolled beside the donkeys with easy, languid steps, cool and untroubled.

Gradually the valley floor came up to meet them, their own path rising more slowly to converge. The scraps of domestication, the hovels, the goats, the sheep-pens, dropped away and the valley narrowed into a deep cleft through which the water fell down from the heights above them, the path following close, crossing and recrossing. They had to traverse huge, smooth boulders and climb up over tree roots and moss, sometimes up the stream-bed itself where the water divided and fell in cascades on either side, one in shadow, deep and cool, and one glittering in the sun. Laura was hypnotized by the water. She lagged behind, and stood gazing into a pool where the water was held up by a huge lip of white rock and formed a basin deep enough to dive into, ice-green and tantalizing. It was a secret place, overhung by rocks and ferns and the slanting trees high above, but the sun shone into it so that the pebbles on its floor shone like jewels. The thought of sliding her sticky, aching body into the embrace of that transparent bowl made her tremble with longing, but her father's voice echoed from above, ricochetting off the sides of the cascade with a tinny insistence: 'Laura! Laura! Laura!' She had to struggle to catch up, slithering and scrambling up the donkey path to the high pastures where the ground suddenly opened out and the mountains stood out boldly above the trees. The rushing cascade was here a wide, burbling river. Goat-bells jangled from the slopes above and the scene was domestic once more, with stone huts and cheese-stores huddled under a stand of pines. This was where they were to stop for the night, to make a base for climbing from.

'Giovanni and Pasquale are taking me and the boys for a hike up there tomorrow,' Philip said to Laura, gesturing with his hand towards the peaks at the head of the valley. 'You can stay here with Hilda and amuse yourself until we come back.'

He was bright red and flopped out under his straw hat, but unperturbed by his lack of condition. Laura thought of wiry, lithe Uncle Harry, and knew he would have fitted here, goatlike on the rocks and easy with the guides, right by instinct. Her father still had all the aura of smart drawing-rooms with him, and looked incongruous even sitting on the ground, but he seemed unaware of the absurdity, calling for the picnic hamper to be unpacked and the wine bottles uncorked.

Giovanni and Pasquale unloaded the donkeys and set up two big shady tents under the trees. They made a fireplace and a cooking fire, drawing water from the river in blackened, iron pots. They talked quietly between themselves in the strange Corsican French that even Simister could not understand and ate apart, spitting olive pips into the fire.

The English party revived with the food and drink and rest. Philip dozed and Gervase, well-wined, forgot his awkwardness and was funny and cheerful. The high valley was new and exciting; the clear air and view of the high peaks, blue-hazed and ethereal in the afternoon heat, was more stimulating than the thick, resinous forest below: even Laura could see their attraction. But she was content with her father's plans. She wanted to go back to her secret pool with the men away and float her body in that crystal water, and lie in the honey-scented sunshine listening to the goat-bells. Hilda was planning to press flowers and wash her hair.

In the evening the two guides cooked them meat over their fire and made a thick soup full of noodles, which Simister said tasted of goat. They sat round the fire in the dusk and watched the last of the sun flaring on the highest peak at the top of the valley. The tip shone like pink glass, and to the east over the forests the stars were shining at the same time. And with the going of the sun the smells of the flowers and shrubs that carpeted the valley mingled with the woodsmoke, drawn by the dampness. Laura was reminded of her mother, seeing the green hellebores which grew wild and which her mother cultivated; she thought of her mother at home with Uncle Harry in her arms, freed from the eternal boredom of her father. Divorced by distance, she could consider it coolly, no longer distressed. Travel broadened the mind, and now anything seemed possible, lying by the pinewood fire: her father and Hilda Bell and even herself and Gervase, if he were drunk enough to charm ... she was very aware of her physical body, having extended it so strenuously during the day. It was rested and fed but still unsatisfied in a curious, wakeful way. The night was strange and she was strange with it, jumpy with longing and curiosity, spiked by the new experiences of the past few days.

She slept with Hilda in one of the tents, the men in the other. They woke very early to the smell of woodsmoke and the boys talking as they went down to bathe in the river. It was cold, the sun not yet touching the valley, a glitter of frost on the rocks. The guides were boiling up coffee-water, Philip grumbling as he groped for his damp clothes.

'I want to go too,' Hilda said, looking at the day.

She told Philip, and Laura could see that he wanted her to come.

'But we can't leave Laura alone here.'

'Why not?' Laura said. 'You're coming back tonight?'

'Yes, but it's not right.'

'I'll stay with her,' Gervase said. 'I've got a headache. I would rather stay.'

Philip looked doubtful, but there was no precedence for the etiquette of such an occasion. They needed both guides for the donkeys, which were going higher, and Laura was not going to volunteer to be one of the climbing party, for she had already decided it would be tedious, tempered to her father's incompetence: hot and gruelling and frustrating. With Uncle Harry she would have gone willingly.

'I will be quite happy alone,' she stated, but Philip would not have it.

'Gervase, my boy, if you will, I would be grateful.'

Laura was slightly cross but said nothing; she could easily give Gervase the slip and amuse herself on her own.

Giovanni and Pasquale caught the donkeys and loaded them up and the three climbers set off behind the guides up the valley. It was very quiet when they had gone, even the goat-bells high up and distant, the fire fluttering softly between its stones. The sun was creeping gradually down the valley, but the dampness of the early morning was refreshing. Without wind Laura knew it would be too hot by midday. There were no clouds in the sky and the rock walls above were already shimmering and hazy in the atmosphere. Laura thought of her private rock pool and decided to bathe when it got hot. She would tell Gervase she was going to look for flowers, an occupation unlikely to attract him. He was reading, lying prone by the fire with a cup of coffee at his elbow.

'Have you really got a headache?' Laura asked him.

'No. I just said that. I can't stand the thought of climbing with Simister. He's such a show-off. And those guides watching. I'm an ass at that sort of thing.'

'You must be better than my father.'

'Yes, but he won't care about being so bad.'

Laura lay on her back and thought about Tiger and Uncle Harry. What a pair they would make on the rocks! She remembered Tiger's long, clinging toes going up the tree-trunk and the way he could balance on nothing. Uncle Harry had often said climbing was largely balance—balance and stamina. Tiger had the animal grace and the delicacy of movement that would fit the job; he would be beautiful to watch. With Harry and Tiger for companions she would have climbed gladly.

By midday the heat was crushing. They lunched off goat's cheese and fruit and a bottle of wine out of the stores under the rocks. Laura only took a glass, topping it generously with water from the stream, but Gervase said it was good for headaches, and laughed, and drank a good deal. He had done nothing but read all morning, apparently content. He had never desired company, all the time Laura had known him. After he had drunk too much he fell asleep, sprawled in the trampled flowers and dried goat droppings, and Laura waited until his breathing was even and relaxed, and slipped away to climb down to the desirable pool.

It was not far away. Coming on it from above, she emerged from the trees on to the warm slabs of rock from which the water ran over into the basin below. It was as beautiful as she remembered it, more so from above, the water dropping down to make eternal ripples across the emerald surface below, rhythmic and cool. The rocks were unshaded, hot to the touch. Laura climbed down, feeling the coolness of the deep water coming up to meet her. She was longing to feel the water on her body, although she was not much of a swimmer: to discard her rough, sweat-stained clothes and feel the cold current running through her hair and over her sticky thighs and breasts. She reached the lower ledges and went to the lip of rock where the water brimmed over out of the basin. The deep pool was at the upper end, under the highest rocks, but it shallowed out before the water fell again, and smooth stones reached down like steps. Laura struggled impatiently out of the dusty skirt, stripped off her socks and boots and blouse and shook her hair free of all its pins and combs so that it fell in a dark dusty cloud down to her waist.

Without hesitation she lowered herself down over the rock shelves into the icy embrace of the pool. It was the most delicious sensation she had ever experienced, the current of the mountain water running over her dirty, stained body, spreading her hair out in a wide fan across the glassy surface behind her with a feeling of purification which seemed at that moment as powerful as a religious purging. She gasped and cried out with the agonizing joy of it, and held her nose with her fingers and ducked down, feeling her hair streaming up above her and the sharp cold stones rolling under her toes. It was an ice-green cathedral, sun-shot and remote, a thousand light-years away from anything that had happened in her life before. She surfaced into the sunlight and laughed, and groped out for the smooth shelves of rock, resting her head back and letting her body float up and feeling the warmth come to it again from the burning sky above. She wanted to head out for the deep pool and swim down into the violet

(160)

shadows, but she was afraid of drowning herself. She could only swim a few strokes, and it was too lovely to die, the elements at her command, burning rock and icy water to hover between. She lay where she was touched by both, her arms stretched out and her head back, luxuriating in the delicious sensations. The thought of gritty Simister and her perspiring father floundering on the high rock walls in the burning sun gave her an even greater sense of satisfaction. It was worth coming for this alone, she thought, and shut her eyes and felt the sun spearing her lids, the water cooling her brain. She lay for a long time, and perhaps dozed, for the physical sensations and the murmur of the falling water were soothing and hypnotic.

Something tiny and sharp spitted the water above her thigh. She opened her eyes and saw Gervase sitting on the high rock shelf above the pool watching her. He was smiling, not with malice or excitement, but in his gentle, wine-struck content, resting his chin on his drawn-up knee. Laura was startled momentarily, angry, and then resigned. It was only Gervase, better than Simister or a bandit. And she felt no embarrassment, for conventions of upbringing had no place here. She did not move, but looked back at him and smiled.

'Why don't you swim too?'

Her voice echoed off the rocks, repeating the question. Gervase shrugged, but started to unlace his boots. He took them off, and his socks and shirt, and sat there in just his breeches, looking down. Dappled by shade from the trees, tawny-legged and black-haired, he looked like a satyr. He was thin and angular and still. Laura had a sense of being quite divorced from everyday life, watching him, and he her, the natural basin of the pool and its netted roof of leaves a world apart; as if nothing had ever happened before this moment, as if Gervase was not someone she knew, but a presence that came with the physical sensations of her body in the transparent water. There was nothing to hide, for she knew nothing, was scarcely Laura at all.

Gervase stood up and stripped off the rest of his clothes. Then he stepped forward on to the edge of the rock, stood poised for a moment, looking down, and dived. The deep pool splintered as his body entered, taking him, and Laura saw the white shape twist abruptly to miss the rock wall beyond, and glide up towards her, fast with its own momentum but completely under control. It was as lovely as Tiger's somersaults, delighting Laura in the same way. As Gervase surfaced beside her, she was laughing. She had not moved, supporting herself with her elbows in the shallow water, and Gervase turned over on his back and lay beside her. It seemed to her that he was not Gervase at all, for she accepted him with no inhibitions, no preconceptions. He said nothing, but smiled again, and looked at her body. She looked at his, at his genitals awash in the softening ripples of his dive and the dark hair swilling over his skin like weed over white sand, reaching up; the hollow of his navel and the arch of his ribs where the flesh undulated over the bones like the surface of the disturbed pool. He was a part of the water like a white lily growing, she thought; there was nothing that was not right. I am mad, she thought then, remembering how it was in fact. But the fantasy was more true than the fact. This is what my mother taught me, she thought; this is the truth.

After a long while Gervase sighed and sat up. Then he pushed himself off the rocks and swam down into the deep pool at the other end. Laura sat and watched him. He turned about under the water, white bubbles streaming behind him, bursting out of the shadows into the white sunshine. Laura was jealous of his ease and beauty, for she could not use the water as he did, although she loved it equally. She could do nonsense like embroidery and play the piano, but she could not do this elemental, powerful thing, although her body was as strong and as willing.

Gervase came back to her, as if he knew what she was thinking, and held his hands out to her.

'I will take you.'

She was not afraid and followed him. He lay on his back and put his hands under her breasts and towed her out from the lip of the rocks. The water turned ice-cold beneath her and under the mesh of their mingled hair she could look down to the boulder floor far below and see their shadows moving there like lurking whales. He kicked with his legs and his body came up to cradle hers, his thighs taking her. Her face was above his, her heavy hair wreathing it, coiling over the surface of the water. She bent her head to kiss his open lips, and the water swilled across their warm tongues and into their mouths. Laura thought she was going to drown, for kissing, seeing his face go down and his eyes beneath the water, green as mossy stones, and feeling herself follow, the buoyancy dissolved. But he caught her chin with his hands, kicking himself up, and laughed and choked. Laura, scared, clung to him, and he swam back with her into the warm shallows.

It was different then, the magic dispersed. She was cold suddenly, and frightened.

'What's wrong?' he said.

'Nothing is wrong.'

But she wanted to be dry again, and clothed, defended, untouched. A cloud had come over the sun. She pulled herself out of the water and crossed to where her clothes lay in a heap. She had nothing to dry herself on, and could do nothing till she dried. Gervase lay prone in the shallows, his hair waving backwards and forwards in the wash of her exit. He was white and still as driftwood.

She dressed uncomfortably and wrung out her hair, her back to Gervase. When she was ready she looked at him doubtfully, for he had not moved and lay as if he were drowned and dead.

'I'm going back now.'

He did not answer, or move, but his eyes were open and watching her, his cheek on the rock where it sloped from the water.

'Are you all right?' she asked him.

'No.'

She shrugged. 'Well—'

She had not invited him, she wanted to say; it was on his own head, what had happened. He was back to the sullen, exasperating Gervase, as she had come back to sombre reality. But why? Those moments in the pool had been reality too. She bent down and touched his cheek.

'Don't be sad. It was beautiful.'

But he would not speak, and turned his head away. Laura left him and climbed up the rocks to the ledge where his clothes lay. The pool glittered like a green jewel far below, but it was different now. It would never be the same again. Nor will I, exactly, Laura thought, not sure what had happened—if anything. Tiger had once told her she dramatized too much; he had spoken with his usual asperity. It could well be true.

She climbed slowly back up the steep donkey-track, soon as sweating and hot as she had been before she came down. But the sun was shrouded now by a violet haze and the valley looked grey and heavy when she reached it. A hot breeze fanned the ashes in the fireplace and the flimsy tents heaved uneasily. They were little more than dew-traps and not man enough for a storm. No doubt Giovanni and Pasquale had other plans if the weather grew bad; Laura expected them back before long, feeling hungry. She revived the fire and put some tea-water on to boil. When Gervase came back they could have tea and cakes like proper tourists, and then get the camp prepared for the evening, the firewood stacked and the beds put tidy in the tents.

Gervase was a long time coming. Laura had the tea made, and could hear thunder growling at the head of the valley by the time he appeared.

'I hope the others come back soon,' she said, having decided to be practical and brisk. 'They don't want to be caught out in a storm.'

'They *are*,' he said, and was right, for the first drops of rain started to fall with a fierce hissing on the fire stones. The sky was dark, with no sign of a sunset. Laura retreated with her cup of tea into the tent she shared with Hilda, and Gervase followed her. He sat and stared gloomily at the scene. Laura could think of nothing to say to him.

The rain started to fall more heavily, the clouds creeping down from the tops until there was nothing to be seen but shrouded trees disappearing into premature dusk. The tents both leaked badly. Gervase kept the fire fed, and the wreathing, dancing flames were the only spark of cheer in the landscape. Even if the weather had stayed fair, it was far past the time the climbing party had expected to be back.

'Do you think something has gone wrong?' Laura said at last, convinced that it had. 'Because if it has, there's no point going on sitting here doing nothing.'

'No.' Gervase threw another log on the fire.

Laura, wet already, went to explore the more solid edifices in the neighbourhood, and found them extremely primitive, mostly animal pens full of dung. One hut was clean, with a board bed built about a foot above the earth floor, strewn with bracken. There were some burnt sticks against the wall and the stone was blackened, as if a fire had been built there, but no chimney. There was no window and it was very small, but the door was solid and fitted well enough. No drips came through the roof.

'Shall we move in here?'

They took their bedding and clothes and the sacks of food and case of wine and stacked them carefully in a corner. The rain fell more and more heavily and they were soaked as if they had bathed in the pool with all their clothes on. Gervase took some fire, shovelling it carefully with a spade he found in one of the pens, and sat crouched against the wall, feeding it with the dry burnt twigs on the floor until it looked healthy. He frowned with concentration, gradually building it up, and smoke rose up and started to stream out through holes under the eaves. Laura brought in the logs and started to pile them up inside the door, for the rain had the steady persistence that promised long duration; the clouds were right down and the valley mostly blotted out. The damp brought cold with it. Laura was shivering in spite of the fire and started to look for some dry clothes.

'There's a candle,' Gervase said. 'I'll light it.'

But the fire made a strange, dancing light over the blackened walls and the candle was unnecessary. Laura found some woollen stockings and her old skirt and made a scrambling change of clothes, embarrassed by Gervase now.

'There will never be room for them all if they do come now,' she said. 'And this was the only clean hut.'

'I can't see how they can have got lost, with the guides. Perhaps there has been an accident. There's another way back, if anything went wrong, that might have been quicker.' Gervase sat back on his heels, surveying his fire with satisfaction. 'You're not worried, are you? I like it.'

'Well—' No, Laura supposed she wasn't. She did not feel much more than a passing affection for any of the climbing party, not as if they had been Uncle Harry or Tiger, not enough to get upset. And if she had to be left with any of them, Gervase was the best. He looked more cheerful, having achieved what he wanted, a cooking fire.

They went through the provisions and found the makings of a stew: lentils and vegetables and strips of what looked like shoe leather but Gervase said was goat-meat. He threw it all in together, with dripping and salt and garlic.

'It will take all night,' Laura said.

'We've got all night.'

Laura ate some bread, which was hard and dark. She dipped it in the simmering stew to soften it. Some lumps fell in, and Gervase stirred them round. He put some cheese in, and some wine, and poured some wine into their tea-mugs. It was warm and strong, like the crazy fire against the wall. Laura crouched on the bed amongst the rugs, feeling the sweat begin to rise, and the smoke in her eyes and her hair. Strange smells were coming out of the stewpot. She began to think that what was happening was a dream, and what had happened earlier was another, knowing that her real life was nothing like this at all.

Gervase sat back and laughed.

'It will be ready at three o'clock in the morning.'

'There is no reason why we shouldn't eat then. We've nothing else to do, save sleep.'

'The others won't come back now. It's too late.'

It was dark outside, no stars, and the rain still fell heavily. When they opened the door they could hear the wildness of the river, rolling stones down its bed with a rumbling like thunder. The hut, lit by flames, carpeted by the coloured Corsican rugs the guides had provided, was exotic by contrast. The stones gave back a glowing warmth. Gervase came and lay down beside Laura.

'I'm not going to sleep,' he said. 'I'm not tired.'

Nor was Laura.

'You kissed me in the pool. Then you went away. You can't go away now.'

Laura considered him, the unlocked Gervase. She did not want to go away. She thought of her mother in her lover's arms.

'It will never be like this again,' Gervase said. 'Your mother does it with Harry, and your father with Miss Bell, and you would like to do it too.'

Laura did not answer. It was what Tiger had said. She did not know.

'You are old enough to know,' Gervase said. 'You are not a child.'

Laura shut her eyes and thought about it, and decided that thinking was out of place. She had not thought in the pool, when she had kissed Gervase, and there had been no guilt, but pure pleasure. A momentary pleasure, it is true, but so sweet she would not quickly forget it. It seemed stupid not to pursue it.

When she did not reply Gervase moved towards her. She was lying propped on one elbow, watching him. He moved her elbow away so that she lay down. She was obedient, willing to learn. He came closer and unbuttoned her peasant blouse. She had no chemise, no petticoats, underneath. She was thinking of her mother and Uncle Harry; she could not stop thinking of them, and of her mother's face. It's in my blood, she thought, it's why I want Gervase, although I am not in love with him. I am in love with Tiger. But Gervase will do, because my nature wants it. His hand closed round her breast and he lay over her and put his mouth over hers. She did not move but opened her mouth to him, remembering the moment in the pool. It was strange; she neither liked it nor disliked it. Gervase moved his hand down over her stomach and undid the fastening of her skirt and pulled it down over her hips. It was all she was wearing; she lay now like her mother to Uncle Harry, for Gervase to use, however it was, acquiescent. His hands explored her body, curious and not particularly gentle, and his mouth her breasts, and then her mouth again, growing more urgent. Laura kept her eyes shut, not liking the urgency but remembering the frenzy she had seen, knowing that it was how it went. But it hurt her. Her mother's cries had not been of pain but of joy, but Laura, when it came, thrusting relentlessly into her body, had not expected such vigour. There was no stopping it, the frantic body coupled into hers so that she was jerked helplessly against the bare boards, Gervase gasping and wild over her head. This is what her mother loved, her mother who showed no excitement, no feeling, apart. Laura felt like a rag-doll, ill-treated by her owner, and cried when Gervase withdrew. He lay sweating and panting. Laura tried to lie calmly, but she felt cheated and disappointed. But I wanted it, she thought, amazed. She could not complain. Gervase gradually came back to himself, enough to recognize her feelings.

'You didn't like it?'

'No.'

'Next time—it will be better.'

'Next time? When?'

'After the stew,' Gervase said. 'About four o'clock.'

He went to sleep immediately, leaving Laura outraged. She could not reconcile it. She wanted to ask Miss Bell about it, Miss Bell who had changed out of all recognition, presumably because she liked it. With her father. Everybody, *everybody* liked it. Gervase liked it. He smiled in his sleep, and lay with his arms over his head in the total sprawl of a baby.

Laura pulled one of the rugs over her nakedness and lay looking at the wreaths of smoke in the roof and listening to the rain. Perhaps no one would come back again, ever, and she and Gervase would become wild Corsicans, living on goat in this stone hut and making love every night while the stew cooked. She dozed, and woke to Gervase putting more wood on the fire.

'Is the stew cooked?'

'Not yet.'

He came back beside her.

'I'm sorry, sorry, sorry,' he said.

He put his arms round her and pulled her to him. He smelled of woodsmoke and sweat. Laura lay passively against him, aware of how thin and sharp he was. Her breasts were round and plump against his ribs. He caressed her.

'It's all right here,' he said. 'But at home nothing is right.'

'Why do you say that?'

'Oh—to make good, how it's expected, and do the right thing —it's impossible. At home nothing is natural. School, the way we live there, competing all the time, driven, even in things we are no good at, humiliated. I'm not good at anything.'

'You are good at swimming.'

'Swimming doesn't count at school. Rugger does, and cricket, and Latin. I'm no good at any of those. And girls. I'm no good at girls, not like Simister.'

Whatever had gone wrong earlier, Laura was quite sure it would have been far worse with Simister. Simister!

'Simister's awful.'

'Would you have kissed Simister in the pool?'

'No.'

'But Simister is good at girls. He knows how to make them happy.'

Laura could not argue, if Gervase was convinced. Now, lying against him, and Gervase, the wine slept off, back to his self-despair, Laura felt tender towards him, with an overwhelming compassion. His whole life was something she could not put right. She could see how it was for him, but there was no cure. One was always up against the people who made the conditions—Gervase, herself, Tiger. But Gervase's conditioning had been the most cruel. Mindless idiots like Simister survived the system. Tiger had survived because of Harry and she was going to survive because she was lucky. But Gervase . . .

'But school is finished for you now. You are going to live in London. You can do what you please.'

'I'm going into the Foreign Office. That's not what I please. It will be like school again, trying to be good at things I hate. Competing. Saying all the right things. Failing.'

'Don't. You are being stupid. It's all right *now*.'

'You didn't like me. I was no good to you.'

'Oh, be quiet.'

She lifted her head and put her lips over his, to stop his talking. He was sweeter when he was sad. She moved his head down to her breasts and lay holding him, stroking his hair. It was soft, without oil, like a baby's. She kissed it. She wanted to make him happy; he was so hopeless. He was crying.

Nobody had ever loved him, she realized. He had nobody at all.

'Gervase—' Even his name was awkward.

She lifted his head and kissed his lips and licked up his tears and kissed his eyes. She lay over him and pressed her body into his thinness and felt his swollen parts against her. It was beautiful, feeling him come to her, but without pain, sadly, gently.

'I can't! I can't!' he moaned.

She hugged him. 'You are lovely! I love you like this!'

He cheered up afterwards, and the smell of stew filled the hut. He got up and put some more wood on the fire and examined the contents of the pot.

'I think it's ready.'

He poured some wine into it, and stirred it again. He was naked, lit by the flames. Laura watched him, full of tenderness for his hopeless malaise. He brought the bowls back to the bed, with spoons and bread and the bottle of wine. Laura realized how hungry she was. The mess smelled pungent and was heavy and thick to the spoon.

'Take lots of wine,' Gervase said, 'And it will taste all right.'

They sat amongst the tumbled rugs eating, and Laura thought of Gervase silent at the dinner-table at home, his manners perfect, his presence scarcely noted. 'He's no trouble,' her mother had always said of him. Afterwards he would disappear until the next appointed meal, no trouble. Her mother had never shown him any affection, not when he arrived nor when he went, although she kissed him and said the right things.

'When you said—nothing is right at home . . . it must be sometimes.'

'When I'm alone I'm all right. At your place nobody bothers me. I don't mind it. It's a great relief, after school.'

'Are you *happy*?'

Gervase considered, and shook his head. 'No. You couldn't call it happy. Just negative: not exactly unhappy, like when I'm at school. Happy is what I am now. I have never felt like this before.'

When they had eaten all they wanted there was still a lot of stew left. Gervase put the pot at the end of the fire and built up the fire again. They slept, heavily and dreamlessly. Laura awoke to Gervase caressing her and the sound of the rain on the roof, and chinks of a grey daylight showing under the eaves. She shut her eyes and pulled the rug over her head and turned to Gervase, feeling him in her half-sleep: her warmth, her plaything, her lover. She did not care any more about the world outside the hut. They explored each other, confidence growing now the initiation was over and the territory understood, amazed at the delights discovered, the secrets their bodies had hidden until now. They giggled and talked and dozed, and later Gervase came into her again, and this time Laura was not outraged, just amazed. She lay thinking about it while Gervase dozed off again. She put some more wood on the fire. She supposed it was about midday, but it was still raining.

When Gervase awoke the fire had burnt down and there was no more firewood. He got up and opened the door. The rain was like mist and the valley was shrouded and dripping softly, gurgling and splashing and murmuring, the smell of resin and earth strong in the damp air. The river ran swollen, twice its former width, crashing through the boulders. The mountains were still hidden and Laura imagined her secret pool stirred and opaque, turbulent, debris blocking its sill.

They gathered some more firewood, not bothering to put on their clothes for the rain. The fire spat at the wet logs, smoking and sulking. The hut filled with smoke. Gervase stacked a pile of logs as big as the first, coughing, and pushed the stewpot back on its hook. They were both smeared with wet bark and soil. They went down to the river, hopping and swearing through the scratchy maquis and juniper, and waded out into the water. It tore at their legs, ice-cold, and sucked the stones from under their feet. They staggered and let themselves fall into the torrent, washed against the rolling boulders like white driftwood, clinging on and fighting for breath above the breakers but laughing at the wildness of it and the fierce cold sucking at their lungs. All the feeling drained out of fingers and feet and the strength was sapped and the blood slowed and they had to struggle back, holding each other, almost at the limit of their strength. They kissed, ice-cold lips and frozen tongues mingling, destroyed by laughter. They were scratched all over, the tiny flicks of blood spreading over their wet skins like flowers. They could not stop shivering. They ran back to the hut, not feeling the spiked bushes and the stones, and found the fire burning freely again with a great fresh snapping of strength, the hut full of leaping firelight and the smell of burning stew. They stood over the fire and shook the water off and felt the heat embracing them. Gervase looked into the stewpan.

'We have enough until tomorrow,' he said.

'Yes. And the fire and the water go on for ever. And the loving.'

'Until the others come back.'

'The others are never coming back.'

Laura combed her hair with her fingers and fanned it before the fire. It felt like icicles. They sat talking, feeding the fire, and Gervase told Laura all the ingredients of his failure: his lack of physical prowess, his lack of clever talk and wit, of sparkle, of brain, pedigree, achievement, appearance, self-respect and muscle. He told her of the pain and tyrannies inflicted by the public school, the total commitment to humiliation and failure for one such as he, who could not compete. He was not alone, but the failures failed in isolation, finding no solace in the company of their fellows.

'It cannot possibly be as bad as you say.'

But afterwards Laura saw that it could, if you had no confidante at all, no parents that counted, no kindly home. She saw then what her own home meant to him: a place welcome for its privacy, but no more. Nobody had ever looked forward to his coming home, not even her. They had always said, 'Oh heavens, Gervase is coming home on Tuesday,' with a sigh of exasperation. And now he was going to start in the Foreign Office, with digs in Holborn at ten shillings a week, one room with use of bath; breakfast and dinner, except at weekends. Alone.

'Why can't you stay at Granny and Grandpa's? Or go to India to your parents?'

'My parents say I can go out there when I've passed my exams at the Foreign Office, and Granny and Grandpa think it will make a man of me to go and live in digs. I can go to them at weekends and be introduced to nice girls.'

Laura giggled. 'Like me.'

They ate the remains of the stew. There was nothing left but some very hard bread and goat's cheese and two bottles of wine. It was still raining. They went back under the rugs and thought about themselves and what had happened. Now the food was running out the end of their idyll was in sight.

'We shall have to go down,' Laura said. 'What if they come and find us like this?'

'We shall hear the donkey-bells first, and get dressed.'

'We've got till tomorrow.'

'Nothing will ever be like this again.'

'No.'

It would not change anything when they got home, Laura thought, for nothing was any different in their everyday selves, which they had discarded for the time being. They slept, and woke in the darkness to make love. For the last time, Laura supposed, and lay holding Gervase in her arms when he slept. He was still in her arms when she woke again. The light was streaming in, bright, blinding sunlight. The door was open and a figure stood there, grinning.

It was Pasquale.

Laura jerked awake with such a sense of shock that it penetrated Gervase and he opened his eyes as abruptly. They lay blinking, the brightness almost a pain. Pasquale came in, not shy at all, but looking round approvingly at their comfortable camp, nodding over the remains of the woodpile and looking into the stewpot. He said something to them.

Laura pulled the rug over her head.

'What does he say?'

'I've no idea.'

'You must get up. Do you think he is alone?'

'Yes, he seems to be.'

Gervase got reluctantly out of bed and pulled on his drawers and breeches. Laura remained hidden, in the darkness. It is finished, she thought. They would remember it like a dream, if at all, a story someone had told them. Gervase was talking to Pasquale outside the door, and Laura could hear the donkey-bell which should have warned them of the arrival. She got dressed and went outside. Pasquale and Gervase were dismantling the sagging tents. The valley steamed and glittered in the return of the sunshine, filled with a burgeoning of fresh growth and life, the water-burdened leaves straightening to the sun, petals uncurling, beetles hurrying underfoot. The goats were back, jangling down by the river. They had not heard the goat-bells either.

'Is everything all right?' Laura asked Gervase. 'With the others?'

'As far as I can make out, somebody has hurt a leg—I'm not sure who. Your father, I think. They went down with him, and it took a long time. I *think* . . . I'm not sure. His French is very difficult to understand.'

Laura was not at all surprised, for bodily grace was not one of her father's characteristics.

Pasquale was squirting wine into his mouth out of his skin bottle. He gestured to Gervase that he should try it, and Gervase made a bold attempt. He caught a little and the rest ran in rivulets down his bare chest. They all laughed. They loaded the bundles of clothes and belongings on to the donkey and left what it could not carry in the hut. The fire had died; chinks of bright sun glittered through the holes in the wall as if it were studded with diamonds. They shut the door and set off down the track behind Pasquale and the donkey. Laura did not know what Gervase was thinking, sober now, walking steadily in his boots and thick stockings. The path was all mud and rivulets and washed-down stones, needing care. They followed the nimble donkey and the stream thundered down beside them; Pasquale whistled, leading the way, and they went down beside the green pool without a word. Gervase never even paused, passing the white ledge he had dived from without even a glance. Laura was behind, watching him, and his eyes were steady on the difficult track; he did not hesitate. She stood, looking down, and saw the pool a cauldron of hasty breakers and whirly debris. She was as confused as the water, desiring a weighty conclusion to a short meditation on this milestone in her life, but nothing came to mind. Her thoughts sheered off like the careering pine twigs.

The way down was long and hot and wearisome. Laura did not even look forward to going home any more, although she had not wanted to come. I am very perverse, she thought. We none of us know what we want.

By the time they reached the Hotel de la Forêt it was evening. Pasquale was still whistling. Only Simister was in the hotel, just sitting down to dinner. He was wearing his suit and supervising the opening of a bottle of burgundy. When he saw them he said, 'Oh, jolly fine! Are you going to change? I'll wait for you.'

'Where are the others?'

'Go and get changed, and I'll tell you over dinner.'

Simister, as usual, was in charge of the situation, ordering the waiter better than either Philip or Gervase. When Laura and Gervase came down dinner was served at once, and the wine poured, Simister testing its temperature with fussy insistence. Laura studied the tablecloth, lifted her eyes and saw Gervase watching Simister, half-smiling. In his suit and stiff shirt, he was back to being a candidate for the Foreign Office.

'We shall have to go home,' Simister said, confirming Laura's fears for the future. 'Your father, Laura, has sprained his ankle and has gone to Ajaccio with Hilda to the doctor. He wants to return home as soon as possible. And a cable has come from Mr Harry to say that your mother is ill.'

Laura had no desire to go back. Her mother was never ill, and if she was she would rather be comforted by Harry than by her husband. Her parents' troubles did not engage her sympathy. Simister explained in his public lecturer fashion what had happened: Philip's total inadequacy on steep rock causing him to fall and the subsequent difficulty of conveying him back to Vizzavona in the bad weather.

'Pasquale was going to go back for you, but it was so difficult we needed him. He said there was a good hut—you would have shelter. At least I thought he said that, in his ridiculous French. But we were worried about you. I thought you would be damned frightened when no one came back.'

'Oh no,' Laura murmured politely. 'We were quite all right.'

She dared not look at Gervase, thinking of the feel of him against her body, swelling and thrusting. She could feel herself blushing. It would not do to remember these things any more.

'We can pack tonight,' she said, very prosaic. 'And go down in the morning if there is transport.'

'Yes, I can arrange that,' Simister said.

'What are you going to do?' she asked him suddenly. 'Now that you have left school?'

'Oh, I am going to South Africa. My pater has got some mines out there. He says I can learn about handling the men, and study the business side.'

'Coal?'

'Diamonds.'

It would be diamonds! Laura thought. She could see Simister handling the men. He already had a bull-neck and his eyes bulged with enthusiasm and arrogance. Dear, dear Gervase.

They went in the morning, driven by Giovanni in the hotel conveyance down through the great arches of the sweet chestnut trees, the first leaves yellowing, village dogs barking, the dust rising sluggishly again after the torrents. They wore their travelling clothes and did not speak much, Simister troubled by the strange mutual self-possession he sensed in Laura and Gervase. They seemed to him very calm about the adventure. Gervase had always been a mystery to Simister, useful for his connections in the holidays and in their younger days splendid to bully at school, but secretive throughout; even through the very worst of the things they had devised he had not struggled or cried or protested; he had a shell and his inner self was never penetrated, whatever they did. Sometimes Simister had felt bad about it, but his pater said life was like that: the survival of the fittest. A man had to have guts to get on, it was Nature's law. School was a testing ground, a grounding for what was to come, and it did not help to be soft with a boy. If a boy got hell knocked out of him it would stand him in good stead later. But Simister, although agreeing, had gone to considerable lengths to make sure he had never been one of the ones who got hell knocked out of him. He knew he was too sensitive to undergo what Gervase suffered. A certain lack of sensitivity could be a help to a man, and Gervase had the edge on him there. Sometimes he could remember feeling uncomfortable at the look in Gervase's eyes, and that proved the delicacy of his—Simister's—emotions.

When they got to Ajaccio they found Philip lying on a chaise-longue on the veranda of the best hotel, waited on devotedly by Hilda. He looked rather better pleased with his holiday since he had hurt his leg, and was quite jovial.

'And what did you two get up to, left alone?' he chaffed Gervase and Laura. 'That wasn't in the plans at all, by Jove!'

But they looked into the distance and said, 'We were quite all right, thank you. We managed very well.'

And if Pasquale had told Simister how he found them, Simister would have believed his understanding of Pasquale's French at fault again, for it was 'devilish funny, considering the man's an actual frog.'

10

When they reached Dover the harbour-master brought them a telegram. It asked them to proceed to Newmarket with all possible haste, as Mrs Keen was very ill. Philip was rather put out, having suffered considerably on the journey and having hoped that the sympathy would be all his when he got home, but he cancelled his plan for staying a night in London and—Simister being equally as good with cabbies as with waiters—they made a quick transit of London and caught the evening train back to Newmarket. Another cab took them home, there not having been time to send a cable to be met. They were all by this time very tired. It was a hot evening, going dusk, and the familiarity of the landscape, the fields of mares and foals, the dusty lanes beneath the canopies of elm, struck Laura with an overwhelming sense of timelessness, of irrevocability: whatever had happened to her, would happen, was of very little account. It made no difference to the pattern of the world, her personal joys and pains. She thought she was returning a changed person, but it was of no account at all. She felt numb, flattened by weariness.

Thorn's was in darkness and only the porch light shone from Dry Meadows as the cab turned in the drive. They had expected to see the bedrooms lit and the bustle of emergency. Simister jumped down, knocked on the door and turned back to help Philip down. The front door opened suddenly, and Harry stood there in the pool of light.

'It's too late,' he said. 'She's gone.'

'What do you mean? Gone where?' Philip said tetchily.

'She's dead.'

They all stood looking at Harry. He was like a shadow, thin and demented-looking. He was not gentle with his news, or concerned for them, not even for Laura, but totally distracted by his own grief. If she had not known that they had been lovers, Laura knew she would have seen it then. She accepted the news without shock; it did not seem out of place. She thought: the green pool in the Manganello will still be there when we have all died, and the horses will race on the Heath a hundred years from now. It will be no different. She stood beside Gervase, who was silent too. He put his arm round her and gave her a gentle hug, and dropped it again, while the others went into a great hubbub of shock and distress. Harry was explaining to Philip. Laura pushed past them and went into the hall and found Albert standing waiting. She went up to him and he put his arms round her and hugged her. She buried her face in his shoulder and the comfort engulfed her; it was coming home in its truest sense, to the one who never changed.

'Sugared almonds won't help this time, my pet,' he said.

'No.'

'It's best, perhaps.'

He took her up to her room. She did not want the others, or to go to her stupid father, who had Hilda; not even to Harry. Albert turned back the bed-covers and helped her with her coat and opened her travelling-bag for her, and said he would bring her some tea.

'I don't want anything. I'm all right.'

She lay on the bed when he had gone and let the shock wash over her, but she had no feelings. If Albert had gone, there would have been a bigger loss. She could remember nothing but her mother's face when Harry had made love to her, and the more she tried to feel some regret for her mother's passing the more ecstatic became the vision and passionate the cries. Laura could not think about it any more, the feeling of distress for that greater than for her mother's death, but she could not sleep either. She lit her lamp again and got out her Fred Archer pictures and spread them on the floor in the light and lay regarding his sad face. He too, they said, loved passionately. She fell asleep, hung over the bed with the pictures spread out, but later she woke with cramp, got up and put the pictures away, put out the lamp, undressed and got into bed properly. She slept heavily, and without dreams.

*   *   *

Cecily's coffin was in the conservatory when Laura went to see her, but Philip had it removed later to his study where it was cooler. She had died of meningitis. She had some of her own white lilies by her head, and looked as cool in death as the front she had put to her life, remote and unearthly. The sight did not pain Laura, only the memory of the same face as it had cried out to Harry; and it was hard now to reconcile the two as the same. This was a porcelain face, a church moulding, less than a photograph. The vigorous growth in the conservatory moved Laura more, that this shell had created such a profusion of strong, arching leaves and bright flowers. Only the weed harebells in the dark cracks under the benches, transparent and frail and unintended, had any affinity with the absent Cecily, as unobtrusive and secretive as she. If Laura had not seen the truth, from the tree with Tiger, she could never have believed what lay beneath the mask. And you have taught me, she said to her mother; I am a good pupil.

She went to see Tiger, but he was in charge of the yard, as Harry 'was all to pieces', and Tiger had to superintend the horses which were racing. He was away all day. Laura did not want to talk to Harry, nor anybody else save Albert, and he put her on to helping with the funeral preparations, which occupied her mind. Her father was shut in the morning-room in a great furore of grief and self-pity, waited on by Hilda; Simister had gone home and Gervase was in his room preparing to be a Foreign Office clerk. Laura had to get the spare bedrooms ready for the relations coming, and order the food, do all the things her mother would have done if it had been anyone else's funeral. She wondered who would run the house afterwards, herself or Hilda. The servants seemed to be wondering the same, for they made heavy aspersions regarding Miss Bell's new duties towards the master in Laura's presence, and no doubt were less guarded when she was out of the kitchen. She knew what they were thinking. Yes, you are right, she wanted to say, just like my mother and Harry. And me and Gervase. The last would really surprise them. But she did not want Albert to know about that, not ever.

On the second evening, the night before the funeral, Tiger came home from Doncaster and Laura saw him coming up the lane, riding a horse, with one of the lads bringing another behind. She went out to meet him. He pulled up in front of her and called to the boy, 'Take them both in. I'll come in a minute.' He dismounted and handed his reins to the boy. He looked very smart, like a real trainer; not flash like some of them but sober and neat, expensive, like Fred. Laura had heard that Harry's yard was doing very well lately, and some people had said it was because of his new partner.

'Not a very nice homecoming for you,' he said.

'No.'

They stood looking at each other, not knowing what to say. There was no need to say anything, in fact; it was all understood.

'They say you're in charge,' Laura said.

'While things are upset, that's all. Mr Keen was—' He shrugged. 'It was unexpected. I think he thinks it was a sort of punishment, for what they had done.'

'What we saw, you mean?'

'Yes. After you had gone, Mr Keen went out every night. He never said anything, he just went. He never does normally. And then she got ill, and he said to me that she wanted to die. He said she willed it. I don't know if it's true.'

'I can believe it.'

'What would have happened, if not?'

Laura shook her head. It was called scandal, she supposed. But she had partaken herself, and it was beautiful. But when other people found out and talked about it, it was shocking. She was frightened for herself and what she had discovered, seeing where it led, to her mother wanting to die and Harry going all to pieces.

'Does everybody know?' she asked Tiger.

'Everybody but your father. The servants and the lads, that is. That means everybody.'

She was not surprised. Scandal indeed. People went beyond the truth, if the truth was not enough, and made the story better. She had been told by Albert that Tiger was thought to be a bastard of Harry's, because Harry had shown him favours. He was known as Tiger Keen, and in looks was not unlike, if one was disposed to favour the theory.

'Are you coming to the funeral tomorrow?'

'Mr Keen wishes it, yes.'

There were so many people at the funeral that they would not all fit into the village church. The London relations came up the long hill in carriages that Albert had hired for them: mostly

Cecily's family whom Laura knew very little of, save that her mother had not cared for them. Cecily's parents were a strange Bohemian couple in flowing cloaks whom Philip disliked intensely: the grandma and grandpa who would take Gervase for weekends to meet the right people. They examined Gervase as soon as they arrived, up and down, and Gervase had no conversation at all. There were several cousins and great-aunts and an aunt or two of Philip and Harry's, but no one nearer.

Albert primed Laura as to who was who. Philip was ill at ease, embarrassed by Hilda who would not leave his side, save in church where she joined the servants. Laura sat with him, and Harry and her grandparents, and Tiger sat behind with Gervase. Laura did not cry, feeling rather a curious sense of release and freedom in her mother's death and a conviction that Harry was right when he said she had desired it. The service, the music, the ritual swilled over her; the bright sunlight fell muted through the coloured glass windows and she sat thinking of the green pool and the water dropping down from the rocks. When she turned round she saw Gervase like a Foreign Office clerk in his black suit and starched shirt, his hair cut and greased down; she stared, it was so strange, seeing his eyes on her and remembering them under the water like mossy stones when she kissed him. Her mother had known.

Harry would not come to the graveside or to the reception. He said it was a racing day and he had owners to see, but Laura knew he went nowhere and Tiger saw the owners and sent the horses down with Arthur.

The reception went very smoothly and Laura had no difficulty in saying the right, conventional things. The relations all assumed that she would now take her mother's place and keep house for her father and she did not demur; only Gervase understood that her future was now as bleak as his own.

'Hilda will take over here, you know that?' he said. 'It is a godsend for her, this happening.'

'She can do so, with pleasure. I don't want to look after my father all my life.'

'What are you going to do?'

'I don't know.'

'I'm going back with the grandparents tomorrow. I start work next week. I hate them, and I shall hate the job. Can I write to you, Laura?'

'Of course.' But it could never be the same again, as it was in the stone hut.

She sat in her mother's place at dinner, and Albert took his orders from her. Hilda sat at the bottom of the table by her father, and Cecily's mother said to her, 'Now Laura is mistress of the house, she will surely no longer need a governess?'

Philip said, 'Miss Bell will take another post, naturally. But she may stay here until she does so.'

Gervase looked across at Laura. They both knew she would stay. So did Albert. When the guests had all departed, and Gervase with them, Philip went to catch up with his correspondence in his study. Laura went out on the terrace, feeling very tired, drained, and more sad than at any time since she had come home.

For the first time she thought of her mother with real affection, looking down across the lovely evening lawns where Cecily had often worked in the summer until the coming of dusk. The stones of the terrace gave out an autumnal warmth and between the cracks the trodden thyme scented the air; it was very calm and silent after the day's upheaval, save for the woodpigeons calling from the trees across the lawn. Laura sat on the wall in her stiff black dress, feeling the warm stones under her thighs, thinking of the thirty-nine years of her mother's life. Perhaps, with Harry, she had known more happiness in the last few years than she would have experienced in another forty with Philip; one could scarcely regret. One was bound by one's nature.

But without her Laura felt incredibly lonely.

While she was sitting there Hilda Bell came round the corner of the house towards the french windows. When she saw Laura she hesitated, but then came on firmly. Laura could see by the way she moved that she was now a fixture. She had a new confidence, a hardness. They had spoken very little since the holiday, Hilda having been completely occupied with Philip on the journey, and having kept out of the way since. But now it was impossible to ignore each other.

'You look tired,' Hilda said. She sat down on the wall beside her. 'I will see to the clearing up, if you wish to go to bed.'

'No, I don't.' Laura's voice came out sharp and cold.

Hilda was silent, but made no move to go. Her nervous despair had completely vanished since the visit to Corsica, and she seemed irritatingly in control of herself. As her whole topic of conversation during the three months before their going had been, 'What is to become of me?', Laura assumed that the change in her demeanour had been brought about by the fact that she now knew.

To confirm it, Hilda presently said, 'Your father has told me that I may stay on here as housekeeper. Has he told you?'

'He had no need. I guessed.'

'What will you do?'

'Become a governess, I suppose.'

Hilda's smug satisfaction stung Laura. She knew she could not live in the house with Hilda taking her mother's place. There was nothing in Hilda save self-interest; if she loved Philip it was for Philip's possessions and money. Laura did not suppose housekeeper was her only aspiration. Given the proper passing of time, she would become his wife. The usurpation made Laura feel very angry, but she realized that she should have been pleased that she was released from the job of being her father's housekeeper, which would have been her lot but for Hilda. The thought of being a governess appealed more, surprisingly. She tried to be rather more gracious to Hilda.

'I was going away, anyway.'

'To London?'

'Yes.'

But Laura knew she would not go to London. Her father could not force her now, being in the wrong over Hilda. She would do what she pleased. What that was, she had no idea.

It became a matter of some urgency to decide as the days went by, Hilda taking her place with surprising confidence. Laura found herself living in the kitchen, at home with the servants' indignation. Albert was unperturbed, carrying on as he had always done, but Peggy and Alice and the day-girl were outraged at having to take orders from Hilda. They complained bitterly to Laura, but Laura was in no situation to change things. Her presence was an embarrassment to everybody.

'I don't want to go away,' she said to Albert. 'Away from this house, yes, but not away.'

'Leave it to me,' Albert said.

Philip made no move to advise her, her contemptuous eyes at the dinner-table each evening undermining his authority. She had made it plain she was not going to London to be groomed for the marriage-market; she would rather be a shop-girl. She had avoided her Uncle Harry and would not ask his advice, for the relationship between them now was painful. She knew that her presence caused him great uneasiness, through guilt at what she knew and through her own resemblance to her mother. It was best to stay away until this bad time was over; she could not believe that it was permanent. More than that, she wanted to put Tiger out of her mind, for his presence had more power than anyone's to disturb her. All she had learned with Gervase she now related to Tiger. She could not see him without fantasies overtaking her, dreams that were akin to the ones she had lavished on Fred Archer, heightened by all she had experienced. They frightened her, verging on hysteria. The fact that Tiger was away such a lot was her only relief, and she determined to leave Dry Meadows before the racing season finished. She could tell nobody about her fears, but Albert sensed her anxiety and told her within a couple of weeks that he had found something that might suit.

'A lady called Mrs Rush—a nice family, they're in racing—a big house on the Ely Road, not far from Mr Archer's—in fact, I believe she is a friend of Mrs Archer—she wants someone to help her. Not a maid, more a nanny, someone she can trust. I think you will like them, if you want to go and pay her a visit. I can arrange it if you wish.'

'Oh yes, I do wish.'

'Very well. Leave it to Albert.'

Laura said nothing to her father, but drove down in her mother's trap on the afternoon arranged by Albert. She passed Falmouth House and had a glimpse of Nellie Archer in the garden with young Freddie Pratt, one of Fred's widowed sister's children whom Fred had taken a fancy to and who had come to live with them. Everyone said he was good company for Nellie with her husband being away such a lot, and their own baby not due till January. Marriage had not dulled Fred's ambition, and Mr Dawson had a new wonder horse called St Simon that was the talk of the racing world. Fred rode him in all his races, and no other horse could get near him: a horse that dreams were made of. Thinking of Fred steadied Laura. Her dream love was an anchor and would never do her harm. She could retreat into that familiar world for the time being; if she was to be a neighbour of the Archers she might even strengthen her acquaintance.

The Rush family home was a substantial new house with large bay windows set behind a brick wall and a leggy shrubbery, approached by a gravel sweep. There were stables behind, and paddocks, and well-trodden paths that spoke of much to-ing and fro-ing. When Laura rang the bell she could hear a commotion inside the house, a boy shouting and a baby screaming and the maid who answered looked put-out, as if interrupted in mid-argument. Laura was ushered into a morning-room strewn with toys and asked to take a seat. A large golden retriever came and put its muzzle on her lap and wagged its tail. All the chairs were torn by claw-marks and shedding stuffing and the atmosphere, Laura considered, was more homely than smart, but the thought pleased her. She did not like the cool beauty favoured by her father for living in.

Lottie Rush had forgotten she was coming, apologized profusely for her unpreparedness, laughed and said, 'It's such a to-do here—I never remember anything. If you would like to work in such a madhouse I would be grateful for your help. We have four children, you see—Charlie is the eldest, fifteen he is and—well—boisterous is perhaps the word, always underfoot, in and out to the stables—I'm always hoping he will leave home and get apprenticed to someone sensible but no, he prefers to help his father, and Bertie likes it that way too. Then there's Ada who is thirteen and the least of our troubles. She goes to school and is nicely behaved except when Charlie sets her off. The two little ones—well, if you could take them off my hands a little life here would be very much more restful. There's Herbie—he's five—and Agnes the baby—you can hear her crying, I daresay. And three dogs and the lads in and out all day—Bertie trains round the back you see and they all think of this as home. I want someone like an elder sister for them really—not exactly a nanny or a governess or a housekeeper, just a sort of extra me, if you understand how it is. I'm afraid I'm not very methodical. We're not at all smart, as you can see. If you want a smart place, this won't do for you, but dear Albert seemed to think you might like us. He said you were too quiet at home.'

Laura was very much taken with Mrs Rush's cheerful lack of affectation and fuss. She seemed to accept Laura without question. Remembering her mother's agony over the appointment of Miss Bell, Laura was amazed that the business could be resolved so easily.

'I would be so glad if you felt you could come. You could always change your mind if you find us unbearable.'

'I'm sure I won't. I would love to come,' Laura said. 'As soon as you wish.'

'Tomorrow?'

'Well—yes—'

It was incredibly simple. Laura drove home excited at her good fortune and went straight to Albert in the kitchen. He laughed at her pleasure.

'You are such a good arranger!' Laura told him. 'She is so nice! Not a bit stuffy. I'm sure I will like it.'

'Well, come and see us sometimes, miss, to cheer us up. We shall miss you and no mistake, always in the way down here. I thought it'd suit you. Have you told your father now? You must put it tactfully. I daresay he won't like it, but I doubt if he'll object to your going.'

'He will be glad to have me out of the way, I think. He can dine with Hilda alone. He will prefer it.'

Albert shook his head scornfully.

'It's a sad pass we've come to here. You'll be better off in a big family—you don't know what family life is, the way you've been brought up.'

It occurred to Laura that she should tell Harry and Tiger where she was going, but she could not bear the thought of going to Thorn's. Albert promised to tell them. Laura announced the news of her post at the dinner-table. As she had suspected her father did not object, although he was not pleased.

'You would be much better off going to your grandparents,' he said. 'I cannot understand why you want to lower yourself in this way.'

'To be a governess?' Laura asked cruelly.

Her father did not reply. Hilda kept her eyes on her plate, her expression not altering. She had cut herself off from Laura since her liaison with Philip, and Laura could now scarcely credit that they had pored over their Fred Archer pictures together, giggling and excited. Every day she was establishing her place in the house more surely, helping Philip now with his work ánd his accounts. Cecily had not been dead a month. Laura could not contain her resentment, and when Percy drove her down the next morning to the Rush establishment she did not trouble to say goodbye. She hugged Albert and kissed Peggy, and Albert said he would call and see her, and to come to him any time if things went wrong.

'I know you will be happy. Things will come right for you, you wait and see.'

Not that there was any waiting to be done in the new household. From the moment she set foot inside the door Laura was busy. The lads were in the kitchen for their ten o'clock bread and cheese, one of the dogs had taken Charlie's boots out into the garden and no one could find them, and Herbie was crying because he wanted to go and play with Freddie and no one would take him.

'Charlie will take you when he's found his boots,' Lottie said.

'No, I'm riding out. They'll be gone by the time I get back,' Charlie grumbled.

'Perhaps Laura will take him, although she's only had her foot inside the door five minutes.'

'Yes, glad to get out again—five minutes is enough,' Charlie said, laughing.

He was an engaging boy, untidy and clumsy but with a natural friendliness that disarmed. His father Bertie was an older version, but with the same directness. Nobody, Laura found, in the Rush family was complicated in the way she had become used to in her own family. They spoke freely, laughed a lot, quarrelled and laughed again. Nobody had laughed in Dry Meadows, save in the kitchen.

She got Herbie dressed to go out, and Lottie said to her, 'Take him to Mrs Archer's, but see if it is all right for him to stay. She said yesterday she would be alone—Fred is in York, I believe. But if she is tired, little Freddie can come back here and stay to lunch. I don't mind. You know Falmouth House?'

'Oh, yes!'

Laura went on her first errand, bemused. Herbie came with her happily and Laura found herself spurred by her old excitement—even knowing dear Fred was away did not spoil the knowledge that she had an introduction to his house, to his wife. The pains of her own experiences in loving could be expunged by this stroke of fortune. Loving Fred was pure pleasure and there was no reality in it to harm her. She could shelter in her fantasy until she felt fit to come to terms with the fractured relationships she had just absconded from: it was a lovely thought. She sent a compulsive prayer of thanks to Albert—he must have known!—and took Herbie into the gates of Falmouth House and up to the front door.

She rang the bell, gazing happily at the immaculate new lawns and newly-planted flower-beds and shrubberies. The house was on a grand scale, reflecting the wealth of its owner. Laura was familiar with its gables and tall latticed chimneys but had never before had the excuse to call, to let herself inside the gates.

The door opened. Expecting to give her message to a maid, Laura was struck dumb by finding herself face to face with Fred himself. He was wearing a dressing-gown and looked somewhat surprised.

'Why, Miss Laura! Excuse me . . . I was expecting my brother-in-law—'

He spoke with the slight deference that was a legacy of Mat Dawson's upbringing and which Laura found so touching in her hero. She presumed he had just come from the Turkish bath, for his hair was wet and he had a towel round his neck. His new house had had one built in, so he no longer had to use the one at Heath House which had been built for the horses when it was the fashion to sweat them a few years earlier.

'Do you wish to see my wife? Would you like to come in?'

It was more than Laura had ever dreamed, to set foot inside Falmouth House. Herbie led the way confidently, and she followed rather more nervously. Fred shut the door and led her into the morning-room and went to call Nellie. They came back together and Fred introduced them.

'Miss Laura is Harry Keen's niece, and used to ride out on the Heath with his horses. She gave me a race once, I remember, when I gave Kimbo a trial—it's just as well they don't let the ladies into this game, else we'd have to look to our laurels.'

Laura felt herself blushing scarlet at this accolade. She shook hands with Nellie, who still, in spite of being obviously with child, looked no more than sixteen, very small and fair and pretty.

'You've come to work for Mrs Rush? She said she hoped to find someone—you'll find her very pleasant to work for, I'm sure.'

'You can ride out for Bertie then,' Fred said. 'We can't waste such talent! You must excuse me, I'll get dressed—I have to get down to Heath House.'

He disappeared and Laura was introduced to young Freddie and several dogs, and admired the paintings in the hall of Silvio the Derby winner and the mare Spinaway. It was arranged for Herbie to stay and for Laura to call back for him in the evening.

'Or Fred will drop him back on his way to the station. He has to go to York later—he's riding there tomorrow. Young Freddie is good company for me when Fred is away—I must say I don't know what I would do without him.'

Fred reappeared, dressed in riding-clothes, and his hack was brought round for him by a groom. Laura went out with him, taking her leave of Nellie, and Fred, getting up on the horse, remarked to her, 'Your uncle's stable is doing well with that new young man of his—what's his name? Tiger? He's a brainy lad. Your uncle was shrewd to promote him, if he only started as an apprentice.'

Looking up into the gaunt face, aware of Archer's curiosity, Laura was smitten suddenly with the memory of Tiger's agony on looking upon the same face on the day of the wedding, the staring expression of shock and distress which he had been unable to hide. She had pushed the memory of it away but now it came back with a vividness that caused her almost as much pain as on the wedding day. She stood speechless for a moment, the shock of it knocking her stupid, her anguish as much for Tiger as for Fred, for Tiger had to suffer the knowledge and Fred knew nothing.

'Please—!' She stopped herself, biting off the involuntary warning, seeing Fred's look of concern.

'Are you all right?'

'I'm sorry—yes—it was just . . .' But there was no explaining. She shook her head. 'A headache—'

'You must look after yourself.'

'And you!' Laura said vehemently.

He laughed. 'I have to,' he said. 'All the time.'

He touched his cap to her then and rode away, trotting fast towards the town. Laura went back to the Rushes' house, shaken and disturbed. There was nothing she could say, save that she had met both Mr and Mrs Archer, and Herbie was staying.

'It must be tonight he's going to York then,' Lottie said. 'I had it wrong. Well, if he's not on a horse he's on a train—poor Nellie scarcely sees him in summer. And when he's at home he's all the time in the bath, and he doesn't eat meals, so there is no sitting at the table, for he can't bear to watch other people eating. And everyone thinks Nellie is so lucky! I don't know how he keeps going as he does.'

Bertie, in for his lunch, said, 'He knows what he's doing, don't you worry. He's a clever man is Fred—he must be to satisfy the punters how he does when his horses carry so much money. It's a rough game when such fortunes are at stake.'

'Yes, but the jockey always gets the blame, however good, if the horse isn't good enough. Look when he didn't win on Galliard this year! There were some cruel things said—Nellie said he was very hurt by it, but he doesn't show anything. He's not at all a hard man, in spite of the life he lives.'

'No, too sensitive for his own good probably. But that's part of his success, because he brings that brain and sensitivity to work on a horse—he doesn't just ride 'em all the same like a herd of cattle, like most of them do. No one understands how a horse thinks like Fred. And he's a pretty shrewd judge of a man too, come to that. For all they crowd round him, and he's always being invited out with their Lordships, his real friends are few and they go back to his childhood, long before he became famous.'

Laura loved to hear conversation about Fred among the Rush family, just as she had loved to listen to the tales her Uncle Harry had regaled her with. Everyone had their Fred Archer stories. But the unexpected meeting brought back all the horrors she had harboured about Tiger's vision and which she had successfully until now resolved to put out of her thoughts. There was no one to share these agonies with, and the force of her feelings about Fred's future made her all the more aware of the crushing responsibility Tiger carried. She might be convinced that disaster lay ahead, but Tiger knew what it was. The burden of that was horrific. She tried to believe that Tiger's gift of prophecy was fallible, but it had not yet been proved so. No horse he had dreamed of as a winner had yet failed to win; and the accident he had prophesied to Fred earlier had duly happened. Laura had no evidence to console her.

Tiger, possibly because of these uncommon responsibilities, had grown into a cautious-tongued, well-respected young trainer in Newmarket. Like Fred himself, he kept apart from the more suspect elements of the racing fraternity, made no boasts for his charges, worked hard and kept his eyes open. It was true, as Fred had remarked, that Thorn's was going up in the world as a training establishment, richer owners and better-class horses gradually beginning to patronize it. Having moved into the Rushes' home, Laura now saw Thorn's and its occupants from a distance, without involvement. She did not visit, and rarely went to Dry Meadows. It seemed better to her, to put a distance of time between herself and all that had happened there. She knew it was not permanent but for herself she felt it necessary. Sometimes she met Hilda or Uncle Harry in town, but she did not linger. Her uncle had visibly aged since her mother's death, but as the weeks went by he came back to his old optimistic cheerfulness, although he never regained the boyish quality which Laura had loved in him. He was almost shy with her now, enquiring only after her well-being with the Rush family.

'As long as you are happy, Laura . . . and the Rushes are a lovely family.'

'Yes, I am. Far better than going to London, which was what they had all decided.'

'Well, all for the best in that department.'

He did not speak of Tiger, nor did Laura enquire. She sometimes saw him on the Heath riding out when she was out with the children, but never close enough to speak to. She saw Fred more often, hacking backwards and forwards to Heath House, and his invariable greeting never failed to raise a blush of delight. When the season was finished the gaunt, strained look went from his face and he filled out, back on big dinners again, to his natural weight over ten stone. Every year it was harder for him to get it down again in the spring, and he spoke freely now of looking for a ride in the Grand National and turning to jumping where he could ride without wasting.

'But he never will,' Bertie said. 'He can't live without the racing he knows. Jumping is another game altogether.'

'He takes terrible liberties with his constitution,' Lottie said severely. 'He should have more regard now he's a married man.'

'You won't change him.'

'Wasting like that killed Tom French.' Tom French was the young jockey Fred had succeeded at Mat Dawson's.

'It's killed a lot of them, I don't deny it.'

Laura was distressed by these conversations, but was convinced that Tiger had seen something far more violent than death by wasting. The expression on Tiger's face was something she had learned to live with, and sometimes she thought the memory of it and what it meant was largely the reason she preferred not to meet Tiger, for it came between. She was reminded of his knowledge whenever she saw him, and she came to realize that it now governed to a large degree her spirits and her behaviour. By no power could she come to believe that it was a figment of the imagination, or something to be sceptical about.

'You're very serious-minded for a young girl,' Lottie said to her. 'If you have a young man, I would be perfectly happy for you to meet him, you know. If you wish to ask someone to tea . . .'

Laura had had letters from Gervase, and he had suggested he might come up to Newmarket one weekend to see her. He hated London and he hated his job.

'I have a cousin whom I might ask, although he's not my young man.'

'Young Mr Keen?'

'He's not my cousin!'

'I thought—' Lottie blushed and looked embarrassed. 'By adoption—I understand your uncle had adopted him.'

'He's a partner. I don't think my uncle can adopt him, not without his parents' consent, and I know they would not give it.'

'I thought—having taken your uncle's name—'

'No. It's only to have a name—he doesn't want his own known. I don't know what it is.'

'How strange! But by all means ask your cousin. We should be very glad to entertain him.'

Laura wrote and invited Gervase for the last weekend in January, although she had no idea how she was to entertain him. At the beginning of January Nellie Archer gave birth to a son, but the baby died almost immediately. Nellie was seriously ill and there was much coming and going at Falmouth House, and Laura was grieved for Fred's disappointment and worry. The weather was very bad and none of the horses could be exercised in the icy conditions. The Heath House stable had the valuable St Simon to contend with, who was a demon in the stable even when in work. Even the equable Bertie was worried, but comforted himself by reporting others worse off than himself.

'Fred tells me St Simon gets on the straw track and kicks like blazes. They can't hold him—real fun and games they're having down there. They're worried to death.'

'There's enough worry at home without all that. Nellie is very poorly. Poor Fred has got his hands full.'

'Well, at least he's not away racing. Come the summer and everything will look up again. They've all their lives ahead of them.'

'Yes, that's a man's view,' Lottie said shortly.

Gervase came and stayed at Dry Meadows a night and called for Laura on the Saturday afternoon. It was cold and frosty but a thin sun was shining and, after introductions, Laura decided they should walk on the Heath before tea. They went out, well wrapped-up, Gervase borrowing a pair of boots from Bertie. He looked to Laura very different from the moody boy she had known, in his London clothes and bowler hat, but as he talked she came to see that nothing was different.

'Oh, how I hate it! It is worse than school, if anything, and I am trapped, just as I was at school, for there is no alternative. There would be if I was tough and brave—I could break out and snap my fingers, but I am nervous and stupid as I've always been. I do as I'm told and they load the work on me because I don't complain and they pay me a pittance and I'm expected to be grateful.'

'You should do something else!'

'I've nothing to offer.'

Laura had a sharp stab of memory, of Tiger boasting how valuable he was as he pulled weeds from her parents' gravel drives. Tiger had broken out; Tiger was tough and brave, and had never been grateful. She sighed impatiently.

'I can't help you,' she said. 'Unless you ask Bertie for a job.'

He irked her now, with his insistence on his own lack of qualities.

'You will have to drink a lot of wine and cheer up,' she said. 'Tell me what you thought of life at Dry Meadows. I never go there, you know. I cannot bear to see Hilda taking my mother's place.'

'Yes, I'll say! She orders everybody, including your father. She has put on weight, and she chucks it about, and your father says, "Yes, dear," every two minutes. I hate to tell you this, Laura, but it's the truth. As soon as a decent interval has elapsed I am sure she will become your step-mother.'

'I am sure you are right. I shall never go back.'

'Then you are homeless, like me.'

But Laura, embraced by the Rush family, did not feel homeless. Undecided about her future, perhaps, but not without warmth and affection—although it could well be true that she appeared to reject it. Laura knew that that was what Lottie meant when she had told her she was serious-minded. The events of the past few months had made her so. She walked soberly with Gervase back across the Severals wishing that she could fall in love with him and make him happy and settle down to a comfortable life in London. But the happy solution was impossible, for it was not in her nature. Sympathetic as she was towards Gervase, she found his pessimism unbearable. It was a relief to come back into the warmth and hubbub of her adopted home and sit round the fire with Ada and Herbie, toasting muffins, and listening to Charlie telling Gervase tall stories of his racing life. Certainly Charlie did not lack self-esteem. But Gervase, hemmed in by his repressions, found it hard to respond and was back to the awkward, stilted manner of his youth, which Laura later had difficulty in defending to Charlie.

'What a stick your boy-friend is! A proper Londoner, I'd say. Not much life about him, Laura—you'd do better—'

'When I want your advice I'll ask for it!' Laura said tartly.

But she was relieved when the time came to escort Gervase back to the station. They stood on the platform in the cold, dying daylight, watching a porter lighting the lamps and the few carriages bringing up the London passengers. It was growing foggy and Laura could picture Gervase's arrival in the dank smoky gloom of Liverpool Street station, his dismal cab ride home to the empty room and cold grate in Bloomsbury. Their breath hung on the still air. Gervase's face was drawn, his eyes desperate.

'I shouldn't have come,' he said. 'It makes it all worse.'

Laura could think of no comfort.

'When we came away—away from that hut, that day with Pasquale . . . and the sun was shining and we went back down that valley—do you remember? We passed the pool where we had swum together. And I could not bear to look at it, because I knew that nothing would ever happen like that to me again, not ever. I knew that if I had looked down from those rocks, I would want to throw myself down—not to swim, but to finish it, so that I could go out with nothing spoilt, while everything was so beautiful. I know you think I am stupid. But I can say this to you, because at least you understand. I know you cannot do anything about how I feel, but I know you understand. And often I wish I had done that and now, tonight, I wish it more than ever.'

'Oh, don't!'

Laura could hear the train coming down the line from Cambridge, muffled, invisible. They were standing underneath a lamp, drawn to its light like moths, and when she looked up at Gervase she saw the lamplight reflected in his eyes like the firelight in the stone hut. He bent down and put his lips on hers. They were both ice-cold, but not with the sparkling mountain water of the Manganello, only with the January winter and the state of their souls. Laura put her arms round his neck.

'Please don't! Don't be so sad!'

'Oh, Laura, it's awful,' he said, not like a Foreign Office clerk but like the twelve-year-old who had gone pale and silent when the day came to return to Rugby.

The train arrived in a turmoil of steam and misty lights, and Laura went to the carriage door with Gervase and saw him in. He leaned out of the window and kissed her again, and transferred all his despair into her dull heart. When the train had pulled out she was alone on a deserted platform, shivering and angry and close to tears.

'It's not my fault!' she thought indignantly.

She went out into the yard to the trap and Lottie's pony patiently waiting, and pulled the rug off his loins and climbed up and wrapped the warm rug over her knees. The cheerfulness of the pony turned for home steadied her a little: it was the weather, she thought, getting Gervase down. It was enough to get anyone down. She turned out of the station approach, pulling up cautiously for the fog, and as she did so a horse and rider came up to her from behind. It was Tiger on one of the Thorn's Hall hacks. She kept the pony halted, aware of a feeling of pleasurable excitement which quite overlaid the emotions Gervase had aroused in her.

Tiger looked as cold as the weather itself.

'Is Gervase courting you now then? Has he proposed yet?'

He pulled up the hack and sat beside her, scowling. It was some time since Laura had seen him at close quarters and she was put out by his greeting. Although he looked so presentable and civilized these days, his manners to her had not changed since he was a little circus brat.

'Is that how you speak to your owners?' she asked coolly. 'I was told that you were quite a gentleman these days.'

'I could scarcely go higher in the world than when I worked for my parents.'

Laura presumed that this was a witticism, although his expression had not changed. He nudged his hack on to keep pace with her as she drove out.

'Why are you entertaining Gervase? Why did you kiss him like that?'

'Because I am sorry for him. Why are you spying on me?'

'I was talking to the station-master, arranging for a mare to be boxed on the train tomorrow. I could not help seeing.'

They trotted down the High Street side by side, the fog encircling them. It was a long time since they had been alone together, and the fog cut them off from the whole of Newmarket.

'He is my cousin.'

'You were kissing him as a cousin?'

'Yes, I was. He is like a brother.'

'You have never thought of me as a brother?'

'No.'

'You must never do that.'

Laura digested this, trying not to read too much into it. The only time Tiger had declared his love for her had been under the tea-table at the Epsom races four years ago, and when he had taken her out the one time down by the stream she remembered that he had asked, 'Could you love me?' She had always supposed that she did love him, but since her days in Corsica she was afraid to think about it.

She did not reply, afraid of being rebuffed, but Tiger kept pace with her, riding alongside. There was nobody about; they passed only one carriage, and left the blurred pools of the street-lamps behind them as they continued out of town. Laura left the pony to make his own way, listening to his hooves crunching in the icy ruts.

'We miss you at Thorn's,' Tiger said. 'Your uncle wants you to come back, but he is afraid of you, because of your mother.'

'How can I come back? There is no place for me.'

'You could marry me when I come of age.'

'Really? Is that a proposal?'

'I'm sounding you out. If you want to marry Gervase, there's an end to it. I'm not going to compete.' He spoke the last word with his usual scorn.

'You have to—to court a girl—' Laura was half excited, half exasperated.

'You made me turn somersaults,' he reminded her. 'I can't keep doing that, just to please you. I wouldn't mind kissing you.'

Laura remembered lying with Gervase under the rough peasant rugs, the explorations they had made and the pleasure they had discovered. The kissing twenty minutes ago on the railway station had brought no memories of it at all. Tiger rode on and leaned down to her driving reins, pulling her pony to a halt. Then he slipped off his horse and opened the door of the trap.

'Get down.'

Laura did as she was told. She stood in the middle of the road and Tiger came up close to her. It was so dark and foggy she could see nothing of his features, but she felt his cold hands take her face and lift it up, almost roughly.

'I do want you, Laura. I love you. I still love you.'

He kissed her, not very tenderly. She felt no response, but only amazement at the turn of events.

He held her away and said, 'Pretend I'm Fred Archer.'

'Tiger—!' The suggestion was painful. She shivered, not entirely with cold, and he kissed her again, more gently this time. 'Are you still in love with him?'

'Yes, I always will be, but it's not real. You know that.'

'Poor Laura.' He did not say it in any mocking way, but with great sorrow. 'But afterwards, you will marry me?'

'Afterwards?'

'When we are old enough, when I am free of my parents.'

She did not think he had meant that, but she could not question him. She knew she never would.

'I probably will.'

'If I have time, I will court you in the proper fashion. If you wish it, that is.'

'Like a gentleman.'

'Yes. No somersaults.'

'Oh, Tiger, I love you when you turn somersaults!' And she kissed him passionately, much to his surprise.

Whether her arrangement with Tiger constituted an engagement Laura had no idea. She certainly told no one of their conversation and presumed that Tiger too said nothing even to Uncle Harry, for Harry did not mention it on any of their occasional meetings. Once the cold weather eased off and the new racing season started Tiger had no time for courting and Laura saw little of him, but she was not worried by the uncertainty of the arrangement. Nothing with Tiger would ever be without its question mark.

On the morning of the Two Thousand Guineas Mr and Mrs Archer gave a breakfast party and Laura was invited along with her employers. Harry was there but Tiger was working. He sought Laura out where she stood alone, taking in the elegant throng that swarmed in and out, the beautiful room decorated for the occasion with great vases of flowers, the trim maids and menservants opening the ever-flowing bottles of champagne. The tables were loaded with food and Nellie Archer was being the perfect hostess, but Laura's eyes were on the slender figure of Fred, back down to racing weight, talking with Captain Machell and the Duchess of Montrose.

Having taken a glass of champagne, Laura said impetuously to her uncle, 'Has Tiger ever spoken of what he saw on the day of Fred's wedding?'

'No, my dear, he hasn't. The only thing he ever said, and it was on the evening of that day, when he was asleep in my study—he said, "Don't ride St Mirin". Whether that was connected with the business I don't know, but it seems unlikely, and so far I've never heard of a horse called St Mirin. And I must say, as time goes on, it is very hard to believe . . . well—look at all this! Most of 'em here have got handles to their names, and old Six-Mile Bottom there—'(Laura knew that this was the nickname of the large, sporting Duchess of Montrose)—'since her husband died, she loves to be in his company, and little Lady Hastings dotes on him—the Hastings have a nice little colt with Mat this year that they want him to ride, and he's a choice of three for the Derby, would you believe! All the best—everything comes his way, you have to admit. It's hard to see what could go wrong.'

'But Tiger's never been wrong.'

'We don't know, Laura. He says nothing about it. He tells me winners now and then, but more and more rarely. He's a grown man and all these gipsy ways are getting to be past habits. And no bad thing, for the responsibility of it is a terrible burden. It's a strange gift and one to be well rid of. Look how he suffered because of it! Put the idea behind you, Laura, and enjoy Fred's success.'

It struck Laura at the breakfast that Nellie looked tired and drawn, and Lottie confirmed this by telling Laura that she was pregnant again.

'They do so dearly want a child! Such good news! I am sure they will be lucky this time.'

And in the afternoon when Laura went to watch the big race she knew that nothing had changed from the afternoon she had put her bet on Charibert; her eyes were just as loyally fixed on dear Fred, now changed out of his sober dark morning suit into the gaudy silks of Captain Machell, and his nature changed with it, attending wholly to the job in hand. It was true, as her uncle had pointed out, that his following, his popularity was immense. Watching the great throng that fawned on him, cheered him, bet on all his mounts, she knew that her own devotion was not unique at all. She was just a pebble on the beach. He was kind to her as he was to all his admirers, never impatient, never proud. She put her money on him, although he had told her to bet on another. His tip won and he was second on St Medard, so to Laura he was right all ways round. He could do no wrong.

11

Lottie poured out the tea for the morning break and said to Bertie, 'Why did Fred have to go to Liverpool when he knew Nellie's time was near? Somebody else could have ridden his horses, couldn't they?'

'But babies come when they think they will, if yours are anything to judge by! And this is the Autumn Cup, not just a selling race. Of course he has his commitments to follow! He's riding the Duchess's horse and it's near enough favourite. He can't let down his owners, baby or no baby.'

'It's as bad as being married to an army man! Nellie will be glad the season is nearly finished and then, if they have the child they want, perhaps he'll have the sense to give up and let his poor body have a rest.'

The doctor had not forecast an easy confinement for Nellie and after the tragedy of the first baby there was some anxiety. Fred's sister, Mrs Coleman, had come to take charge, but Nellie had started her pains after Fred had left to ride at the Liverpool meeting. Living nearby the Rush household could not be unaware of the events taking place at Falmouth House.

Bertie growled, 'A man is well out of the way at such a time. I reckon Fred timed it well.'

'Oh, you men!' Lottie despaired. 'All the pleasure and none of the pain! You think hard before you get married, Laura! It's not all roses, as young girls always think.'

She was half-laughing, holding Agnes on her knee while Laura sat at the table putting a quick darn in the little girl's only clean pair of socks.

'Yes, it's high time Laura got herself a young man,' Bertie said. 'I'll look out for a likely fellow if you like.'

'Laura's in love with Fred,' Lottie said.

'Married ladies and all are in love with Fred, but that's neither here nor there. Laura should have a nice young fellow of her own. Eh, Laura, how about it?'

Laura merely grinned, used to the jibes and teases of the Rush menfolk. She saw Tiger on the Heath sometimes, leading the string, and occasionally he would come and speak to her if she was close enough, pushing Agnes in her perambulator or trailing Herbie and his friends. But such meetings could scarcely be considered as courting. Occasionally she rode out with Bertie's string on one of the hacks that took kindly to a side-saddle, and if they met the Thorn's Hall horses Tiger would come across and speak to her.

She snipped off her cotton and put Agnes' socks on.

'There, how smart you are! Go and find your boots now and I will take you out.'

'And I must drive to Exning and take Aunt Sarah that crochet silk she wanted.' Lottie put the little girl down so that she could fetch her outdoor clothes. Laura found the days slipped past, and had no time to be bored or discontented, for the job she did hardly counted as paid employment. It was like being the eldest sister. When she had news from Tiger or Albert about Miss Bell's reign at Dry Meadows, she realized that she owed Miss Bell a deeper debt of gratitude than she had ever imagined; the thought of being her father's housekeeper was chilling. Her hatred of Hilda Bell had evaporated and when she met her that morning in the High Street she could greet her with something of the old cordiality. Hilda was surprised, but responded gratefully when she had recovered from the shock.

'They say Mrs Archer has gone into labour. Is it true, Laura?'

'Yes, I believe it's so.'

'Let's hope there's no upset this time. Poor Fred, losing a boy! I suppose you see a good deal of him now, down here. I do envy you, Laura, in that. Mr Keen is not at all interested in talking of racing, let alone visiting the races. I expect you know that.'

'Indeed I do! If you remember, he employed you to take my mind off dear Fred.' Laura spoke without acrimony, smiling at the recollection.

Hilda blushed. They were on very delicate ground, and Laura broke off the conversation before they should fall into a mutual embarrassment. But as she pushed Agnes back home she knew she was coming to terms with what had happened, and her resentment towards Hilda Bell had changed into eternal gratitude. She could even think of her father's behaviour without bitterness, for his deceit in Corsica was only a fraction of Cecily's over the years.

By tea-time word came of Nellie's safe delivery of a girl. A telegram had been sent to Fred and he was on his way home. Everyone was relieved and Lottie spoke freely: 'After last time, thank God for that! I was frightened for her, I'll not deny it.'

Bertie teased her. 'She's timed it well! Fred will be set on going out with hounds in the morning. He'd have been cross to have missed it, if he'd had to wait on doctors.'

'You'd think he'd be sick of riding!'

'What do you bet me, that he's out with the drag tomorrow?'

'I don't bet!'

'Well, it's how he always spends his winters. I doubt Nellie will change it.'

The day's anxiety was over. When Laura went to bed she thought of Fred making the long, boring train journey home from racing; she was used to hearing his hack come back from the station late at night and often wondered at the length of his days and the prodigious energy he was able to generate out of his sparrow's diet. In the morning, she thought, if hounds were meeting nearby she would take Agnes and Herbie to watch. It was something they all enjoyed. With luck Lottie might allow her to take a hunter out herself one day. She had mentioned it a couple of times and tomorrow might jog her mind. Laura fell into a dream of hunting with Fred beside her, as once she had ridden in the trial . . . and slept.

In the morning the weather was fair enough; Herbie clamoured with excitement at the prospect of going to the meet.

'You should be going on a pony, not with a nursemaid,' Bertie said. 'I'll have to get you one, the rate you're growing. How about a pony for Christmas, Herbie?'

Laura took the children to the meet, Herbie bouncing with excitement at the thought of his Christmas present. It was cold, sharp, the season in its last week and the Heath tawny with autumn, the great wide skies of Suffolk which Laura had missed so much in Corsica steely and invigorating from horizon to horizon. Laura had a not unfamiliar tug of passion for this uncompromising landscape, scoured by horizontal rain, the prancing young thoroughbreds nipped by frost and fired by gleams of winter sunshine; the idea of a life without this perennial backdrop was strange to her. If her mother had not died, she found it hard to believe that she would have now been exiled in London. It was terrible to be grateful for the events that had delivered her from this fate, but she was forced to acknowledge that what had come about had all been to her advantage. At the meet, greeting the racing devotees of hunting mounted on their ex-steeplechasers ready for the start, she shared Herbie's excitement at the spectacle. Her only undoubted disappointment was the absence of Fred Archer. News of the birth of his daughter was on everyone's lips.

'Who'd have thought it would have kept him at home!' they ribbed. 'See what domesticity does for you!'

Laura stayed until hounds moved off, went back to do a little shopping for Lottie, and headed back home. By the time she got to the gates drops of rain were falling, and the shrubberies were flailing to the scudding clouds.

'Run, Herbie, before we get soaked!'

Agnes laughed in the perambulator as they bounced up the drive and into the haven of the big porch. Laura opened the door and went into the warmth and uncommon quiet of the house. Someone was crying in the kitchen. She stood listening, the exhilaration of the wild hustle home dampened by a cold apprehension. Even amid tears and tantrums, the house had never had quite this feel before; Laura was aware of it, and was prepared for the shock before it came.

Bertie came out into the hall and spoke gruffly. 'There you are then. We've had bad news while you've been away. It's poor little Nellie Archer.'

'What do you mean?'

'She's been taken bad.'

Laura saw Tiger's face and heard his voice crying out, 'No, no, no!' She lifted Agnes out of her pram, cuddling her in her arms.

'What happened? Everything was all right at the birth.'

'Yes. It was very sudden. They say Fred was getting dressed for the meet and his sister suddenly ran in and shouted, "Nellie's dying!" She had a convulsion, it seems, and now she's unconscious. There are three doctors there, and they've sent for Dr Latham too, from Cambridge.'

Laura followed Bertie back into the kitchen, burying her face into the warm, cuddly body in her arms. Agnes wriggled and laughed, glowing and energetic as a young puppy. Lottie was sobbing at the kitchen table, and the cook and the scullery maid were sniffing over the vegetables.

'Oh, Laura! Bertie's told you—poor dear Nellie! And Fred—what will become of Fred if she dies? He loves her so!'

For Laura it was the same as when Harry had announced her mother's death: no warning, the shock of it coming like a cold hand, freezing tears, speech, emotion. She tried to resist it.

'She might come out of it all right! All these doctors—they must be able to save her.'

Lottie looked grim. 'It's how it happens, Laura. I've seen it before. It's a tragic thing. And this time a fine, bonny baby and the telegram boy backwards and forwards all day with congratulations . . . poor little girl! She's only twenty-three.'

While they waited for news, Laura wondered whether this was the tragedy Tiger had seen, that it wasn't something happening to Fred himself but to Nellie. The thought brought her a sense of relief, and this in turn caused her as much pain as the original news.

'Less than two years since they were married; it doesn't seem possible,' Lottie said. 'And all that good fortune, everything a couple could possibly wish for—' She turned automatically to help Laura take off the children's outdoor clothes. 'Money and fame are nothing, by comparison. How we are cut down to size, when something like this happens.'

They waited all day for news. Dr Latham drove past and stayed. Four doctors were in the house, and members of the family and friends went backwards and forwards all day.

The following morning Charlie went up early and learned from the head-groom that Nellie had died in the night.

Laura asked permission to go up to Thorn's Hall, and Lottie allowed her to borrow the trap. She drove past Falmouth House with its blank, curtained windows and the visitors' carriages waiting, turning her face resolutely to the road ahead, clicking to the pony.

When she drove into the yard at Thorn's and pulled the pony to a halt Arthur came out to see who it was.

'Why, Miss Laura! You're a stranger here these days!'

He came up and opened the trap door for her.

'Good afternoon, Arthur. Is my uncle in, and Tiger?'

'Yes, miss. They're inside.'

She went in as she had always done without ceremony, and found her uncle and Tiger sitting at the kitchen table over mugs of tea and bread and cheese. They both looked up in astonishment.

'Laura!' Harry's surprise turned into undoubted pleasure. Tiger got to his feet, half startled, and Laura watched his expression like a hawk as she spoke.

'I had to come up and tell you that Nellie Archer died last night.'

Tiger's face blanked out. Watching for it, Laura saw the animation go like a light turning out, the eyes veil over in a curious, catlike way. She had seen it before without actually studying the phenomenon, but now her eyes did not leave his.

'But she was delivered safely—we got the message yesterday,' Harry said uncertainly.

'Yes, the baby is well. But Nellie had a convulsion yesterday and never recovered consciousness.'

'Poor soul! And Fred—Fred will be heartbroken!'

'Is that what you saw, the day of the wedding?' Laura asked Tiger.

Tiger did not reply. His face was like a mask. It was as if he did not exist behind it; he looked at her, but seemed not to be present. Laura felt frozen by the expression, the answer meaning so much.

'It *is* what you saw! Tell me it is!' She could not help the urgency breaking into what she had meant to be a calm plea. It was like throwing a pebble at a stone wall.

Uncle Harry said, 'Laura, don't! Tiger mustn't speak of these things—it will do nobody any good.'

'Why not? If there is no more catastrophe to come, he can say so, surely? And then we need never think of it again. Please, Tiger, say it's not Fred too!'

It was as if all the grief she should have felt for Nellie was engulfing her. 'Please tell me! Say it isn't Fred!'

'Laura!' Harry took her by the shoulders and sat her roughly down in his chair. 'It's not fair. It's not wise either. Leave him alone.'

'Who is St Mirin?' She wept.

At this Tiger's mask quivered.

'Who said St Mirin?'

'You said! You said, "Don't ride St Mirin." '

'I never!' Tiger cried out vehemently. 'I never said that! You make up these things!'

'Be quiet, both of you, for heaven's sake,' Harry groaned.

'She's always asking questions! All her life—getting me to tell her things she knows she doesn't want to know! I will tell you nothing. I saw *nothing*—I know nothing—I don't *want* to know!'

This last was uttered with such despair that Laura was shocked into silence. She realized immediately that her ignorance was blessed compared with Tiger's knowledge, had always been so. She was horrified by the obvious pain she had stirred in him for, from happily eating bread and cheese in front of the fire, he was now standing, white as a sheet, in a state of far greater distress than she had experienced from the beginning. The mask was shattered and his eyes were full of tears.

'Oh, Tiger, don't! I'm sorry, I'm sorry!' Laura flung her arms round him in a passion of self-reproach, childlike in her transparent emotion. It had all happened before, their hurting of each other through this awful talent of Tiger's; her relationship with Tiger was a bed of nails. She hugged him, but he turned away and sat down at the table again, his head in his hands.

'Go away,' he said. 'It's much better here without you.'

'Oh, hush,' said Harry. 'What a stir-up in two minutes! You don't mean that—not that you don't deserve it from him, Laura. You should have learned by now—some things are better not mentioned, not even thought of. Say no more, for God's sake. Just pour out another cup of tea.'

Anxious to make amends, Laura did as she was told, and put some more coal on the range. The kitchen looked shabby from how she remembered it, the rag rug in holes, chair cushions faded to drab, plates chipped. Was she engaged to Tiger, she wondered? She felt confused and wretched, seeing the misery she had reduced him to.

Arthur called Harry out to speak to a visitor and Laura sat at the table alone with Tiger. She watched him gradually returning to himself, blow his nose, scowling, rub his hands wearily over his face. She put her hand out and caught his and pulled it to her cheek impulsively.

'Truly, I'm sorry. I didn't mean to hurt you.'

'How much do you love Fred?'

She shrugged. 'It's a dream. You know it is. I love him, but it's not real.'

'You are not the only one. But when it's over you will love me. There will be no one else.'

Laura wanted to ask him if he knew, if he had seen it, what he meant by 'when it's over', whether he was asking or whether he knew, but she dared not question him again. She looked into the fox-gold eyes, no longer shuttered, but bright with an emotion she hoped was love, but could not enquire. She knew nothing, not even if she loved him, not if he loved her. He got up from his chair and came to her and pulled her to her feet. He put his arms round her and bent her head back and put his lips down to hers.

'Pretend I'm Fred,' he said. 'And kiss me. Kiss me as if you love me.'

She kissed him, remembering Gervase, thinking of Fred, whispering Tiger's name. This was not how he had kissed her before, tentative and experimental; this was a wild, sensual kissing that her body responded to as if she was back in the firelit hut, and gave her shock enough to break away. It was the thought of Fred that stopped her—to think that she had come to tell Tiger of Nellie's death, and was now experiencing such joy in the face of Fred's sorrow: it was as wicked as all her other confused motives and unbidden feelings. Her confusion was endless. Where truth and dreams began and ended she could not tell. But she loved to feel Tiger's arms round her and his bony jaw against her cheek, his lips seeking hers again.

'No, please—!'

'*Yes*, please,' he muttered. 'You are always wrong. I love you, Laura.'

'Oh, Tiger, yes, I love you too.'

She put up her hands to stroke his hair, his eyes, his cheeks, but the outside door slammed behind them and they had to part abruptly. It was impossible to appear composed, to hide the sudden passions that Tiger had aroused in that moment, and Laura had to turn away and gather up the dishes, so that Harry would not see her face.

'After all this to-do,' Harry said to her, 'did you know it was Tiger's birthday today? He's nineteen—or so he tells me. I've no choice but to believe him. Two years today and he will come into his independence. I thought perhaps it was the reason for your visit.'

'I didn't know! He never told me. Not his name, not his family, his birthday, not anything.'

'Well then, you know now. And his name is Tiger Keen. You christened him yourself, half from you, half from me. Give him a kiss now, for my sake, and wish him a happy birthday.'

Laura laughed then. She turned to Tiger challengingly, thinking he would not accept Harry's invitation, but he came to her un-smiling, and kissed her again on the lips, as if Harry was not there at all. Laura felt his body quivering for a moment against hers, then he thrust her away.

'Happy birthday, Tiger,' she said, with all the presence of mind she could command. His eyes were positively glittering now; he did not look gracious at all but had the expression that had prompted her to choose his name at their first meeting. Harry looked surprised, but was uncertain of making a comment on the liaison he sensed.

'It's lovely to see you again, Laura. Will you make it a habit?'

'Yes, I will come more often. It's better now.'

'That's splendid. I will write a letter to poor Fred. God knows, I feel for him.'

Laura drove home, exhausted by her conflicting emotions. There was still a good deal of coming and going at Falmouth House and in the evening rumour came that Fred was almost out of his mind with grief. In the days following he never left the house, and was reported not to sleep nor eat nor speak to anyone. The tragedy threw its shadow over the whole community and the extremity of Fred's reaction doubled the concern. People said he had tried to commit suicide. Laura lived on a knife-edge of antici-pation that now the ultimate tragedy was about to happen, but the days passed uneventfully and when Lottie spoke to Fred's sister, Mrs Coleman, she discovered that plans were being made to take Fred abroad to try and break him out of his black depression.

'They think it's the only course to take. He can't go about anywhere here without people sympathizing and staring, and he's in such a state, she says, they're at their wits' end to distract him. She says he's going to America with Captain Bowling, and they're going down to Cheltenham first to make arrangements with his family and his solicitors. And meanwhile there are so many letters to answer—she showed me—from just about all the Lordships in the land and one from the Prince of Wales as well, and shoals from people who can scarcely write or afford the stamp by the look of it. It's quite amazing.'

Laura knew she could not intrude on such a situation, and saw Fred only once on the day of the funeral, a glimpse of him in the carriage that followed the hearse, accompanied by his brothers-in-law, dressed in unrelieved black and looking more frail and drawn than ever he had brought upon himself by wasting. From the funeral, where he was reported by the newspapers to be 'visibly affected by grief', he went straight to the station to travel back to Cheltenham with his own family. His following, accustomed to his habitual nerve on the race-course and stoic reserve in the face of adversity, were awed by this total surrender by their hero.

Lottie was more understanding.

'Can you wonder at it, coming at the end of the season when the man is worn to a shadow?' she complained. 'They all think he is a machine—riding over two hundred winners a year for the last four years and champion jockey every year since he was seventeen. But he's only flesh and blood! And he's never worn his heart on his sleeve, we all know that. He never loved any girl but Nellie, never even looked at another. I can remember when he used to walk her home from parties when he was just a boy—the Dawsons used to order him, because he was always trustworthy, when he was just one of the apprentices.'

'Those were the days when he used to cry when he didn't win,' Bertie said. 'I can remember that too. And I remember him winning the Cesarewitch on Salvanos when he was only fifteen, riding at five stone and a bit, and that colt was a bolter, a difficult ride, but old Mat knew he was capable, even then.'

'Well, there's no one who doesn't wish him his happiness again. Let's hope the trip will get him back to a proper frame of mind, for all his loss.'

Fred duly departed, and word came of the press conference he was forced to give on board the ship when it docked, before he could even get foot ashore, and of his being entertained in New York by Governor Vanderbilt. He travelled all over the States and did not come home until the following spring.

That winter, having broken the ice with her visit to Thorn's Hall, Laura started to go back there regularly on her days off. Sometimes she called at Dry Meadows too, mainly to see Albert. Hilda would invite her to dinner and once or twice Laura accepted, but the cold atmosphere of her own home after the lovely jumble of the Rush household depressed her, serving only to increase her feeling of debt to Hilda. Thorn's Hall was much better, as it had always been. Laura took to renewing the cushion covers and rugs, choosing new curtains, and getting Harry to employ a young woman to help Martha keep the place clean.

'A woman's touch is what we could do with,' Harry said. 'Your improvements make a difference.'

Tiger, sitting before the fire cleaning his boots, said, 'Would you like me to marry her?'

'Yes,' Harry said.

'Will you marry me, Laura?'

'Yes, I wouldn't mind.'

'That's fixed then.' He went on cleaning his boots.

Harry looked at Laura dubiously. 'That's very romantic, I must say. Is this a surprise to you?'

'No. He has suggested it in his manner at times, but not exactly asked. We can't yet, after all. Not for two years.'

'The idea pleases you?'

Laura laughed. 'Yes.'

Harry leaned back in his chair and Laura saw that he was moved by this strange exchange more than he wanted to show. He said nothing, but looked as if he would easily burst into tears. He had never mentioned to Laura his love for her mother, but Laura knew the thoughts that were going through his mind. She moved across the room and kissed him gently.

'We will never go away from you. I will look after you as well as Tiger.'

'I could do with it, and that's a fact. I don't have the enthusiasm I used to have, not since your mother went. Nothing has been quite the same since then. I wonder what she would have said to this?'

'She would have wanted me to marry whoever I loved.'

'I don't know that your father will like the idea.'

'What's wrong with me?' Tiger asked.

'You're a gipsy,' Laura said.

'My family aren't gipsies. Rogues maybe, but not gipsies. I'm good enough for you.'

'Ask my father then, and we can be properly engaged.'

'I'll put a word in,' Harry said. 'I doubt if he'll object, although he might not be pleased. He's no room to complain: he'll be marrying himself before you're ready.'

Tiger went to Philip and Philip found it hard to remember him as a homeless waif, confronted by this slender, confident, handsomely-dressed youth who was successful in his job, had very fair prospects ahead of him and answered to a sum of money in the bank that was larger than Philip's own. There was in effect nothing he could object to.

'Your family . . .' And he hesitated, for there was no hint of ill-breeding in the figure before him . . . what could one say? Believing him to be a gipsy, Philip was aware only of a self-possession verging on arrogance and features undeniably intelligent and attractive.

'I look upon Mr Keen as my father, sir, and he wishes me to be his heir. I have you to thank for my good fortune and shall always be grateful to you for taking me in.'

Tiger had rehearsed these lines with Harry the evening before but they were the truth and he had no compunction in using them. Philip had shown him compassion, although Tiger had never doubted that he would have got by without his intervention.

'What is your family name?' Philip persisted.

'I have taken Mr Keen's name, sir, and have no reason to recall my own.'

'Well, we shall have to go into all that later, but for the time being I can see no objection, if you continue as diligently as you appear to be doing now. I would have wished Laura to marry into a different profession, I don't deny, but that is a personal opinion and does not really affect the issue. You have my permission to become engaged.'

'Thank you very much, sir.'

Tiger reported back as to what a model contender he had shown himself to be. 'It was like talking to an owner.'

'He is an owner,' Harry said. 'He's the owner of Laura. Yes, it's been very good practice for you. Owners must always be shown respect; owners are always right. It has done you no harm to learn these lessons. You have done well and if this marriage comes about no one will be happier than me.'

'If? Why if?'

'I sometimes think life is as uncertain as racing. I am less optimistic as I grow older, when I see what happens. Look at poor Fred, for instance.'

Wrapped up in his own thoughts of Cecily, Harry regretted his carelessness instantly. He started up to make amends, but Tiger forestalled him.

'It's the truth!' His face was contorted with the dread which Harry had come to recognize. 'But not for me and Laura! When it's all over with Fred, then Laura and I shall be married, and nothing will ever come between us!'

And Harry could only be thankful that Laura was not there to hear him, for it was the only acknowledgement Tiger ever made of what he knew and Harry never ceased to regret his own carelessness in prompting it.

'This fiancé of Laura's is very elusive,' Charlie said. 'Ask him to dinner, Ma, so we can all have a look at him. We'll see if he's good enough for her.'

'Don't be so cheeky, Charlie! Would you like to invite him to dinner, Laura, with your uncle? They would be very welcome. I've been thinking myself it's high time we sent an invitation.'

'Yes, I'm sure they would be pleased to come.'

'We can hear all about this move Harry is making,' Bertie said. 'It's not everyone who has a brand new house to go to when they're married.'

'I think the stables come first,' Laura said. 'That's all they talk about—very little about the house.'

Harry's string having flourished during the last year or two, he had decided to buy a yard in the Bury road on the outskirts of the town, a much bigger and more convenient place. Laura regretted that she was not to live at Thorn's, which she loved as a home, but realized how much more spacious and convenient the new place would be. Tiger and Harry were improving the yard and, as there was only a small cottage to go with it, the adjoining plot had been earmarked for a new house. When it was finished, and Tiger was of age, they would get married. So far only the foundations were laid.

'It won't be Falmouth House,' Harry said, 'but it will do you proud, I promise. It's my dearest wish, to see you two married.'

'Poor old fellow, you're not considering retiring?' Laura was surprised how much Harry left to Tiger now in all respects. At one time Tiger, riding work every day and knowing the horses so well, had been tried out as stable jockey. He was still small and slight at twenty, but—at a few pounds under nine stone—he could not easily do the weights required. When Harry insisted and he got down to eight and a half, he rode in a few races but then pleaded to be excused the job.

'I will do whatever you wish save starve,' he said. 'I can stand anything but that.'

Since then he had taken more and more of the stable decisions and was now an accepted member of the exclusive Newmarket racing fraternity, attending race-meetings in the formal attire of the trainer with lads to order and jockeys to instruct. When he came to dinner at the Rushes' with Harry, Laura, greeting him in the hall with a chaste kiss, had a sudden, crazy vision of him in his silver spangled suit turning somersaults in the dome of the circus tent, and she laughed out loud, so that everybody looked at her.

'Oh, you are so respectable! Like somebody else.'

He looked put out and said, 'What would you have then? My mucking out breeches?'

'You look like Gervase,' she said.

He glowered furiously and Harry said, 'You're making mischief, Laura. I remember when you rode astride, wore pigtails, and accosted Mr Dawson himself to ride out with his string. You're just as respectable as Tiger yourself these days, but I would say it's an improvement, meriting congratulation.'

'It's called growing up,' Lottie said. 'I'm hoping Charlie will take to it soon.'

Laura, looking into Tiger's angry eyes, had an upsurge of longing to be back in the loosebox with him kissing her; she wanted to be strolling down the grassy fields with him with the smell of meadowsweet on the evening air and her arms round his thin, sharp body. Since they had become engaged he had taken infinite pains not to be alone with her. He kissed her as if she were his aunt. He worked so hard he was hardly ever able to take her out or, when he did, it was to the races, in a big crowd. She knew he wanted it that way until they could be married, although he had not said so; he had given her a diamond ring and put shutters up, retired into a shell she could not pierce. It was a time of waiting. She was not sure whether they were waiting until they could be married, or for something else, and her mind shied away from considering the possibilities, preferring the state of limbo in the relationship which gave no pain, at least. There were some things she could not bear to think about.

They went in to dinner and the talk was all of racing. Laura was very much aware that her state of limbo, as she considered it, was not at all to be despised, for she felt more at home in her adoptive family than ever she had at Dry Meadows, and with the addition of Tiger and Harry her circle was complete. She was happy, sitting beside Tiger, listening to Charlie's tall stories and the laughter that greeted them. It was a warm summer evening and the long french windows were open on to the lawn, the heady smell of syringa drifting in and the moths blundering into the light. Tiger did not speak much, save when asked for an opinion, and when the conversation came round to Archer's victories Laura saw the strange withdrawal cloud his expression, a stillness fall over him, an invisible barrier to the company. Sometimes she thought this reaction of his was a figment of her imagination; she was acutely conscious of it, but believed it might be conjured up by her own instinctive dread of what he knew. It was part of his shuttered-up attitude to her. 'I make it all up,' she told herself. 'Nobody else is worried by it. They have not noticed.' But there was no way of knowing. Nobody else had any inhibitions about discussing the eternally fascinating subject of Fred's amazing dominance when it came to the riding of winners. In the summer after Nellie's death he had ridden the winners of four out of the five classic races and a total of two hundred and forty-six winners during the season, and in this, the season following, he had won the Derby again on the apparently invincible Ormonde and his percentage of winners was equal to the previous astonishing year. When the men talked of these victories with such enthusiasm, Lottie pursed her lips and said sharply, 'And what is he doing to himself to get these results? If Nellie were still alive, she would not let him treat himself so cruelly.'

'That's not true!' Bertie argued. 'He's been doing it for ten years or more now and his weight problem is nothing new. She never tried to stop him—she had more sense than to think she could succeed.'

'He's just a bundle of nerves these days. They all say at Falmouth House how difficult he is to live with, flying off the handle all the time. Poor Dickie left him—said he couldn't stand it any more, after eight years. Starving the whole time . . . it's to be expected, but it doesn't help if you have to live with it.'

'He drives himself all the harder since Nellie's death because it's all he's got to take his mind off it. And his constitution is accustomed to it—in fact, Dr Wright's told him that if he ate normally he would probably get dropsy.'

'Rather that than go the way poor Tom French went, and he was only Fred's age.'

'Tom French died of consumption.'

'Brought on by wasting,' Lottie said. 'Do you wonder at it? I've seen them out there in October and November—Fred as often as any—in nothing but a silk shirt and cotton breeches and the east wind like a knife and the sleet coming sideways so's you can hardly stand against it!'

'It's true that Fred is riding overweight a good deal this season,' Harry said. 'He has a job to do eight and a half now.'

'Tiger didn't stick it for long—and he had the makings of a good jockey. Didn't fancy starvation, eh, Tiger?'

Tiger shook his head faintly, eyes down. Laura knew his condition wasn't her imagination by the way Bertie looked at him, taking in the white, absent expression that Arthur called 'one of his gipsy turns'.

'Come on, Lottie, give him a second helping. I reckon he's still suffering from Harry's treatment.'

'He's all right,' Laura said softly. 'He doesn't want any more.'

She put out an instinctive hand to his hand lying on the table, to give him her protection, not unaware that he had a reputation around the stables for his strange temperament, but Lottie smoothed the occasion by suggesting a game of croquet after dinner: the evening was too fine to sit indoors.

In the ensuing discussion on the best way to beat one's opponents, Tiger gradually recovered from his 'absence' and by the time they went outside he was back to normal.

'Croquet!' he muttered at Laura as they went to the summerhouse to collect the sticks. 'Even Gervase never played croquet!'

Laura laughed. 'Turn somersaults instead. They'll be no end impressed!'

'Somersaults! Is that all you want from me?'

And, hidden from the others by the rhododendron shrubbery that made an arbour round the summerhouse, she turned fiercely to him and said, 'No! No! It's not all I want!' As if her abrupt change of mood simultaneously charged Tiger with a similar electricity, they kissed wildly. There was nothing experimental or prudish about the contact between them; no fantasies came between, no delicacy of convention, only an overpowering surge of mutual passion which was ended abruptly by Charlie's arrival round the hedge and his surprised apology.

'Oh lord, dreadfully sorry! I should have guessed—'

Laura broke away, shaken, hard put to it to come back to her senses.

'Honestly, carry on, I'll get the old stuff, no trouble,' Charlie said obligingly, blundering into the untidy summerhouse and loudly throwing chairs and tennis racquets aside, but the moment was broken and neither Tiger nor Laura cared to resume, dazed by the strength of passion that had so briefly and unexpectedly overtaken them.

Later, some time during the game when they were briefly standing close together, Tiger said to Laura, 'Is that how you really feel for me, or were you—'

'I wasn't pretending, if that's what you think! Yes, I feel like that! It's you who keep your distance—like an uncle—Uncle Harry and Uncle Tiger—'

She hit the ball such a crack that it disappeared under the yew-hedge and into the kitchen garden.

'It's not *cricket*,' Lottie complained.

'You mustn't kiss me like that again. It's not cricket,' Tiger whispered, and laughed.

And Laura found that the evening was ending in a daze of yellow bursting stars, like old times. She realized she did not look ahead to her marriage with Tiger, nor acknowledge her love for him, because she was frightened of what came between, frightened for him as well as for herself. It was as if this unspoken, dreadful thing must be exorcised before they could enjoy their love. And then she told herself the feeling was ridiculous, like a superstition, and all brought about by too much unhealthy dreaming, a wild imagination, her unstable adolescent experiences, a legacy of her mother's predilection for loving through pain and sorrow and despair. But however she tried to convince herself otherwise, she could not rid herself of the certainty that her instinct was true.

Several days after the dinner party Archer rode a horse called St

(217)

Mirin, belonging to the Duchess of Montrose, in a race at Ascot. The horse won uneventfully. In September and October he rode him again at Newmarket, winning each time. Laura, having lived in dread of the Ascot race, realized afterwards that she had no idea of what her fears had been—only that the superstition that she had woven around Tiger's hallucinations had the power of the devil to frighten her. Tiger himself had given her no warnings, no reasons to fear.

Shortly afterwards Fred travelled to Ireland to ride Cambusmore at the Curragh. The newspapers reported the enthusiastic reception that awaited him, and how the royal box had been reserved for him and his party at the theatre with the compliments of the manager and of the cheering crowd that waited for him afterwards and escorted him back to his hotel. Of more interest to Bertie and Charlie was the news that he had accepted a ride on a fancied horse carrying a weight of eight stone seven.

'Cambusmore is in at nine, and he was talking of having to get weight off to ride *him*.'

'Yes, but he's accepted the ride on St Mirin in the Cambridgeshire and St Mirin's only got eight six, so he must think he can do it. The Duchess reckons she's in luck from the handicapper—as well she might! The horse stands a good chance at that weight.'

'But Fred will never get down to eight six!'

'Well, it's a fact that he's accepted. The Cambridgeshire is about the only race he's never won—you know what it means to him. And the Duchess is crazy for him to ride for her, she dotes on him so.'

'If she loves him as they say, she has a strange way of showing it,' Lottie said. 'I haven't noticed *she* has ever experienced the pains of dieting, from the look of her. To encourage Fred in this is wicked. I've a good mind to go and tell him what I think when he comes home.'

'He doesn't care for anything save winning. The horse stands a good chance so why do you think he will take any notice of you?'

'He has his little girl to think of,' Lottie said. 'He dotes on her well enough! For her sake he should not take such liberties with his health. The weather is cold as charity—he'll sit boiling himself up in that wretched bath of his all morning and then go out there virtually naked, and expect to come to no harm! I wonder what his sister will have to say about it?'

But no one argued much with Fred these days, Laura knew, even those who looked after him.

This conversation, and the confirmation that Fred was to ride St Mirin in the Cambridgeshire at eight stone six, was her first real intimation of the danger he faced. She could not speak of it to Tiger, nor to Harry, although the whole of Newmarket was saying Fred would never get down to such a weight. He had ridden the horse Isadore at the Curragh but had been unable to get lower than eight twelve. When he came home everyone remarked how bad he looked.

'Even at that, and another six pounds to lose!' Lottie said. 'Of what, I should like to know? He's down to skin and bone as it is.'

The weather was bitter, the sky overlaid with heavy grey clouds. The horses galloped like demons over the Heath, chivvied by the sour wind. The town was preparing for its last invasion of the season: the Cambridgeshire attracted a vast influx of visitors content to brave the elements up on the Heath for the pleasure of the last big gamble of the year. St Mirin was not much fancied, word having gone round that in a private trial with his stable companion Carlton he had been easily beaten. But Fred had not been riding him.

'Fred can get far more out of him than the boy who rode him in the trial,' Bertie said, and told Laura to stick with Fred for her bet.

'I always do,' Laura whispered, appalled by what was happening.

Fred rode a winner for the Duchess on Monday the day before the Cambridgeshire. They said he looked like death. He had not eaten a morsel since the Friday night. That evening, driven by a compulsion quite outside her control, Laura walked up to Falmouth House. It was dark and bitterly cold and raining. Laura held her face up to the wind and saw faint stars coming and going. She went into the gates and up the wide, winding drive. Dogs barked in the house and from the stableyard, and she knew she could not turn back, but did not know what she was doing. She knocked at the door, and when a manservant answered she stood, mute, like an imbecile. She had nothing to say. The man flinched at the cold wind and asked her inside, so that he could close the door. Laura stepped inside and the warmth, the aura of rich comfort, embraced her. The house was beautiful. Fred lacked for nothing save his wife.

Fred was not alone—why had she thought he would be, when so many people longed, like her, to be in his company? He did with little sleep, and did not read books of an evening, nor doze in his armchair. Several racing men were there—she knew most of them—and his sister Mrs Coleman, who came to greet her.

'What do you want, my dear? Is anything wrong?'

Laura shook her head, looking at Fred. It was true what they said about him, that he looked like death. He was going to ride at eight stone six the next day, but he was smiling with Captain Machell. His friends were drinking port, but Fred had a glass of his mixture in front of him. People who had tried a spoonful had been laid out for a week, but Fred took it every day by the glassful when he was wasting. It was renowned throughout Newmarket, the famous Archer's mixture, concocted for him by Dr Wright.

Mrs Coleman gave Laura a very curious look, and no wonder, Laura thought, for the instinct that drove her was incomprehensible even to herself, let alone Mrs Coleman. But in the company, seeing her so strange, the woman did not press her. Perhaps she was used to women forcing their attentions on Fred —there was precedent enough, Laura was well aware—but when the racing men left she gathered up the glasses and took them out to the kitchen, leaving Laura alone. Fred came back into the room and said to her, 'Well, Laura, will you be on the Heath tomorrow?'

'Yes,' she whispered.

'Are you all right?'

'Yes.'

'Did you come with a message?'

'No.'

She looked up at him standing in front of the fire, at the characteristic stoop of his shoulders and the whip-thin torso in the evening suit, the half-amused, half-enquiring smile and the tired, sad, grey eyes. There was nothing she could say at all. She stared at him and he shook his head and turned away. He picked up the glass which Mrs Coleman had left and drained it. The manservant came in and said, 'Will that be all, sir?'

'Yes, I'm going up now.'

He turned back to Laura and said, 'Shall my man see you home, Miss Keen? It's late.'

She stood up abruptly. 'Oh, no! I'm quite all right—I'm sorry to keep you! I didn't mean to disturb you. I'm so sorry.'

Confused, she went with him out into the hall. She was glad she had come now, his kindness in not turning her impulsive intrusion into a dreadful embarrassment giving her back her wits and courage. He saw her out himself. There was nothing she could say beyond goodbye and good luck, but she knew there was no good luck for him any more, and that he knew it himself.

She walked home very slowly, not feeling the cold nor seeing the dark skeletons of the trees and the stars between the branches. In the morning the clouds were as dark and low as the night before, the wind freezing.

*　　*　　*

She went to Harry's new yard; he had a horse saddled for her and they rode to the course together, through the town and the crowds and out on to the brow of the Heath where the road to Cambridge curved away beside the wall of the new, bare cemetery. Laura huddled down against the cold, eyes watering. Harry said little, heavy in spirits. Tiger had stayed behind. Harry had some excuse for him, but Laura had known he would not come.

The Prince of Wales had a filly in the second race. It was the first time Laura had seen Fred in the royal purple, scarlet and gold, and the resplendency of the colours served to accentuate his pallor and air of frailty as he came into the Birdcage. The Prince kept him talking for several minutes, then the trainer gave him a leg-up and he rode out and away at a canter over the bitter grass towards the start, until he was a speck of colour far in the distance, the other runners trailing behind.

The Prince's filly duly won by half a length amid roars of patriotic delight—'Cleverly! Cleverly!' Harry said with satisfaction, although his money had been on Clear the Way.

'We'll view the runners for the big race and then ride up to the Red Post to see the finish. It's the best place.'

When the numbers went up on the board, St Mirin was announced to be carrying one pound overweight.

'There, well, in spite of all he can do, eight seven is his limit these days, and that's a miracle, the height of him, and a dreadful sacrifice from him to get there. The Duchess should never have encouraged him.'

They watched from their hacks over the heads of the crowd as the nineteen runners came out into the paddock. St Mirin was a big bay colt, moderately fancied, but his stable companion Carlton was said to have the legs of him and had been made favourite. Laura watched them led round, warmly blanketed, their lads blue-nosed and pinched.

'There's Melton, who Fred won the Derby on last year.' Harry pointed to a beautiful little bay. 'Carrying nine stone odd. Fred should have stuck with him.'

'Melton doesn't win these days.'

'More's the pity.'

'It's too late now.'

Laura had a sense of irrevocability; she was a spectator of events she could not influence. She watched Fred come out wearing the Duchess's scarlet silks with nothing else underneath as Lottie had forecast, and stand looking at St Mirin as he was brought up to him. She could not take her eyes off him; she was shivering. Fred did up the girth and the boy pulled the rug off over the horse's quarters. St Mirin swung about, the cold wind in his nostrils, the crowd barging and shouting round him, but the lad held him and Fred was up and in the saddle so lightly the horse scarcely knew it. As the runners filed out of the paddock and made out towards the distant horizon over the dark winter grass, Laura set off with Harry away from the stands in the opposite direction. The finish was almost back into town, heading for the cemetery. The wind came at them and their horses shied, nervous of the wide open spaces and the bitter elements. 'Stary' was the word used to describe the bleak unsheltered grasslands, and some horses were too sensitive to thrive in Newmarket and had to go to kinder, softer hills and friendlier downs to find their true form. Laura, riding quietly, knew that today she was that sort of a creature, and would happily have ridden away from her stary haunts, that made her afraid.

They waited by the Red Post with a small crowd of trainers and owners on their hacks, anxious and shivering. The great shouting from the stands soon reached them, to be followed quickly by the pulsating crescendo of approaching hooves. The bright blobs of colour and the wide phalanx of flying horses crystallized abruptly into individual heads and faces; Laura saw St Mirin come away clear in front, Fred sitting right forward in his characteristic finish, reins loose and heels going, and then, while the wild relief was bursting from her lips to echo the general cheering, she saw another horse make a spectacular run up to the leader and battle on doggedly to reach St Mirin's girth . . . shoulder . . . neck and neck—an outsider.

'Who is it?'

They pulled their horses round and joined in the mad canter down to the post on the tail of the stragglers.

'It was Sailor Prince,' Harry shouted to Laura, 'but God knows if he made it.'

Nobody knew. They met the horses coming back, played out, heads down, and Fred went past, white-faced, spattered with mud and horses' sweat and acknowledging no one. Harry pulled up sadly, watching them go.

'If Fred was beat,' he said to Laura, 'it was by as little as that extra pound weight he was carrying.'

When the numbers went up, Sailor Prince was the winner by a head, a forty to one outsider. Carlton, the favourite, was third.

'I want to go home,' Laura said.

It was starting to rain and they turned back over the churned grass, silent, feeling their horses' eagerness to go. No accident had occurred; Laura knew that Fred would not ride St Mirin again; the season had only another week or two to go and she had nothing to worry about any more, but her spirits were like lead.

*　　*　　*

Fred rode races for the rest of the meeting and rode work in the morning as usual and the following week went to ride at Brighton and Lewes. The weather was abysmal. Everyone said he looked terrible and rumours came from Falmouth House of his deep depression. The second anniversary of Nellie's death was very close; he had had an exhausting season and the shedding of ten pounds to ride St Mirin were said to be the cause of his condition. He came home early from Lewes, feeling ill, the first time he had missed a race through ill-health since his arm had been so badly injured six years ago. Two days later he was reported to be suffering from typhoid fever, and a bulletin was issued to the public stating that his high fever gave cause for alarm.

Laura, seeing Dr Latham's gig go past—the Cambridge doctor, called to give a second opinion—and Fred's brother Charley on his hack, the Dawson carriage from Warren house and the institution nurses in uniform from Cambridge all making for Falmouth House, went to look for Tiger.

'He is going to die,' she said to him.

'So are we all,' Tiger said coldly. He looked as bad as Fred when he rode St Mirin.

'Tell me the truth! It is so close now—I know it is!'

'Why will it help you to know? He is not going to die of typhoid, no. Go away, Laura. You bring all this pain on yourself because you are so nosy. You never change.'

His words soothed her. She believed him implicitly. She went back, relaxed and happy, and on Sunday afternoon walked up to Falmouth House to enquire after the invalid's health. Not bold enough this time to walk up to the front door, she asked the head groom in the stables, and was told that Mr Archer was holding his own nicely. On Monday morning the under-gardener said he was much better. Sunday, the seventh of November, had been the anniversary of Nellie's death, and Laura was greatly relieved to have this day safely passed.

Lottie made no bones about it. 'Thank God! It seemed like fate, his getting so bad right to the day. It will be all for the best in the end, I daresay, as he will realize how foolish he has been to weaken himself the way he did. Next year he will have more sense.'

'Only if he retires,' Charlie said. 'And can you see him living without it? He's been a martyr to the cause since he was seventeen—he was wasting even then, Ma—you forget!'

'All jockeys retire! Why should he be any different?'

'Not at twenty-nine. And he *is* different. You know he is.' Charlie spoke scornfully. 'No one will ever ride two hundred and forty-six winners in a season, like he did last year. Not again.'

Laura agreed with Charlie, but now the crisis was over she felt ashamed of her stupid obsession with Fred's fate over the last couple of weeks. She started to think about planning a date for her wedding as Harry had been suggesting: in the spring but before the Two Thousand Guineas. The house would be ready; her father had agreed. A few months later, a seemly three years after Cecily's death, he was going to marry Miss Bell. He had not told her himself but Albert had told her. 'He'll get around to telling you, I daresay, so look surprised at the news, else I shall get into trouble.' Laura was going to ask Albert if he would like to come and work for her when she was married if Tiger agreed; he was too good for her father. Lottie had organized her into making a start on her trousseau, and had said she would arrange the reception. There was still a good deal to think about and she had been remiss in neglecting to make plans. She went to find an almanac in Bertie's study, and pored over next year's dates, sitting at the desk in the front bay window. Charlie was looking through the files, checking on an entry for the Liverpool Cup.

'What date is the Two Thousand Guineas?'

'End of April—a Wednesday. You want a Saturday for a wedding. I can't see you, Laura . . . a married lady.'

'Why not?'

'You're too scatty.'

'Oh, no, I'm improving all the time.'

'You look more at home on a horse than pushing a pram. Hey, what's up?'

He looked out of the window, pulling the nets aside. 'Someone's in a hurry.'

Laura looked up and saw a horse go by, cantering fast.

Charlie said, 'It's one of the grooms from Falmouth House.'

Laura laid down the almanac. All her new, optimistic resolve was quenched within seconds. She felt suddenly, physically, cold, as if Charlie had opened the window. She looked at the clock on the mantelpiece. It was just gone half past two: Agnes was having her nap and Herbie was in the kitchen with the cook making brandy snaps. The smell of gently warming sugar and treacle seeped across the hall and in the grate the flames of a bright coal fire were fluttering with a comfortable afternoon noise—disaster seemed out of place.

'What is it?'

'How should I know?' Charlie asked. 'He's in a devil of a hurry, that's all I know.'

'It's Fred.'

'Fred is getting better.'

'No.'

Laura stood up. 'Tiger knew.' There was no doubt in her mind now. She tried to make her voice reasonable and calm. 'Something is wrong. Will you go and enquire?'

'You're jumping to conclusions, aren't you? It's a bit inquisitive, to barge in and say, "Where the devil was Pask going in such a hurry?"' Charlie laughed, but his expression was not without concern.

'We'll keep an eye open and see who he's fetching,' he suggested. 'Honestly, Laura, you look like you've seen a ghost. Long engagements are bad for the nervous system, I've heard it said. Sit down now, and fix that date. I'll watch for developments.'

He stood in the window, his hands in his pockets. Laura went and stood by the fire to stop her shivers, but took the almanac with her, leafing unseeingly for wedding dates. Oh, Tiger, she was thinking, what did you see? *What did you see?*

Ten minutes later Dr Wright's gig went past at a spanking trot making for Falmouth House.

'Hmm.' Charlie looked at Laura dubiously. 'Perhaps he's had a set-back.'

'Will you go and see?' Laura asked softly. 'Please, Charlie.'

Charlie shrugged and went out.

Laura knelt down in front of the fire, her skirts billowing out across the hearth-rug, hugging her cold body with her arms. The flames were like icicles. She longed for Tiger and his fierce embrace and his comfort, for she knew there would be no comfort from Charlie. Tiger already knew. He would be thinking of her now.

It was a quarter past three when Charlie came back. She heard the door slam in the kitchen, a shriek from the cook. She heard Lottie's feet flying upstairs. Someone was shouting in the stable-yard, and in the street someone else rode past at a canter, but she did not see who. She was staring into the flames. Charlie came in behind her and shut the door.

'You were right,' he said quietly.

She did not turn round, but braced herself for what he would say.

'Fred has shot himself. He is dead.'

So. It was true: violent and unlikely. Charlie came up behind her, knelt down and put his arm round her.

'I'm sorry.'

'Yes, I knew.'

'He put the pistol in his mouth. It was quite instantaneous and they say there's not a mark on him. He did it very well, like he did everything else.'

'Dear Fred, why?'

'Because of Nellie, I should think. Two years ago yesterday. And his weight. Always his weight.'

Charlie was deeply moved. Laura saw tears in his eyes, but she could not cry. She felt as if she had already been crying for weeks and was wrung out, a skin without heart.

* * *

Not only the town of Newmarket but the whole country was stunned by the event and the death was reported widely in newspapers all over the world from America to Australia. In London the presses could not turn out papers fast enough for the demand. Questions and blame dominated all conversation; the evidence at the inquest was minutely examined, the verdict argued over: 'The deceased shot himself whilst in a state of unsound mind, the weak state and high fever having disordered his brain to such an extent as to leave no doubt that he was insane at the time he committed the rash act.'

'Rubbish,' said Bertie. 'He knew what he was doing all right.'

'The nurse said he was perfectly rational.'

'It was tragic the gun was there, all the same.'

The loaded revolver was kept in a drawer in the bedside table. It had been given to Archer by a grateful owner, and he had kept it at hand in case of burglars, the house being stuffed with valuables, equally the gifts of grateful owners.

'They were happy to near enough kill him without the help of a revolver,' as Lottie remarked, 'asking him to ride at those weights.'

'He did what he wanted,' Bertie said. 'Including kill himself when he could see it finishing. He was overweight for half his races this last season, not just for the Cambridgeshire.'

'If Nellie had not died, he would not have done it.'

'No, poor Fred. He did love her.'

On the morning of the funeral the rain fell heavily from a leaden sky. The street was busy with traffic, and had been so all the week, backwards and forwards from Falmouth House, but now as midday approached it was growing quiet. Lottie came in and drew the curtains across.

'The town is crowded with visitors, and yet they are all so quiet and still, waiting, it gives the saddest feeling.'

Laura was aware of it without being told.

'Bertie says we shall follow the cortege in the carriage when it comes by. Will you come with us, or are you going with Tiger and your uncle?'

'I shall come with you.'

She had not seen Tiger since Fred's death. Harry had said that he had gone home to Nottingham to see his family, which she preferred not to think about, remembering the harsh young men at Epsom and the brutal self-assurance of his father. She was not convinced that Tiger had the command of them, although by his age he was no longer bound and presumably had nothing to fear. If he still had dreams, he never spoke of them, and had not forecast a winner for over a year.

'And good riddance to winners,' Harry had said forcibly. 'Along with the rest of his dreams—we can well do without.'

But Laura was anxious to have him back, more so now that this public exhibition of grief was about to overtake them all. She needed his strengthening presence and ascetic tongue to temper the funeral mood; she was exhausted with doom and needed to look beyond. The tolling of the knell from All Saints came faintly across the grey landscape from the town; the rain had ceased but the sky was still dark and heavy.

For the last time Laura watched Fred go past the gate. There was nothing to be seen of the coffin for flowers, and carriages full of flowers accompanied the hearse, heaped high in a profusion of white and gold and purple, of lilies and roses and chrysanthemum, of lilac and violets, orchids, camellias, ivies and ferns. The scent was overpowering, reminding Laura vividly of her mother's conservatory; it lingered in the raw air long after the hearse had passed and the interminable procession of carriages filled the road in both directions as far as the eye could see. Laura rode with Lottie and Bertie and Charlie, their carriage falling in behind. The pavement even up to their house was scattered with knots of spectators, but as they came into town the crowds became dense, standing silent and bare-headed on either side of the road. All the shops were shuttered and the hotels closed.

At the top of the town the police had to control the large crowd at the cemetery gates, but there were too many carriages to be accommodated and the after part of the procession came to a standstill halfway up the hill. The coffin and family mourners passed into the small chapel alone, but the police were unable to hold the gates against the press and had to retreat to defend the graveside as best they could.

'He's used to being mobbed by crowds,' Bertie said. 'It'll not worry him.'

Laura, staring stonily out of the window, saw Tiger coming back down the road alone, picking his way between the carriages. She tapped on the window and he saw her and came up and opened the door. She was so relieved and excited to see him she scarcely had the grace to excuse herself. 'Please, do you mind—?'

'No, go with him, gel, and get cheered up,' Bertie said heavily. 'It'll do you no harm.'

Laura jumped down and Tiger shut the door behind her. They struggled through the crowd and escaped into the street that led up to the station.

'You'll never get any closer to the churchyard now,' Tiger said. 'We'll wait till they've all gone home and go up tonight and say goodbye, and then it's over and done with, Laura. There's nothing between us now, nor ever will be.'

'There never was.'

'Oh, yes. For me as much as for you. For me more, for you said yourself that yours was a dream, but mine was always the truth.'

'You must never see anything else!'

'No. It's finished now. I went to see my grandmother in Nottingham and she said my gift—that's what she called it—had run its course. It was a child's gift, she said, as hers had been. She gave me her blessing, and to you as well—more than I can say for the

(229)

rest of the family. My brothers beat me up and my father locked me up for three days until my grandmother convinced him I'd never give him another winner, then he gave me a few cracks round the head for good measure and sent me packing. We won't ask them to our wedding, Laura—they're not nice.'

He laughed.

'You shouldn't have gone!'

'I knew I had to, to make a clean start. It was worth it. I knew what it would be like—and that wasn't second sight, believe me, that was just *knowing* them—but it had to be done, else I'd never have felt free.'

'Uncle Harry would have gone with you if you'd asked.'

'I wouldn't have him abused, I've too much regard for him. Come home with me now, and we'll make some plans. We've nothing to stop us.'

They went round the back of the stricken town to Harry's new yard, and into the cottage. It was empty but the fires were burning and one of Martha's pies was cooking in the oven.

'There are no plans to make, only the date, and I've decided that.'

Laura felt relaxed and free for the first time in months. Four days before the Two Thousand Guineas she would marry Tiger in All Saints and come here to live with the two people she loved most. Her house was up to the eaves and the bays on either side of the front door stared placidly across smooth lawns into the stable-yard. Chestnut trees masked the building from the road and sandy horse-rides led out through the back on to the gallops.

'We shall do well here,' Tiger said. 'You can ride work like you used to, and have babies in between, and we shall win the Derby and grow rich. I used to be afraid it wouldn't work out. I was afraid of your loving Fred, and afraid of my family.'

The afternoon grew dark early and the throngs of people in the town silently dispersed, the lads back to feed their horses, the distinguished visitors to the station or the hotels, the owners to their trainers to chat and drink, and the village people to trail back along the lanes, huddled in their Sunday black against the raw afternoon. Laura watched the carriage lamps bobbing up the Bury road, savouring her new abode, her town status, her life-to-be. When Harry came home she had the table laid and the kettle boiling, and she was touched to see how his face lit up at the sight of Tiger.

'You've been home?'

'Yes, sir.'

'I guessed it! Vanishing without a word—it could only be! I was thinking if you didn't come back after today I would follow you up there and fight your father for possession. He tried to keep you? You *have* been fighting by the look of you—'

'His habits are still as rough, yes. But once I convinced him that I no longer dream winners he was glad enough to kick me out.'

'The day is not entirely in vain then. We need some cheering news, believe me. Dear God, what a tragic business! This is what you saw way back on the day of the wedding?'

'Yes. I could have given the evidence Mrs Coleman gave at the inquest, word for word, of how he shot himself, three years ago. Even to the expression on his face. When I saw it, it was exactly as it came to be in fact, and yet at the time he was standing there with his bride on his arm, smiling, and everyone was cheering and throwing rice. And the image never faded, not like dreams fade. It stayed as sharp as it must be now for Mrs Coleman, who tried to stop him. Perhaps now he is in his grave it will fade away.'

'You have everything to look forward to and no time for thinking back. It will go.'

Later in the evening Tiger went out to do the evening inspection of the yard. He told Laura to put on her riding habit which she kept at the cottage, and when she went out he had saddled two horses. They were not hacks but two of the horses in training, flighty-eyed in the lamplight.

'You have been a governess too long,' he said. 'I want my old Laura back.'

'Who is she then?'

'The one who did not know her mother had a lover. That changed you.'

'It frightened me.'

'Frightened you of loving? You weren't frightened when I used to kiss you in the stables.'

'No.'

'No one can thrash me for it now. Come here.'

He kissed her. She knew what he meant by the old Laura and it seemed quite suddenly that she was back to that sweet state. And he was the same cocky waif who had so fascinated her with his opinion of his own value while pulling out dandelions on the terrace, before she knew that her mother loved her uncle instead of her father. He was still proud but the dandelion days were over and he was not too proud to say how much he loved her.

'More than myself, Laura, by far, and I have never loved anyone else, only Harry, and Harry is a man. I have never loved another woman in all my life.'

'I have loved Gervase,' Laura said suddenly.

She did not know what prompted her, save the longing to have her innocence before Tiger complete, back to the old days he had just said he desired. Loving Gervase had been a part of finding out what she wanted, and she wanted Tiger. How could he complain?

'I know,' he said.

'Did you *see*?'

'No. It wasn't necessary. I knew when you came home. But that day at the station I thought you were still loving him.'

'No. That day I was finding out that I didn't, nor ever would. I had decided that, and then you appeared, instantly.'

'Poor Gervase. I did well, didn't I, timing it so perfectly?'

'You are supposed to be mad with jealousy.'

'I could never be jealous of Gervase. I am glad if you made him happy. It might be the only time in his life. I have never seen him happy.'

They led the horses out and Tiger gave her a leg-up. They rode side by side up the Cambridge road and left the lights of the town behind them as they breasted the great expanse of turf. The westerly wind met them, raw and rain-flecked, but bearing with it the exotic scents of hot-house flowers: camellias and orchids and tuberoses. The Heath had never known such a token of love and respect as lay on its cold edge, the great heaps of flowers glimmering white in the darkness where Fred had been laid beside his wife and infant son. Tiger and Laura rode slowly down beside the cemetery wall, guided by the scent, their horses frightened by the strangeness, tossing their heads nervously. There were no trees, only the low wall to mark the cemetery from the Heath—like a harbour wall, Laura thought, and the graves like ships come in from the sea. But Fred's ship was made of flowers, and the ethereal pile palely throwing out its scent to the bleak landscape was more eloquent of affection than any ornate marble which might follow. Laura knew she would remember this unlikely, wildly-fragrant mountain until she came to lie in the same place herself. Nine feet down under the Newmarket turf, Fred was within earshot of the hooves on the race-course; the same wind that had knifed through his gaudy silks would blow these bright petals to mush on the autumn grass by the last race of the season. Fred had changed to hearsay and lesser mortals rode unscathed.

Their horses pulled nervously at their bits.

'It's stary,' Laura whispered, feeling like her horse, the wind taking her.

They went away at a canter, across the road and over the dark turf into infinity.

'These are the first hooves Fred will hear in his grave, Tiger's and mine,' Laura thought. 'Of all the hooves that will race across the Heath by his grave, ours will be the first.'

And she went with the great raking stride of her race-horse in Tiger's wake, wishing the lovely drumming of their gallop to Fred's cold ears for comfort.